CloudWorld

David Cunningham
CloudWorld

faber and faber

First published in 2005
by Faber and Faber Limited
3 Queen Square London WC1N 3AU

Typeset by Faber and Faber Limited
Printed in England by Mackays of Chatham plc, Chatham, Kent

A CIP record for this book
is available from the British Library

ISBN 0–571–22366–4

2 4 6 8 10 9 7 5 3

David Cunningham
CloudWorld

faber and faber

First published in 2005
by Faber and Faber Limited
3 Queen Square London WCIN 3AU

Typeset by Faber and Faber Limited
Printed in England by Mackays of Chatham plc, Chatham, Kent

A CIP record for this book
is available from the British Library

ISBN 0-571-22366-4

2 4 6 8 10 9 7 5 3

To my mother and to my father's memory.

When I behold, upon the night's starr'd face,
Huge cloudy symbols of a high romance,
And think that I may never live to trace
Their shadows, with the magic hand of chance

When I have fears that I may cease to be
Keats

Imagine . . .

Imagine a planet entirely covered in clouds. Imagine an ocean of cloud, stretching away in all directions, as far as the eye can see, for ever shifting and changing . . .

Imagine peaks rising out of the clouds, their gentle slopes covered in fields and orchards. Imagine a citadel standing on each peak – a citadel built in layers, each layer wider than the one above and encircled by a fortified wall. A palace sits on the topmost layer . . .

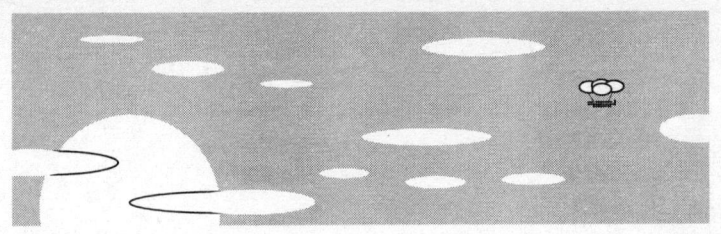

Imagine floating far out over the cloudscape. The rising sun sheds a ripening orange glow across it. A flying vessel appears in the distance. Tiny figures move around its broad, open deck, which hangs beneath a cluster of bulbous air sacs. Driven by its twin impellers, it speeds onwards, brushing the cloud tops. It passes behind the swollen peak of a cumulus cloud. But, when it emerges, trailing skeins of cloud vapour, it seems to be in trouble. Smoke wreathes it. Cinders fall from the underside of its bleached wooden hull. Its air sacs pucker and sag.

On its deck crew members now run back and forth. Some collide with one another. The smoke thickens, making it almost impossible to see. A tall, grey-bearded man staggers on to the deck. His hair is disordered and he is dressed in a long, sleep-crumpled robe. He gazes around him in vexed bewilderment for a few moments then moves amongst the crew, shouting orders to them. He grows wraith-like in the smoke then strays out of sight. The deck tilts sharply. Flames swarm up the rigging, towards the air sacs. The vessel begins to sink . . .

...A thousand miles westward, where the sun has not yet risen, a boy wakes in his bed from a nightmare and gasps in the pounding darkness.

CloudWorld

Heliopolis

Marcus moved through the palace garden, alert to the footfall of approaching guards. He crept between two small artificial hills, in a narrow, gently sloping gully that brimmed with late blooming plants – heart shaped fremanji, clustered white jasmine and lolling clumps of elhuemeria. Their mingled fragrance was so intense it made him feel almost light-headed. Though they offered good cover, progress through them was difficult. So, forsaking the gully, he crawled up the hill on his left, where the vegetation was thinner. Reaching the top, he flattened himself against it.

At fourteen, having been raised, like all cloud dwellers, in clear air and plentiful sunlight, Marcus was olive skinned with pale blue eyes, though also a little on the short side. His gaze sharpened by a lifetime spent watching countless tiny changes in the appearance of the clouds, he peered out over the undulating landscape of the huge garden that surrounded him. Brawling streams wound between the other low hills. Waterfalls poured icy torrents into deep, sheer-sided pools, which were fringed by ornamented pathways.

Though it covered several acres, the palace garden – called the Hortoreum – was enclosed by a high, battlemented wall. Just visible beyond the wall was the white dome of an observatory, rising amid a jostle of turrets, spires and minarets. The armoured sentinels who patrolled the wall paid no heed to what was going on in the Hortoreum. Cloaks fluttering, they stood with their backs to it, intent upon gazing out over the cloudscape. Their golden armour – the breastplates beaten into exaggeratedly muscled contours – glittered in the sunlight.

Far above them, tethered to the battlements by thick rope ladders, parasails rode the powerful air currents. Each parasail consisted of a canopy more than twenty feet wide with a wooden cage attached to it. The canopy's convex shape provided lift while a sentinel stood in the cage beneath. Hands gripping the bars, he scanned the horizon for any signs of an approaching aëro:cruiser – one of the citadel's many flying vessels. The whole assembly swayed back and forth, cage creaking, ladder flexing.

Meanwhile, on the far side of the Hortoreum Marcus spotted a guard whom he recognised. His name was Savis. He was tall and tanned and, like Marcus, he wore a sleeveless tunic and loose cotton trousers, for ease of movement. A sword hung from his belt, as did a small hand-held weapon, called a crossbolt. It was T-shaped, with a carved wooden handle, and was loaded with a row of stubby bolts, which could be fired in rapid succession – some tipped with fine-grained gunpowder that exploded on impact. Savis was inching along one of the wrought iron gangways that were fixed to the

4

battlemented wall. He thrust a spear through the gaps in its grid-like floor, trying to root out anyone who might be concealed in the foliage below, which was especially thick on the fringes of the Hortoreum. Presently another guard, whose name Marcus didn't know, joined Savis. They exchanged a few words then continued with their search. Marcus cursed inwardly. How was he going to escape from the Hortoreum without being caught when the perimeter was swarming with guards?

A bee, drowsy in the late autumn sunlight, emerged from a lolling clump of fremanji a few feet from Marcus. It weaved towards him and circled his head a few times. He flapped his hand at it. As he did so his elbow dislodged a small rock. It tumbled down the other side of the hill, gathering more rocks on its way, along with a large volume of soil. This miniature landslide fell into the stream at the bottom in a prolonged series of splashes. Marcus winced at each one. Savis's head jerked up, as did the other guard's. Their eyes darted across the Hortoreum.

You're too exposed here. Move! Marcus thought.

He shuffled back down the hill. He had gone only a few inches, however, when a large pair of hands clamped themselves around his ankles and wrenched him the rest of the way. His face now caked with soil, he looked up to see another guard – Medaq – standing awkwardly on the hillside, scowling down at him. He rolled sideways just as Medaq hurled his spear.

The spear plunged into the ground next to Marcus's head, its shaft quivering with the impact. Medaq frowned irritatedly at having missed. He stamped a foot on Marcus's chest to pin him down and reached again for the spear. Improvising desperately, Marcus grabbed it. It was too deeply lodged for him to pull it out. Instead he bent it as far as possible then released it. The shaft struck Medaq in the face. He staggered backwards, hands clasped over his nose, and gave a muffled bellow of surprise and anger.

The instant Medaq's foot was off his chest, Marcus rolled down the rest of the hill and plunged back into the cover of the undergrowth. He blundered forwards in a crouch, not sure if he was anywhere near an exit point, but keen to put as much distance as possible between himself and his attacker.

Eventually the undergrowth thinned and he stumbled into a narrow, fast-running stream. He straightened up and looked around to get his bearings. The exits were at the Hortoreum's corners and he was closest to the south-east corner, so that had to be the way to go. No sooner had he decided this, however, than he saw Savis appearing over the brow of one of the nearby artificial hills about ten feet above him. He turned to run, but Savis threw himself down the hillside and cannoned into him.

They both fell, face first, into the water. It coursed around their thrashing arms and legs. Spluttering, his shoulder aching, Marcus tried to scramble upstream. But the stream-bed – carved from alabaster – was smooth and hard to grip. Grabbing him by the collar, Savis hauled him back. They struggled for a while. Savis tried, with difficulty, to hold on to the squirming Marcus with one hand while drawing his sword with the other. He shifted his legs wider apart to steady himself, planting them on either side of the stream. Seeing him do this gave Marcus an idea. He squirmed with renewed vigour.

Savis's feet slipped a little and his fingers loosened for an instant on Marcus's collar. Marcus wrenched himself free. But, instead of trying to scramble away again, he allowed himself to fall backwards into the stream, arms flat against his sides. The rush of water bore him swiftly downstream. He shot between Savis's legs and out of reach. Savis whirled round, snarling in frustration. He lost his footing again and dropped his sword.

Marcus hurtled downstream on his back, feet first. Instead of heading south-east, towards the nearest exit, he was now being carried back towards the centre of the Hortoreum. But at least he had eluded Savis and, inadvertently, drawn him away from the perimeter.

It's not over yet! he told himself.

For a few moments he found himself gazing up at a blue sky, streaked with thin cirrostratus clouds. Then glossy vegetation rose on either side of the stream and overlapped above, concealing him from view. It created a tunnel of soft green light which, in spite of his immediate circumstances, felt almost soothing.

A few moments later something nudged his left shoulder. He tilted his head back, trying not to let the water lap over his face. It was Savis's sword, bobbing downstream. Slender and fast moving, it had caught up with him already. He reached diagonally across his chest with his right hand and grabbed it.

Now equipped with a sword, he was borne onward, away from his assailants. He felt buoyant with relief until he remembered that this stream fed a waterfall, which in turn poured into the largest of the Hortoreum's pools. Craning his neck, he looked ahead of him. Sure enough, the waterfall's foaming edge was approaching rapidly. He could scarcely avoid going over it. But then any guards patrolling the rim of the pool would be bound to see him. Just as this thought occurred to him, swords thrust down through the canopy of foliage. The blades glinted in the slender beams of sunlight they created, their owners ranged along either side of the stream, searching for him.

Twisting desperately between this succession of lancing swords, Marcus felt the water growing more turbulent around him. A few seconds later he tumbled through the spray-choked air and plunged into the pool. As the cold water closed over his head, he knew that he couldn't simply thrash his way back to the surface – his attackers would be watching for him to re-emerge. He had taken a deep breath as he fell – and, having lived all his life at high altitude, he had strong lungs. So he kicked towards the bottom of the pool then twisted round and looked back up, parting his fringe. Far above he could see guards grouped on either side of the waterfall, peering anxiously into the pool, their outlines distorted by the rippling of the surface as the cascade gushed into it.

His lungs began to ache.

What to do?

Just then he remembered that there was a narrow but deep cleft in the rock, just behind the waterfall, that stretched almost all the way to the bottom of the pool. His vision growing speckled and hazy from the effort of holding his breath for so long, he swam towards the spot where the surface was most churned. He kept on swimming until his head bumped against something solid. Then he surfaced, chest heaving.

He looked around. Sure enough, he was inside a damp, glowing space with three walls of smooth rock and one of streaming water. The sun, shining through the water, filled the space with rippling shadows. His knees nudged against a sloping ledge. He climbed up on to it, trying to ensure that no part of his body poked out through the cascade.

Safe, if slightly precarious, on the ledge, he slowly realised how cold he felt. For a while he just stood there, shivering and staring blankly at the water as it tumbled down right in front of his face.

Focus! What'll the guards do next?

They would probably scuttle down the hillside and fan out around the pool, poised to grab him, no matter where he emerged. Then again if he didn't emerge they would work out fairly soon where he was hidden. The best plan might be to swim for the far side of the pool, where the undergrowth was thickest, then take his chances: pick an exit and dash for it.

Crippled by indecision, he leaned back and closed his

eyes and therefore missed the exact moment when a spear was thrust through the cascade. It was not until he heard an odd scraping noise that he opened his eyes again and saw its tip being swept against the wall in an exploratory way right above his head. The shaft was angled downwards. This suggested that the person holding the other end of it was bending over the edge of the waterfall and pushing it inwards to flush out anyone hiding in the space behind it.

Marcus remained motionless. His eyes were fixed on the spear's tip as it withdrew a little and started to waggle around, right in front of his face. It grazed his cheek lightly, then paused and held still. Some newly awakened instinct told him what to do. With a small hop, he plunged, feet first, back into the water just as the spear was thrust forward, stabbing into the portion of the wall where his head had just been.

Underwater again, Marcus swam hard for the far side of the pool. Reaching it, he stayed deep while looking up to check if anyone was there. The toes of a guard's sandals hung a few inches over the edge of the pathway. Palms flat against the side of the pool, Marcus pushed down to the bottom, paused, crouching, for a second then launched himself back up. Thrusting his arms above his head, he grabbed the guard's legs and wrenched at them with all his remaining strength.

The guard toppled into the water. Ducking sideways to avoid being driven back under by his falling body, Marcus hauled himself up on to the gravel pathway that fringed the pool. The guard surfaced, spluttering, and clawed for the edge. Marcus knew he couldn't afford to look round and check how many other guards had seen him. Already he heard them shouting to each other to cut him off. Bolts whizzed past his head. He plunged into the undergrowth.

He had gone only a few paces when the short blade of a dagger flicked like a snake's tongue out of the fremanji bush in front of him. The guard who wielded it parted the bush with a broad sweep of his free hand then stepped forward, smiling. It was Savis again. Marcus tried to back away. But the guard he had wrenched from the edge of the pool appeared behind him, dripping and expressionless. There was no escape. The dagger pressed into his throat, just above the breastbone. Kneeling, he closed his eyes ...

Clear air turbulence

'Well done, Your Highness,' said Savis, smiling. 'You may not have escaped, but you led us quite a dance this time.'

He removed the dagger from Marcus's throat. Its blade was dull and, like all the swords, spears and bolts he had been threatened with in the past half-hour, it was tipped with cork to prevent serious injury. Marcus rose to his feet again. He massaged his shoulder. Savis, so menacing only a short time before, grew instantly solicitous.

'Is it sore?' he asked.

'A bit.'

'I'm sorry, but the general does always tell us to make the sparring session as realistic as possible.'

'It's okay. I'm sure he'll be pleased you follow his orders with such gusto.'

They re-emerged from the undergrowth. More guards had gathered around the pool. They greeted Marcus with an approving murmur and a scattering of applause. Embarrassed, he placed one hand flat against his stomach and gave an ironic little bow. Then the guards parted, falling silent, and another man strode between them – more imposing than the others and somewhat older. His jaw was strong, his nose broad and angular, with a thick bridge. He wore his iron-grey hair cropped. His eyes were deep-set, but glinted also with shrewd watchfulness. This was General Titus Grath, supreme commander of the citadel's armed forces. As he approached Marcus he tucked a watch on a chain back into the pocket of his tunic.

'An interesting display,' he said. 'You still had four minutes fifty-seven seconds to reach an exit when you were caught, which isn't bad.'

Marcus smiled.

'Praise indeed,' he said. 'Thank you.'

'It was, however, somewhat unorthodox,' continued Titus. 'Do please bear in mind that a sparring session, no matter how, uh . . . *improvised*, should ideally contain some actual sparring instead of just being a series of ingenious escapes.'

'I know, general. But you did tell me to make the most of being small and agile when fighting a much larger opponent, remember?'

Titus nodded.

'Indeed I did,' he said.

He steered Marcus away from the pool. Together they climbed a winding path that led to one of the Hortoreum's elevated viewing points. Though not wide, it contained an ornate semicircular bench and an octagonal sundial on a marble plinth. As soon as they were out of earshot of the others, Titus grew more relaxed.

'Just remember,' he continued, 'that no matter how much you may despair of ever growing any taller, the day will come – perhaps sooner than you think – when you'll be the same size as a foe you encounter during a training session and you have to be prepared for that. In the meantime, I think we'll step up your regime of hand to hand combat. I'd like to see you taking on more than one swordsman at a time.'

From the viewing point Marcus could see across the battlements to the cloudscape beyond. It looked unusually calm this morning, with only faint ripples in its surface, while extreme distance lent a bluish tint to the cumulus clouds massed on the western horizon. He strained his eyes towards them.

Noticing this, Titus said, 'Then again perhaps your mind isn't entirely on such matters at the moment.'

'I'm sorry,' said Marcus. 'It's just . . . How long is the *Regulus* overdue now? Three days?'

'Only two.'

'Isn't that two days too many, though?'

'Not necessarily. It isn't unusual this late in the season for aëro:cruisers to alter their course if they spot a tumult brewing in their path.'

'But wouldn't that mean that it might be in danger?'

'No, because the *Regulus* has more powerful telescopes and better lookouts than any other aëro:cruiser. Just the slightest change in the shape or texture of the clouds can tell them what conditions will be hundreds of miles away.'

'But I heard once,' Marcus persisted, 'that tumults at this time of year can spring up out of nowhere. And then there's those bolts of lightning . . . what are they called?'

'Steropys?'

'That's right, steropys. Can't they fire up out of the clouds when they're in tumult?'

Titus sighed.

'Sometimes, Marcus, you have altogether too vivid an imagination. As far as I can remember, no aëro:cruiser has ever been lost in such a way.'

'Have there been any telegraph signals?'

'No, but bear in mind that the *Regulus* may not yet be within range. Or electrical discharges in the cloud depths could be interfering with the transmission.'

'Still, don't you think the delay could be a bad sign?'

Titus sat down and gestured for Marcus to do the same. Then, placing a hand on his damp shoulder, he said, 'How long have you known me?'

'All my life.'

'Exactly. I've been teaching you to spar since you were five years old. And how often in that time have we seen each other, do you think?'

'Almost every day. I mean, my father has been away on state visits so much I've probably spent more time with you than with him.'

Titus nodded.

'And for my part I've always tried to . . . well, to take his place in his absence, I suppose . . . to teach you the things he would want you to know – about courage and resourcefulness, if nothing else.'

'But you *have*, you've taught me so much.'

Marcus paused. He would like to have gone further. He would like to have told Titus that he measured himself against him in many ways. But doing so would somehow have felt disloyal to his father.

'In that case,' replied Titus, smiling, 'believe me when I tell you that your worrying about him does you no discredit in my eyes, particularly since you lost your mother so young. But if I thought that his safety was imperilled in any way I would tell you. Remember, I've been a soldier all my life. I'm trained to deal in brute realities, not entertain false hope – nor offer any where none exists.'

'So you aren't worried at all?' Marcus asked.

'Not too much. But I promise you this: if the *Regulus* isn't back by tomorrow morning we'll meet in the observatory and scan the horizon. If we still don't see it, I'll send out some ornithopters. The range of the largest is only a hundred miles or so, but we can rig them with telescopes so their pilots can see quite a bit further.'

'I'd like that.'

'Good,' replied Titus, standing up and tugging smartly at the hem of his tunic. 'In that case I hope *not* to see you tomorrow morning, if you get my meaning.'

'Yes.'

'Always assuming Madam Asperia is willing to liberate you from lessons for an hour or so.'

Marcus glanced down at the sundial. 'I'd better go, actually, or I'll be late for her. Thank you, general. Thank you for talking to me.'

'You're very welcome. Just remember we're all preoccupied with the king's absence.'

Marcus nodded then hastened back down the path and across the Hortoreum. As he reached one of its vine-woven pergolas, from which a spiral staircase descended to the rest of the palace, he reflected that no matter how blunt Titus was he had a heartening knack for making everything seem better.

The staircase led to an octagonal courtyard. Fluted columns stood sentry around the walls and a fountain splashed at its centre. Sunshine, pouring in through the domed skylight, threw the water's sparkling reflection across the walls.

From here Marcus hurried along a series of cool, bright corridors. Every one was lit by more skylights. They threw sharply etched rectangles of light on to the marble floor at regular intervals. When he reached his apartments he looked around for Asperia. The drawing room, although large, was quite simply furnished. Patterned rugs sprawled across the marble floor, which was dominated by a low, glass-topped table with cushions scattered around it. The domed ceiling was covered in a blue fresco, streaked with white that was intended to echo the sky. On the far side of the room silk curtains hung in front of a curved archway and stirred gently in the breeze. But Asperia hadn't yet arrived.

After changing into dry clothes, Marcus slipped between the curtains and went out on to the balcony to resume his vigil for the *Regulus*. It was late autumn in the northern hemisphere, a time of warm afternoons and crisp evenings. Soon, with hardly any warning, the first winter storms, called 'tumults', would begin. Powerful winds would thrash the cloudscape into a swollen, ragged mass. But, for the moment, the season had a deceptive tranquillity about it, as if it would never change.

King Antior Hyperios had been away for three months on a diplomatic tour of the northern citadels. Marcus still found it difficult to fathom the exact purpose of his father's tours. Apparently they consisted of the king arriving at a foreign palace, being greeted by the head of state, shaking the hands of assembled dignitaries, being fed numberless huge meals, then leaving and travelling on to the next palace.

'They are vital because they contribute to the bonds of goodwill between us and our neighbours,' Marcus's tutor Asperia had told him.

As far as Marcus could see each time the *Regulus* floated back into dock, the only thing the tours contributed to was the width of his father's waistline. But he knew that he had a lot to learn about politics.

And, indeed, about many other things. Though he was bright and inquisitive, his powers of concentration, as Asperia never failed to remind him, left much to be desired. He found it hard to remember any piece of information that didn't immediately grab his attention, especially if it was conveyed to him in the form of a lesson. On the other hand, he tended to be very curious about things he was supposed to just accept.

Take Heliopolis, for instance. Its population numbered many tens of thousands, but its society was rigidly divided. The Farmers lived in the lowest layer – the one closest to the fields and orchards. A fortified wall encircled it. Shelving upwards in disordered rows above the wall were the Farmers' cottages. Each cottage had shuttered windows facing out over the cloudscape, and a sagging roof with many tiles missing.

The Farmers grew all the fruit, vegetables and crops that fed the rest of the citadel. They also kept many aviaries, since fowl was the only meat that its citizens knew in their world above the clouds. The food they produced was stored in a cavernous warehouse, called the Laborium, at the centre of the layer. Here, within cool stone walls, lit by tallow lamps, they cleaned the fruit and vegetables, ground the wheat and plucked and prepared the fowl.

In the next layer lived the Artisans. The Artisans made all the furniture, all the clothes, all the implements, all the *things,* used by the citizenry of Heliopolis. At the heart of their layer was a huge communal workshop, called the Factorium. And, like the Farmers, they lived in cramped, ramshackle cottages that were stacked on top of one another and stretched all round the outside of their layer. Confined every day within the Factorium, amid the constant din of manufacture and the heat of the furnaces, they cultivated tiny roof gardens to sit out in after work. They and the Farmers exchanged goods by barter, but both were also compelled, by law, to send the majority of what they produced upwards, to feed and furnish the layers above.

Above the Artisans lived the citadel's Administrators – known as Admins for short. Their layer had a sheer circular wall that was featureless except for the tiny, identical windows carved into it. Like the Farmers and the Artisans, the Admins spent their days in tireless activity, though its end product was a bit harder to discern. They sat in dimly lit rooms conducting studies into how efficient those below were and drafting proposals on how methods of production could be changed through rigid planning.

('You mean improved?' Marcus had asked Asperia once.

'No, just changed,' she had replied dryly.)

Once the Admins had exhaustively discussed these proposals in committees, working parties and steering groups, they were amended, copied again, then sent up to the ministers in the palace. The ministers filed most of them away unread. No one could fathom why the Admins bothered doing any of this. Nor could anyone remember how they had acquired their role in the first place. Their necessities of life were provided by the layers below and in return they sent down an endless stream of memos and questionnaires. Asperia suspected the Admins felt obliged to create as much upheaval as possible in order to justify their existence – if things continued to run smoothly for a while people would realise that none of them was needed. Marcus would usually have continued to plague her with questions on this topic. But there was something about the unending tedium of the Admins' work that exhausted even his curiosity.

Much more interesting to him were the men and women who lived in the next layer: the Cloudfarers.

Cloudfarers were regarded with awe throughout the citadel because they did something that was unimaginable to most of its citizens: they travelled out across the cloudscape. Most of the Cloudfarers came from families that had lived in the layer for generations, bred for this noble role. But occasionally children from the Farmers' and Artisans' layers who displayed special strength and alertness were granted the honour of training for the corps – leaving their families in the process. In turn, only the most accomplished Cloudfarers were selected for the Praesidion Guard, which maintained the security of the palace.

The Cloudfarers' layer had a smooth, circular wall like the Admins' layer. But this wall sloped inwards. Lots of attic-style windows were set into it, with squat, thinly smoking chimneys protruding from each one. And into several different sections were cut broad, flat landing stages, where the citadel's aëro:cruisers took off and landed.

All this Marcus had learned from Asperia. During their lessons together she explained to him, in minute detail, how each layer was organised and how they all fitted together into the great society of Heliopolis. But he had never been allowed to visit any other part of the citadel and she told him nothing about how the inhabitants of each layer actually *felt* about their lives. As far as she was concerned such matters were irrelevant – citizens in the lower layers were expected to fulfil their appointed roles unquestioningly, just as generations of their ancestors had done.

Marcus gazed down at the Cloudfarers' layer. Below it the other layers, with their fortified walls, shelved away like vast, curving steps to the fields, which in turn sloped gently into the cloudscape. He remembered how he had watched with a mixture of envy and awe, three months earlier, as the *Regulus* rose into the air from the landing stage, slipped its mooring lines and floated out from the citadel. Its white, bleached hull, emblazoned with the royal crest, had glowed in the early summer sunlight.

On numerous occasions in his young life Marcus had pleaded with his father to take him along on a state visit. But Antior had always refused, albeit gently and with an air of keen regret. Didn't Marcus realise that to have both the king and his heir travelling over the cloudscape at the same time went against the constitution of Heliopolis? If something went wrong it would leave the citadel without any monarchy and destroy centuries of tradition. And nothing – nothing in the world – was more important than tradition.

Now, the landing stage was empty, save for the occasional Cloudfarer who walked out across the apron to the edge, scanning the western horizon – like Marcus – for signs of the returning *Regulus*.

'Cloud gazing as usual?' said a familiar voice.

Marcus started and looked round.

Asperia was standing behind him, clutching an ominously large book to her chest. She was in her early-sixties. Her face was finely etched with lines that testified to a lifetime spent squinting in strong sunlight. (Though she insisted that she'd had fewer lines before embarking on the ordeal of educating Marcus.) Her long dark hair, streaked with silver, was plaited, swept back and coiled on top of her head. This style only added to her already considerable height, which Marcus rather suspected was the whole point of it.

Her face wore its usual expression: lips drawn taut, eyebrows raised, as if she were preparing to disapprove of the next thing he said or did.

'Good morning, madam,' he replied. 'Actually I was looking out for my father.'

'Oh,' she said, her expression softening a little. 'Well, don't worry. I'm sure he'll return soon. In the meantime I have to feed you a few more scraps of knowledge so you can have forgotten them all by tomorrow morning.'

Wedging the book under her arm, she turned and went back into Marcus's apartments. A sudden gust of wind caused the curtains to part obligingly for her. Grumbling under his breath, Marcus followed.

She dropped the book on to the glass-topped table. It landed with a thud that portended a very dull morning. Then she lowered herself carefully on to the cushions and put on her reading glasses. Flopping down on his side of the table with a sigh, Marcus sat in a bored slouch, waiting for her to begin. She was forever scolding him about his insufficiently regal posture.

'Now,' she said, licking her long, slender index finger and turning a page, 'this morning we shall continue with languages. Specifically the language of Selenopolis

– the citadel to the north east of us, from which your father is, I'm sure, safely returning even as we speak. All right. Lesson Six: articles of clothing.'

'Madam?'

'Hmm?'

'What's the point of me learning the names of clothes in another language?'

'One day, when you ascend the throne, you will go on state visits yourself and when you do you'll need to be able to speak to the monarchs of other citadels in their own tongues.'

'But I don't even know how clothes are made in Heliopolis. Wouldn't it be better if I learned that first? Perhaps we should go down to the Artisans' layer and . . .'

'You don't have to know how clothes are made in Heliopolis,' Asperia reminded him. 'Your clothes are made for you by Heliopolis's finest tailors.'

'But surely knowledge of my own citadel is more important?'

Asperia suddenly looked tired. She took off her glasses and rubbed her eyes.

'I see,' she said.

'What?'

'It's going to be that sort of tutorial, is it?'

'What sort of tutorial?'

'One of those tutorials where every time I ask you a question you ask me a question in return?'

'Do I do that?'

'I rest my case,' she said. 'Right. Basic vocabulary.'

Marcus opened his mouth to protest once more.

'You may one day have to inform a visiting dignitary that his trousers are falling down!' Asperia suggested. 'Who knows what the future might hold? Now, repeat after me please. Shirt: *pirõnchyé*.'

'Asperia?'

'What?'

'Do the tailors always stay in the Artisans' layer?'

'I assume so.'

'But don't they come up to measure people in the higher layers for clothes?'

'No. Everyone's measurements are sent down to them, just like yours are. Now repeat, please. Shirt . . .'

'But wouldn't it make more sense for them to come up here and measure us, rather than employing lots of people to do it, then take all the measurements down to them?' Marcus asked, picking at a loose thread on a cushion so that he could pretend not to see the black look Asperia was levelling at him across the table.

'Possibly,' she replied. 'Now repeat . . .'

'Have you been to the Artisans' layer?'

'No, I'm glad to say. Now . . .'

'Why not?'

Asperia slammed the book shut. A cloud of dust burst from it and drifted into the air above their heads.

'Why not? Because I find that noise, gloom and lack of space don't hold as much fascination for me as they evidently do for you! So . . . may I continue with the tutorial?'

Still preoccupied with the loose thread, Marcus nodded.

'Thank you. Now ...'

'But what I'm really trying to say,' Marcus piped up, 'is that it seems wrong to me that these people clothe me – they know what I look like better than I do, probably – yet I'm not allowed to meet them. I never get to meet anyone outside the palace. I mean, if I'm going to be king one day, surely I should see how people live in other parts of the citadel so I'll understand them.'

Instead of shouting at him, Asperia crumpled slightly, as if the effort of continuing to be annoyed were too much for her.

'Why are you so concerned about this?' she asked.

Marcus shrugged. Even by his normal standards, he was being tirelessly inquisitorial. Yet he couldn't help himself. Perhaps, he thought, the length of his father's absence had left him too much time alone to question everything.

'All right,' she said. 'This is what I think. You feel that you should get to know the citizenry better. That's commendable. But has it ever occurred to you that *they* may not want to get to know you better? They may prefer to think of you as someone mysterious, someone different from them, living far above the clamour and confinement of the rest of the Polis, looking distant and regal on a balcony. Now, may I continue?'

'All right.'

'Good. Oh, where was I?'

'Shirt: *pirõnchyé*,' Marcus reminded her.

'Ah yes. Repeat please. Shirt: *pirõnchyé*.'

'I just said it!'

'Well, you can say it twenty more times for insolence!'

Marcus glared at her, then closed his eyes and repeated, 'Shirt: *pirõnchyé*. Shirt: *pirõnchyé*. Shirt . . .'

He had not gone far when he heard a deep, grave voice say, 'Good morning, Your Highness.'

He opened his eyes. Synvadis, the citadel's prime minister, was standing over him. He possessed an effortless and unsettling knack for suddenly materialising in rooms without appearing to have come in. One minute he wasn't there and the next he was. It was disturbing if you happened to be speaking about him, because you were never quite sure what he'd overheard before you noticed him.

'Sleek' was probably the word that best described him. His long, slightly mournful face, with its hooded brown eyes and flaring nostrils, was elongated even further by his goatee beard, trimmed to a point at his chin, and his hair was wound into a ponytail that vanished under the collar of his robes. The robes were scarlet with seams of gold woven into them. This befitted a man of the prime minister's importance, Marcus supposed, though he noticed that no one else in the palace – except his father – dressed in such finery.

There was an awkward silence. Synvadis was a man of few unnecessary words. When speaking to him Marcus usually found himself babbling to fill in gaps in the conversation. Asperia had scolded him about this on many occasions. It was most unregal, she said. A prince or king did not make small talk. That was other people's task.

Marcus could see her point, but he found the habit hard to break. Sometimes he wondered, despairingly, if he really had what it took to be a monarch – at least a monarch in the traditional sense, like his father.

The silence persisted. The curtains at the archway swelled then deflated again, curling around the edges, as if the air passing through them had suddenly grown stale. The room grew noticeably colder.

'Can we help you, prime minister?' enquired Asperia.

'Thank you, madam,' he replied. 'I am here to see His Highness. I have some legislation requiring royal consent in the absence of King Antior.'

Synvadis produced a thick roll of parchments from inside his voluminous robes and spread them out over the table. Marcus peered at them. They were written in a cursive, slanting script that was difficult to read.

'My father will be back any moment,' he pointed out. 'At least I hope so. Couldn't you wait for him?'

'Sadly not, Your Highness. They must be ratified immediately.'

'I see. Oh well.'

Marcus reached for a quill pen and a pot of ink at the edge of the table.

'There seems to have been an awful lot of legislation recently,' he observed.

Synvadis laughed like someone who hadn't quite got the hang of it yet. When Marcus had finished signing the documents ('The last one's a bit smudged, sorry,' he said), the prime minister slipped them all back under his robes.

'It is the way of these things, Your Highness,' he explained. 'We spend a large part of the year discussing and drafting legislation, then a relatively short period turning it into law.'

'I see,' said Marcus, nodding.

Synvadis and his ministers were scarcely less officious than the Admins, but they wielded much more influence. Though the king was the supreme power in Heliopolis, he relied upon tiers of advisers – known collectively as the Executive – whom he consulted on a whole range of topics, from economics to citadel defences to diplomatic relations. Marcus recalled his father complaining that he spent most of his time closeted with the ministers, fending off countless proposals for new laws that they wanted him to pass. Marcus wondered if his absence had perhaps encouraged them to get a little out of hand.

'I am deeply sorry, of course, that His Majesty cannot be here to ratify this legislation of which he was so strongly in favour,' continued Synvadis, with an unconvincing sigh. 'But it must be sent down to the Administrators to be duplicated post haste.'

'Hmf!' commented Asperia.

Both Marcus and Synvadis stared at her. Marcus knew that there had been friction between her and Synvadis in the past – with two such strong personalities it could scarcely be otherwise. The chambermaids who looked after his apartments were tireless gossips and he listened eagerly to their tales about who in the palace was arguing with whom and which courtiers were in or out of favour with the king. According to them, Asperia felt that Synvadis patronised her because he was jealous of the influence she had over Marcus's education. For his part, Synvadis was supposed to resent Asperia's insinuation that he meddled in areas that didn't strictly concern him.

But, in spite of their differences, Marcus had always sensed a respect, albeit grudging, between them. This was the first time he'd ever seen them openly hostile.

'I'm sorry, what was that?' Synvadis demanded.

'Oh, nothing,' replied Asperia. 'I just have a slight cough.'

'You should take care. With the change of the seasons the smallest cough can become dangerous.'

'Oh, rest assured I take many precautions.'

As Marcus continued to watch, mesmerised, they nodded meaningfully at one another. Then Synvadis, with a deep bow, which seemed insolent for some reason, swept out of the room. Asperia continued to frown at the door for some time after he exited it.

'*Pirõnchyé!*' said Marcus loudly.

'Hmm?'

'That was twenty times. Didn't you hear?'

'Oh . . . yes, of course,' she said, finding her place. 'All right, since languages don't seem to be grabbing your attention, we'll move onto nephology, since you always seem to enjoy the study of clouds so much. Now where were we last time? . . . Ah yes, thermostrati. These are small, funnel-shaped clouds. They're barely noticeable, even to an experienced nephologist, but they're thought to be one of the sources of clear air turbulence.'

'Of what?'

'This is when, in spite of apparently peaceful conditions, a sudden discord in the middle air can knock you completely off course.'

Fascinated, Marcus settled down to listen, his earlier restlessness forgotten.

The tutorial continued until lunchtime, punctuated towards the end by forlorn rumbles from Marcus's empty stomach. Asperia pretended not to hear them. She also ignored the fact that his eyes kept straying back to the restless curtains, which peeled apart every now and then to offer a tantalising glimpse of the azure horizon.

For all their clashes, Marcus knew that much of Asperia's sternness was an act. When Queen Maeterina died in childbirth, the king was at first too overwhelmed by grief to look upon his first-born. This flushed, squalling scrap of humanity was at once the focus of all his love, but also the cause of his beloved wife's death. It took months of cloistered solitude before he could reconcile these facts. When at last he emerged from mourning, he decided that what Marcus needed was a steady female influence in his life. Her principal role would be to educate him, but also to take the place – in some respects at least – of his mother. He considered a range of possible candidates and eventually chose Asperia. She was a female Academician. Childless, in her fifties, she lived alone in a small apartment on the lower floors of the palace. Her area of research, to which she had devoted her life, was the social history of Heliopolis. There were other scholars whose eminence far exceeded hers. But Antior sensed that Asperia would be more conscientious and, in her own somewhat flinty way, more nurturing than any other. Overruling certain disgruntled ministers – who had sponsored different candidates – he not only appointed her, but offered her a free hand with Marcus's education.

So Asperia, though desperately fond of Marcus, was also deeply sensible of her duty towards him. She wanted him to become the best-informed monarch Heliopolis had ever possessed: concerned about his people's welfare, while also accepting of the citadel's traditions. But she knew that his mind was like one of the vivid butterflies that filled the air in the palace garden – restlessly flitting from one thing to the next and never settling anywhere for long. It was because of this that she pushed him so hard.

During the tutorial's final minutes Marcus sat hunched over a written test to demonstrate how much he had remembered. As he completed it there was the sound of a commotion from outside. The door burst open and a steward raced in. Sliding to a halt on the polished floor, he almost collided with the table. Marcus and Asperia gazed up at him in astonishment.

'What is the meaning of this?' snapped Asperia.

Florid faced, the steward placed one hand on the edge of the table and bent over, panting. He did this, Marcus suspected, just a little longer than was strictly necessary, to avoid delivering unpleasant news. As he waited for the man to speak he felt drenched in panic.

'I am sorry, madam,' the steward gasped, 'but we've just received a very faint signal from the *Regulus*. It seems to be in trouble . . . *serious* trouble . . .'

III

The *Regulus*

Asperia immediately departed with the steward to discover more about what was happening. Ignoring Marcus's strenuous protests, she told him to stay where he was. He spent the next hour fuming and pacing around the drawing room. During the few moments he wasn't fuming and pacing around the drawing room he was fuming and pacing around the balcony instead.

A mixture of dread and anxiety writhed within him. He couldn't believe this was happening. From the moment he'd first grown conscious of the world he lived in, as a small child, it had been dominated by three people. On a daily basis he saw Asperia, who taught him history, meteorology, languages and nephology. Several times a week he sparred with Titus and a group of specially selected Praesidion guards, adoring the exertion and freedom of their sessions together, after hours shut in tutorials. Then, last thing every night, his father came and sat on his bed, often looking tired and preoccupied, to hear about what he had learned that day. These three people aside, it was a fairly solitary upbringing. Although his father could spend little time with him – immersed as he was in affairs of state – Marcus always felt loved, always felt the warmth of his concern. He could even summon up the feeling from memory when they were thousands of miles apart. Now it threatened to fade, replaced by an encroaching coldness. The walls and floor around him, though unchanged, looked somehow more insubstantial already.

These thoughts were interrupted by the arrival of Anan, a young steward, his arms piled high with freshly laundered bedding. He looked serious (everyone who entered Marcus's apartments looked as if they had paused before entering to assume the gravest possible expression), but untroubled. He clearly hadn't heard the news about the *Regulus*.

'Apologies for the interruption, Your Highness,' he said, eyes lowered as he headed for the bedroom.

'No, no, it's fine,' Marcus assured him. He smiled, eager for some company to distract him from his anxieties. 'How are you, Anan?'

Anan paused and turned back towards Marcus. He frowned, at a loss what to say.

Marcus sighed. He tried as hard as he could to get on with the palace's innumerable guards, maids, stewards and seneschals. But it wasn't easy. He had long since noticed that most people behaved strangely in his and his father's presence. They grew very self-conscious, concentrating mainly on avoiding eye contact and the use of apostrophes. Asked how they were, they would reply, 'I am well. It is most kind of you to enquire,' while staring at their feet. On the other hand, many of the more senior servants appeared to have a far greater sense of their own importance than Marcus did of his. Any attempt at friendliness with them was sternly discouraged, as if it were an affront to *their* dignity.

'I am well. It is most . . .' Anan began, staring at his feet.

'No, Anan,' Marcus said gently, 'I really am asking you how you are.'

Hugging the bed linen to him, Anan said, 'I, uh . . . I have recently changed my shift pattern. I'm doing more late shifts. So that always takes a while to adjust to . . . and it's a little tiring. Also, I see my family less now. Um . . . how are you, Your Highness?'

Marcus yearned to confess his fears. But he knew that until the fate of the *Regulus* was confirmed it would be deemed inappropriate for him to discuss them with a junior steward. None the less, just to have Anan's company and to be able to speak to him about anything was a comfort. It allowed him to ignore the dread that he felt stealing upon him, seeking out all his hope and happiness with deadly intent.

'Oh, all right – spending every day learning things I'll probably never need to know and rehearsing for battles I'll never be in.' He paused then added, with a self-deprecating laugh, 'You know, the usual.'

Anan nodded, smiling just a little.

'I suppose it must sometimes feel like a great burden so early in life . . . preparing for the throne, I mean,' he ventured. His tone rose questioningly at the end, betraying amazement at his own daring in saying this.

'Well, there certainly doesn't seem to be any time off from it,' replied Marcus. 'Often I wonder what it would be like to be free, with nothing to do, just for a day . . . I can't imagine it really.'

'Yes, when I was your age I lived in a tiny apartment in the lowest floor of the palace with my parents and three brothers and sisters. I would have loved to have all this space to myself. But on the other hand, my friends and I were pretty much free to do what we wanted. No one was bothered what we got up to because no one expected much of us.'

Marcus gestured for Anan to sit down.

'I envy you,' he said. 'Not just your freedom but the friends you had. You know, when I was younger Asperia used to organise "play" for me with some of the ministers' children.'

'Really?' asked Anan, surprised.

'Yes, but it wasn't much of a success. I mean, after all, "play" can't really be organised, can it? Least of all by adults. During every game the other children kept away from me as much as they could. I think they'd been ordered to do it because their parents were terrified of what might happen if any of them injured the king's son.'

Anan smoothed down the bed linen that now covered his lap.

'Well,' he replied, 'it's not really my place to say . . .'

'No, go on,' Marcus urged him.

'When you're young maybe you need to get into scrapes. Maybe you have to realise that it's okay to make mistakes as long as you learn from them. And I suppose it's easier to do that if you're not important.'

Marcus nodded.

'Any time I push to do something Asperia doesn't want me to do and maybe it turns out to be wrong, she always says, "There you are, you see, *you* insisted on that and see what's happened now" – I mean, I know she means well, but it's almost as if she's triumphant or something when I make a mistake.'

Anan considered this.

'Hmm, I often think . . .' he began.

Just then, unnoticed by either of them, a more senior steward – Curtus – entered. Seeing Anan sitting talking to Marcus, he did a convincing impression of a man who had just been shot in the forehead by an invisible crossbow bolt. His eyes widened and his head jerked back. He even staggered slightly.

'Anan!' he exclaimed. 'How dare you sit in His Majesty's presence. Have you no idea of decorum?'

Anan leaped up, crimson faced. He scurried into the bedroom with the laundry, emerged seconds later without it and scurried out of the drawing room, bowing and mumbling apologies all the while.

'No, it's all right really,' protested Marcus. 'We were just talking about . . .'

Before he could go any further, Curtus, turning to him, said, 'I'm terribly sorry, Your Highness.'

'But it's . . .'

'I don't know what the man could have been thinking of.'

'No, really . . .'

'I'll ensure he is properly reprimanded.'

'No, don't, it's . . .'

But Curtus was apologising so rapidly and strenuously that he didn't hear a word Marcus said. He continued to utter an uninterrupted stream of apologies as he backed out of the door. And, as always, Marcus was left to nurse his fears in silence and in solitude.

When Asperia returned at last he unleashed a salvo of questions at her. She made no attempt to answer them; nor did she tell him to calm down. Instead she clasped him in a brief, tight embrace. This surprised him so much that he too lapsed into silence as she led him across to the sofa and sat beside him, holding his hand. She looked at him with a smile that wasn't really a smile at all, her gaze wandering over the contours of his face as if she were seeing it for the first time.

'So . . . what's wrong?' he asked.

'The message was very faint, very hard to make out, but it seemed to suggest that the *Regulus* was venting gas and sinking into the cloudscape.'

'Does anyone know how it could have got into such trouble?'

'Not really. It could have been a tumult, but the vessel's lookouts should have been able to spot one long before it happened. It could have been steropys, but they're usually associated with tumults. Then again it might be some other phenomenon that we've never encountered before . . . though that seems unlikely.'

'How soon before a rescue mission can be launched?'

'I don't know. Synvadis doesn't seem keen. He feels that any mission launched so late in the season – when the cloudscape is already turbid – would be doomed to failure.'

'If the *Regulus* doesn't reappear, does that mean that Synvadis will become Regent?'

Asperia nodded.

'Until you come of age he will have absolute power over Heliopolis and all its citizens. After that . . .'

She trailed off. Marcus could tell she was troubled by the same question as he, though neither of them wanted to admit it yet. In spite of all the justifiable reasons not to stage a rescue mission, was Synvadis reluctant because he wouldn't want to give up power again if the king *were* found? And when Marcus finally came of age would Synvadis, with his love of influence, be willing to step aside as regent?

'But surely if there's even the slightest chance that the *Regulus* could have survived . . .' he said.

'I know, I know. But remember we have no idea what – if anything – lies in the cloud depths. I mean, all sorts of experiments have been done in the past, lowering nephologists from aëro:cruisers to measure the clouds' composition. But we didn't have the capacity to send them down more than a league or so. And at least the scientists lowered from aëro:cruisers have come back. Anyone who has ever tried to climb down into the clouds from the edge of the fields has never been seen again.'

Marcus nodded, tears of frustration glazing his eyes. The cloud depths were an abiding mystery to all those who lived above them and many different myths had sprung up to account for the existence of their world. The most famous told how, before the beginning of time, there had been only a chaos of cloud. Omnium, a magical being who inhabited this formless region, grew bored and gathered the clouds in certain places. With his incredible strength he pushed them together until they became massy and rough. Having created these islands of solidity and fertility that floated in the sea of cloud, he placed living creatures on top of them. Though Heliopolis still held public holidays in celebration of Omnium and worshipped him in its chapels, only the most aged citizens clung to such beliefs.

None the less, cloud dwellers throughout the hemisphere had no more scientific way of explaining their world. Most modern theories in Heliopolis proposed that the citadel and its surrounding fields sat on rock that stretched down into the clouds. Though these ideas were widely accepted, no geologist knew how far the rock stretched or what, if anything, lay below. To add to the mystery, not every citadel in the hemisphere was built on a single peak, like Heliopolis. Some sat on a much greater mass of land that swelled into several precipitous peaks and nestled in the valleys between them. Others clung to the edge of craters that brimmed with freshwater lakes called calderas. The lakes had rocky shores, while the craters' slopes were smothered in lush vegetation. They often reared out of the clouds in clusters, with rope bridges slung between them, connecting several citadels.

In spite of all this, Marcus knew that if the *Regulus* really had sunk into the cloud depths the chances of finding it again were almost non-existent. He covered his face with his hands then drew them slowly down it, hollow-eyed with worry. He had no memory of his mother. And now the image of his father, after so extended an absence, was already growing slightly less clear.

'I can't have lost him too, Asperia . . . I just can't,' he said.

She drew him closer and put her arm around him.

'I know, Marcus – it's so unfair. I can't think of any words of consolation to offer you. All I can say is that at least he was doing something valuable for the security of his people.'

'What do you mean? Why did he have to be away so long?'

Asperia hesitated fractionally.

'The Hemispheric Wars,' she said.

'But I thought we *won* the Hemispheric Wars,' Marcus replied. 'I mean, I don't know that much about it because everyone always seems so reluctant to talk about that time. But I don't see how something that happened so long ago would keep him away so much.'

'All right,' she said, sighing. 'Let me explain . . . Before you were born a group of citadels to the north of us – including Scythium and néo-Sirus – tried to seize control of the best trading routes in the hemisphere. By "best" I mean the ones where the air currents move most swiftly, so aëro:cruisers can travel fastest when already laden with goods. There are only a few of these routes and they circle the hemisphere in bands, usually running westerly. Anyway, the northern citadels intended to tax these routes, making other citadels pay to use them. Of course this was in violation of every treaty. As you're aware, no citadel has ever been allowed to control more than a few hundred miles of the airspace around it, strictly in the interests of security.'

'So what happened?'

'Well, we formed an alliance with our closest neighbours to fight off this aggression, but it wasn't easy. Many of the northern citadels have militarised economies.'

'They have *what*?'

'They pour all their wealth into building huge fleets of aëro:cruisers – though I've heard that, as a result, living conditions for any citizen who doesn't work in the Cloudfaring Corps are terrible. Anyway, for five years battles raged all over the cloudscape. Many aëro:cruisers on both sides were lost in the cloud depths with all hands. But eventually we prevailed. Selenopolis in particular was a strong ally. And of course our forces were led by Titus. Many feel it was his tactical genius that ultimately won the war for us. I have heard that he and his officers wanted to guarantee our security by occupying the northern citadels and changing their regimes. But your father, rightly I think, felt that a more secure peace could be achieved by improving relations with them and helping them to rebuild – on non-military lines, of course. So that's why he has had to spend much of his time in recent years on diplomatic tours. But I swear to you, it wasn't his choice to be away so much, or to miss so much of your growing up.'

Marcus guessed that one day he might find some consolation in all this, but at the moment he could see none. His head nodded. A surfeit of tiredness, which until now he'd held at bay, washed over him.

'Come on,' said Asperia, coaxing him to his feet. 'It's been a terrible day for all of us – you more than anyone. You need rest. We'll talk again tomorrow. Now get ready for bed and I'll send the physician along to give you something that'll help you sleep.'

Too enfeebled by worry to protest any more, Marcus stumbled towards his bedroom. Asperia began to gather up the books and papers still strewn across the table, abandoned when she had hurried out after the steward. He paused at the door.

'Asperia?'

'What?'

'I'm not ready for all this.'

She smiled sadly.

'I know, dear. But don't worry ... I have faith in you.'

In spite of the physician's best efforts, Marcus woke in the small hours from a nightmare. In it he had been standing somewhere he had never stood in real life: at the base of the citadel. Below him lay the fields and orchards. Though there was no wind blowing, the clouds raced from the east, surging up in certain places, as if trying to vault one another. Standing with his back against the wall of the Farmers' layer, Marcus felt it press against him. He looked round, alarmed. Cracks bloomed all across its curving surface, hastening to meet one another. With a sense of impotent panic, he realised that the whole citadel was starting to slide down towards the fields and orchards. It gathered speed, felling trees in its path, then broke apart. Mouth wide open, lungs aching, but unable to emit any sound, he was swept down with it, tumbling into the churning void.

He woke with the sickening sensation of having plunged on to his bed from an immense height. Woozy from the sleeping draught, but certain that he would be unable to get back to sleep, he rose, put on his robe and wandered through to the drawing room. It was warm, thanks to the central heating system, which circulated warm air through flues that ran beneath the floor and up the walls. Opening the shutters that covered the archway at night, he slipped out on to the balcony. In stark contrast to the way it had appeared in his dream, the cloudscape was barely moving. Its peaks were silvered by the moon, which shone so strongly that night seemed almost as bright as day – just grainier and less colourful.

Marcus shivered and drew his robe more tightly round him. Out on the balcony the floor was not heated. He felt the chill of the coming winter and of other things, also unsought, also unavoidable. Still he struggled to comprehend what had happened. But, after the initial

45

shock and pain, he felt a new emotion stirring within him. If he was to assume greater responsibilities; if he was to try and counter Synvadis's growing influence; if he was to bid farewell to the few carefree moments that his life still offered – if he was to do all these things, he first had to know for sure that his father was lost. Merely assuming the worst was not good enough.

I have to do it! he thought, startled by the rush of determination he felt. *I have to search for the* Regulus *myself. I have to see where it foundered.*

Warmed by his resolve, he stayed out on the balcony until dawn and watched the orange glow of the rising sun steal across the cloudscape.

IV

The survivor

'His Serene Highness, Prince Marcus!'

Usually, when he heard these words uttered in so portentous a voice, Marcus couldn't help looking around for the much taller, more assured person they must actually refer to. This time, however, he just flinched a little then stepped towards the long cabinet table. It was rectangular and made of marble, with carved end slabs to support its great weight. He bowed to the senior ministers, who were assembled along either side. Then he bowed to Synvadis, who stood at the other end, a curtained balcony behind him.

The cabinet chamber was one of the largest rooms in the palace. Octagonal stained-glass windows were ranged around the top of the walls. Paintings crammed the space below them: portraits of former monarchs and prime ministers. Depending on the season and time of day, the beams of coloured light from the window fell upon a different selection of solemn, venerable faces. Motes of dust swirled in the coloured beams too, shining as if ablaze – here a firestorm of purple, there one of green.

With sighs and grunts, some better concealed than others, the senior ministers sat down and prepared to listen. Synvadis had assumed a melancholy expression, suggesting bravely borne grief at the king's fate. But his posture – shoulders back, head held high – betrayed his excitement at his key role in so important a gathering. He began to unroll the parchment that lay on the table before him. This took a dispiritingly long time. Eventually the parchment spilled over the edge of the table and the curled edge of it bobbed just above the floor.

Meanwhile, less important members of the executive jostled around the fringes of the room. Heads bobbing, they tried to get a better view of what was happening at the cabinet table and muttered apologies, tinged with irritation, as they trod on one another's toes in the process. Asperia was amongst those closest to the front, arms folded, wearing the 'not terribly impressed' look that she had refined through years of practice. Titus stood beside her, watchful as ever, offering the occasional whispered observation, at which she nodded. Even the sentries, who were supposed to be facing out of the room, couldn't help risking a reproof by peering in over their shoulders.

The atmosphere was taut with expectation. Rumours that the king was missing – possibly lost in the depthless cloudscape – had already started to percolate throughout the citadel. The arrival and departure of airships was so visible that the failure of a vessel as distinctive as the *Regulus* to reappear couldn't help but be noticed. Indeed, one of the few times that the Farmers paused in their work was when an immense shadow rippled across the fields, prompting them to look up, mopping their brows, at the hull of an airship passing overhead. Now reports were being received that they and the Artisans had assembled on their respective parts of the great spiral staircase that connected all the layers. Apparently they were pleading with the guards above to be told what was happening. There was a growing fear that if a statement wasn't issued soon they might break with all convention and surge upwards towards the palace, in search of answers.

In some respects Marcus wished they would. At least it might distract all the other people in the room from the fact that he looked as if he were wearing the lightly embroidered shroud of a parasail. His ceremonial robes had not been tailored for him: they were an heirloom, intended to be worn by the prince when he reached adulthood and began to attend official functions. He plucked nervously at them, but only succeeded in getting more lost within their folds.

How was he going to persuade the senior ministers that he had enough stature to take part in such a discussion, he wondered despairingly, when his attire made him look as if he were shrinking with every passing second?

'This meeting of the senior cabinet,' announced Synvadis, in his most sonorous tone, 'has been convened to discuss the safe governance of Heliopolis after the terrible events of the past few days. As is our custom, we shall deal with the implications arising from these events in strict order.'

He consulted the parchment, holding it as far from him as possible, since he was too vain to wear spectacles on so public an occasion.

'Item one . . .' he began.

Having already seen a copy of the agenda, Marcus knew that item one was some footling piece of nonsense inviting the minister of aëronautics to deliver a long and tedious report, complete with schematics, about how the *Regulus* might have suffered a fatal engineering failure which caused it to crash into the cloud depths.

'Item one,' Marcus interrupted, his voice quavering but loud. 'A glorious mission into the cloud depths in search of the king.'

First there were gasps. Then there was a soft rasping noise – the sound of fifty pairs of sandals being shuffled in embarrassment on a marble floor. Along either side of the cabinet table the senior ministers exchanged speculative looks. Long experience of working their way up through the tiers of the executive had taught them that when dealing with the crazy notions of superiors it was better to say nothing that might be held against you later.

'Um . . .' said the minister of security.

'Er . . .' said the minister of agriculture.

The minister of trade was the most politic. He said, 'Well . . .' in so neutral a tone that it might equally have been the beginning of 'Well, I think that's a brilliant idea' or 'Well, I think that's the stupidest thing I've ever heard.' Since he went no further it was impossible to tell.

The only person at the table whose features bore any trace of an honest reaction was Synvadis. And though he was stroking his moustache with thumb and forefinger in a self-consciously thoughtful way, he looked less outraged than Marcus might have expected.

'Your Highness,' he said, once the hubbub had subsided, 'you do realise that many people in Heliopolis – particularly our older citizens – still regard the cloud depths as the realm of Omnium?'

'Yes.'

'You must also be aware that those of us who no longer believe in the ancient myths of creation still accept that the region below the cloudscape is perilous and unnavigable. It is the source of turbulence; it is where electrical storms originate.'

'Yes.'

'So, accepting all of this, you must see that the mission you propose would be regarded at the very worst as blasphemous and at best as foolhardy.'

'Yes, I do see that.'

'Why then do you propose it?'

'Because I must . . . I will not, I *cannot* rest if I have to live with the knowledge that I didn't do everything in my power to know for sure whether or not my father is still alive.'

'Bravo!' said Titus. Several other onlookers applauded, making Marcus blush.

Synvadis sighed and gazed down at the cabinet table for a few moments. Then he said, 'Minister of aëronautics, would such a mission be possible?'

The minister of aëronautics – Flegmatos – rose slowly to his feet. He was much chubbier than Synvadis. But in all other respects, like the rest of the senior ministers, he resembled nothing so much as an inferior copy of him. He had assiduously cultivated the same moustache but couldn't make it curl quite so tightly. His hair was smoothed back with oil, but lacked the same lustrous sheen. A beam of green light fell on his frowning face, making him look not only unhappy, but also slightly queasy at being drawn into a discussion fraught with so many potential pitfalls. He cleared his throat.

'Given that we know its average cruising speed, we could . . . we could calculate roughly the circumference of the area where it must have gone down,' he began hesitantly. 'Having established *that*, we could take a couple of aëro:cruisers to the area's epicentre. The question then is how to search.' He pinched as many of his chins as he could gather between thumb and forefinger. 'The best thing might be to winch down some kind of cage, using the mechanism with which we normally tow returning aëro:cruisers on to the landing stage. Recently we've been doing some research into ways of penetrating further into the cloud depths. We've designed special insulating clothing for the cold and we might be able to use air pipes to protect against the change in pressure. With any luck we could perhaps lower someone more than two leagues. Of course they would need telescopes to look around once they're that far into the cloud depths. Always assuming there is anything down there, which I gravely doubt . . .'

He pondered it a little longer.

'Yes, it may *just* be possible. But very dangerous. And far from advisable.'

Synvadis nodded.

'Thank you, minister.'

'I'm not saying it won't be dangerous,' conceded Marcus. 'But the sooner we do this the greater the chance that we might find my father still alive. The cloudscape is still fairly calm at the moment. But it can't be long before the winter storms begin.'

'Were I to accept that a mission should be attempted – and I'm not saying that I do – which citizen of the Polis could we ask to lead so dangerous a mission?' asked Synvadis.

Marcus hesitated, steeling himself to convey all the cool certainty that he didn't really feel.

'*I* will lead it.'

A murmur of astonished excitement rippled out-wards from the cabinet table. Synvadis looked appalled.

'That I can never allow.'

'I should think not!' put in Asperia.

'But . . .'

'I cannot allow you to imperil yourself,' continued Synvadis. 'You are all that the citizenry has to look to now that the king is . . . absent. Monarchy is essential for the citadel's stability.'

Trying not to flinch from Synvadis's level gaze, Marcus wondered what disturbed the prime minister more: the prospect of losing the heir as well as the monarch (and all the upheaval that would entail) or the prospect of the prince slipping beyond his grasp. Whatever the answer, he sensed that the argument was slipping away from him.

'Is it not true,' he said, pushing his sleeves up yet again, 'that every prince of Heliopolis must, as he approaches adulthood, accomplish some daring feat to demonstrate that he's willing to devote the rest of his life to the responsibilities of kingship?'

'Indeed, but . . .'

'The Prince's Test is purely ceremonial,' interrupted Asperia, stepping forward. 'It is not supposed to involve any real danger. As I recall, your own father's test involved scaling the palace walls attached to at least three ropes, with several sentinels below to catch him if he fell.'

'Yes, thank you, Asperia,' replied Marcus. He wasn't sure if it was such a good idea to let this story get around. Looking back at Synvadis, he said, 'None the less, I *will* go.'

'No.'

'In my father's absence I am the supreme power in the Polis. I *demand* to go.'

'Your Highness, in the king's absence *I* am the supreme power in the Polis. The constitution states clearly that until you come of age it is my duty to run the citadel as I see fit and I forbid this.'

Marcus glared at Synvadis. One could almost see their opposing wills wrestling in the air between them. Titus stepped forwards and in a quiet, measured tone said, 'Prime minister, I agree with you that the prince must not be allowed to venture into the cloud depths himself.

But he must at least be present when the attempt is made. Whatever the outcome may be, it is the only thing that can set his mind at rest, as he says. I, of course, volunteer to go with him and ensure his safety.'

Titus smiled encouragingly at Marcus, who felt a surge of gratitude towards him. It was as if the general, in his tone and posture, embodied all the calm certainty that he himself had struggled to convey. Synvadis, however, looked not only offended by the general's intervention, but disdainful.

'Given that your own Cloudfaring Corps has manifestly failed to protect the king on his homeward journey,' he retorted, 'I wouldn't have thought you were in any position to offer self-serving homilies about the safety of the prince.'

Marcus was not the only person in the room to wince at this. Titus reddened, but refused to be provoked. Asperia, however, could contain herself no longer.

'Whatever lapses may have occurred, Synvadis, one needn't look too far to see who would have most to gain if a mission in search of the king were not even attempted!' she exclaimed, throwing off the restraining hand that Titus had placed on her arm.

There was a collective gasp. Asperia had just given voice to the one great unmentionable topic of the moment – everyone present dwelt in its shadow but refused to acknowledge it.

Synvadis, eyes ablaze with indignation, said, 'How dare you, madam! Do you really mean to suggest that I have . . .'

Just then they were all distracted by a strange phenomenon. The light from the windows along one side of the room flickered briefly, as if something very swift were passing close to them. A few moments later the same happened on the other side of the room. Along with Marcus, Asperia and the others, Synvadis gawped upwards. Only Titus, grim faced, had the presence of mind to stride towards the curtains, wrench them aside and peer out on to the balcony.

'What is it?' asked Marcus.

'An ornithopter,' reported Titus. 'It seems to be in trouble. And it has the crest of the *Regulus* on its wings!'

'Here he comes again,' shouted Marcus, shading his eyes and pointing up at the sky.

He, Synvadis, Asperia, Titus and assorted ministers and deckhands were standing on the apron of the landing platform in the Cloudfarers' layer. The layer's smoothly curving walls reared up on either side of them. In the walls' crisply etched shadows it was distinctly chilly, but as they all gazed upwards the sun still felt hot on their faces. From where they stood they could see nothing of the rest of the citadel – the landing stage seemed to jut out right over the cloudscape. On the left-hand side of it lay a long rail, with a sturdy, spring-loaded mechanism at the rear of it, used to launch ornithopters. Marcus had no time to savour his first chance to visit the most intriguing section of Heliopolis. Right now his and everyone else's attention was focused on the ornithopter that swooped above them.

It was a flimsy contraption. The pilot lay on his

stomach inside a rectangular cage made of lightweight materials. The area around his head was open, allowing him to see out. The ornithopter's wings consisted of wooden frames covered in hand-sewn fabric. With his hands the pilot operated a system of pulleys, which made the wings beat. At the rear of the cage were two pedals. These allowed him also to move the ornithopter's rudder with his feet. Only the *Regulus* contained such escape ornithopters, jettisoned in times of extreme danger.

But this ornithopter's wings weren't moving at all. Frail against the great span of cobalt blue sky, it was simply gliding, buffeted one way and the other by conflicting air currents. As it circled the palace it pitched and yawed wildly. Once it almost crashed into a turret. Frequently it swept low across the trees in the Hortoreum, raking the foliage. Sentinels on the battlements ducked as it shot past.

It came round again, lower this time, and narrowly avoided striking the lip of the landing stage. Marcus saw that the pilot's head was lolling.

'The man's injured,' he whispered to Titus.

Titus nodded, his keen grey eyes following the ornithopter.

'Does it really have the royal crest on its wings?' asked Synvadis.

'I can't see,' said Titus.

'This is it!' shouted one of the deckhands who had emerged on to the apron of the platform. 'Back everyone!'

Other deckhands appeared from the hangar. They hastened over to either side of the platform. Members of each group, crouching to grasp the stubby handle of a winch, hoisted up a net that stretched all the way across the platform. Marcus, Synvadis, Asperia and the ministers retreated inside the hangar. Titus strode forwards to help with the net. The deckhands allowed it to sag slightly – if it were too taut it might catapult the ornithopter back over the edge.

From the hangar's shadowed interior Marcus could see the ornithopter coming round again, in tighter and tighter spirals, perilously close to the city walls. At last it plunged into the net. The deckhands instantly slackened it even more. Growing quickly entangled, the ornithopter tumbled sideways, scattering people before it, then slammed into the side wall. Its wings sheared off and the cage containing the pilot crumpled.

Immediately deckhands rushed over to the wreck. They cut through the net, slid the fitfully convulsing pilot out of the ornithopter and gently laid him on the stretcher. Marcus and the others hurried over too.

The pilot had suffered severe cuts and bruises in the crash. Indeed, his right arm, held up to protect his face, wore a gauntlet of blood. Even more ominously, his lips were encrusted with scabs where they had cracked. When one of the deckhands tried to pour some water into his mouth he could barely part them. His gaze was almost opaque, yet it roved restlessly over everything around him. He convulsed again, racked by a muscular contraction. Marcus got the impression that he was clinging on to life until he could impart his news.

'It's Naulix,' whispered Titus, appearing at Marcus's side. He looked deeply shaken by the man's condition. 'He was one of your father's personal bodyguards on the *Regulus*.'

'Naulix, can you hear me?' Marcus asked.

Naulix's eyes focused with difficulty on Marcus's anxious face. He raised a trembling hand and beckoned him to come closer. Marcus couldn't help noticing that Synvadis, Asperia and Titus also leaned in unbidden, eager to hear what the man had to say.

'What happened?' asked Marcus.

'We were returning from Selenopolis,' croaked Naulix.

'Yes?'

'All was well . . . there was some bad weather ahead, but nothing too dangerous . . . was woken early in the morning by shouts and screams . . . the *Regulus* was on fire . . . its air sacs had torn . . . it was sinking . . .'

'That's impossible!' said Titus. 'The *Regulus* has eight separate air sacs. Even if six are punctured it can still fly with only two.'

'What happened next, Naulix?' asked Marcus.

'I got on deck . . . there was smoke pouring from the hold and we were already in the clouds . . . there was nothing but white around us . . . people were shouting . . . I and others got the king to the ornithopters . . . we jettisoned from the *Regulus* . . . we couldn't see a thing . . . some of the ornithopters collided with one another

. . . we kept on spinning downwards . . . we seemed to sink for ever . . . but then I caught a thermal and began to rise again . . .'

'And the king's ornithopter?' asked Titus.

'I don't know . . . the last thing I saw was the *Regulus* falling away from me . . . it was on fire . . . people were jumping off it on fire, screaming . . . it was falling towards . . .'

'Towards what? *What*?'

Naulix coughed and his breathing became more laboured. He seemed to be chasing every breath. With one last great effort he gripped Marcus's arm and his eyes, which had been growing duller all the time, shone with a sudden desperate clarity.

'There is another world!' he said.

V

The *Noble Quest*

Some hours later, on the evening of the same day,
Marcus stood again on the landing platform, but the
scene around him was very different. The crushed and
buckled wreckage of the ornithopter had been cleared
away. Two aëro:cruisers were being prepared for launch.
They were well over a hundred feet long and a moder-
ately lean forty feet wide amidships. They bristled with
cannons, the squat barrels protruding from square slots
ranged along their hulls. Each aëro:cruiser had a raised
bridge at its prow and a squat tower – the aft'castle – at
its stern, which contained the crew's quarters. Floating
just above the landing stage, they looked ponderous and
weightless at the same time. Their clustered air sacs were
rigid, attached to the deck by rigging and by two thick-
er ropes, called lanyards, fore and aft. In honour of their
forthcoming journey, they had been renamed the *Noble
Quest* and the *Valorous Mission*. Gangplanks led up to
their decks.

The *Noble Quest*, aboard which Marcus would be
travelling, lay closest to him. At its stern deckhands
attended to the impellers. While the air sacs lent the

vessel its buoyancy, the impellers provided its thrust. They looked like two wide metal tubes that were embedded into each side of the hull and ran the length of it. If you gazed into the mouth of one of them, it looked hollow. In fact, its shadowed interior bristled with innumerable sets of variously angled blades.

In the bowels of the aëro:cruiser there were two rows of work stations, with an iron catwalk running between them. Each work station had a sturdy handle – called a circumvolver – protruding from the wall beside it. This circumvolver was connected to a crank-shaft that moved the blades within the impellers. The men who occupied these work stations were called Impellerators. When they turned all the circumvolvers in unison the blades began to spin. By this method – sucking air into the front of the impellers, hastening it along, compressing it, then forcing it out at the stern, where much larger, corkscrew-shaped blades gave it a final boost – aëro:cruisers could reach speeds of up to eighty knots.

Other deckhands stood on a wheeled platform beneath *Noble Quest*'s hull and lifted ammunition and other supplies through a hatch into the bowels of the hold. Occasionally the air was filled with a sonorous roar, as the crew tested one of the caged burners ranged along the centre of its deck. Each time an extra blast of heated gas surged into its air sacs, the aëro:cruiser's already taut mooring lines creaked with the strain of holding it down.

★

Naulix had died soon after sharing his revelation. His body had been taken down to the Farmers' layer where his family lived. Arrangements were already in place to give him an honorary state funeral in recognition of the trials he had endured to bring such important news back to the citadel. The Admins were busy writing and copying his obituary – called a necrologue – for circulation throughout the citadel.

The Heliopolitans cast their dead over the side into the clouds at night, the body wrapped in a burial shroud, after a torchlit procession through the fields. Usually only immediate family members attended the funeral. (It was more or less the sole occasion when citizens from other layers descended to the fields.) But, in Naulix's case, the whole citizenry would assemble on the walls, to sing and pay their respects.

Once Naulix had been taken to his family, Marcus, Synvadis, Titus and the senior ministers had another, much less formal cabinet meeting inside the hangar at the rear of the landing stage. Astonished as everyone else by Naulix's story, Synvadis reluctantly conceded that a search mission, no matter how perilous, had to be attempted. But he remained firm in his opposition to Marcus going on it. And the harder Marcus tried to persuade him otherwise, the firmer he became, assuming all the stubbornness and pomposity of dictatorship that Marcus most feared in him.

Temporarily defeated, Marcus retired, despondent, into the shadowy recesses of the hangar. From here he continued to watch Titus arguing with the prime minister on his behalf. The two men paced back and forth, gesturing angrily to one another, their silhouetted figures framed by the hangar's open door. Gradually Titus wore Synvadis down. Marcus heard Synvadis say, 'For his people's sake I cannot allow him to go.' To which Titus replied, 'I believe it is for his people's sake that he wishes to go.' Finally Synvadis relented, albeit with ill grace, and stalked away to the cabinet chamber, a gaggle of ministers at his heels. Marcus resolved not to fret about the plans he might be hatching there, to put into practice in his and Titus's absence. Such problems would have to wait until he returned.

In the hours since the decision had been made to go ahead with the mission the weather had deteriorated. The wind blew fiercer and colder. The flags on the palace turrets snapped against their poles. The trees in the orchards threshed and jostled. Burnished autumn leaves, torn from them, spun through the air.

The wind had wrought a change in the face of the cloudscape too. No longer merely swollen, the clouds were now churned and ragged, those on the topmost layer rolling in from the north-east. If you stood and gazed at them long enough, Marcus noticed, you got the impression that they were stationary and Heliopolis was ploughing inexorably through them.

'Quite a sight, isn't it?' said Titus, approaching across the apron, hands clasped behind his back. 'You never really get used to it.'

'Yes. I've dreamed of this day for so long. But I can't

really imagine what it'll be like.'

'Nervous?'

'A little, I suppose.'

'Don't worry, it's perfectly natural. Just remember that your father would be very proud of you.'

Marcus smiled, touched.

'What do you think our chances are . . . honestly?'

'Honestly? I have no idea. We're doing something that has never been attempted before. And we're doing it in far from perfect conditions. We'll simply have to trust to the skill of our crew . . . and hope for the best.'

'Well . . . I'm very glad you're with me anyway.'

Titus put an arm around him and squeezed his shoulder.

'So am I, Marcus. So am I.'

They lapsed into silence for a while, both gazing out over the cloudscape. Presently a tall young woman appeared and handed the general a wooden clipboard. The parchment clipped to it was covered in calculations.

'All the required ordnance has been loaded aboard both vessels, sir,' she said.

Though attractive, with an abundance of thick, dark hair neatly tied back, she had strong features, the planes of her face lending her an air of quiet determination.

Gesturing to her, Titus said, 'Your Highness, may I present my second-in-command on our voyage, Lieutenant Rhea.'

Rhea bowed.

'An honour.'

'Thank you,' replied Marcus, always uncomfortable with this kind of obeisance, even though he was well used to it. 'Is, uh . . . everything prepared for our departure?'

'Almost. In fact there are a few final tasks to be supervised, if you'll excuse me.'

With that she bowed again and hastened away, leaving Marcus a little startled at the briefness of their conversation. Titus said, 'She's a little nervous, I think. There are few women in the Cloudfaring Corps and still fewer officers. So she'll be feeling under considerable pressure, as anyone would in her position. But she's utterly loyal and a fine Cloudfarer.'

'I'm sure . . . So have you taken part in many royal tours?'

'Oh yes. I used to be first mate on the *Regulus* – more years ago than I care to admit. I accompanied the king on many state visits. Saw all sorts of other citadels. Some monarchies, like our own or Selenopolis. Some republics like Utn'gard. Some military dictatorships like Scythium and néo-Sirus. It was fascinating. I learned a good deal.'

'I envy you.'

'Oh, I don't know. So much cloudfaring can bring its own problems. It's difficult to settle when you get back. Once you've seen home from a distance it never looks quite the same again. Things that you took for granted before seem so . . .'

He trailed off.

Marcus didn't really understand, but nodded anyway

then glanced over at the *Noble Quest*. Its impeller tubes began to vibrate and the blades protruding from its stern revolved slowly. It nudged forward, until restrained by the mooring lines, as if anxious to be on its way.

'Now, Marcus, a refresher lesson,' said Titus, brightening. 'What is the principle that lies behind the buoyancy of aëro:cruisers?'

'Hot air rises faster than cold.'

'And why is that?'

'Because hot air has, uh . . . less mass.'

'Good. And what generates sufficient hot air to lift an aëro:cruiser?'

'Proleyne.'

'Which is?'

'It's yellow, waxy stuff. You can mine it from seams in the rock below the citadel then mash it into a liquid.'

'And why do we use proleyne?'

'When it burns it produces a gas called selium which is much lighter than air but not flammable or so hot that it scorches the canvas of the air sacs.'

'And what else can proleyne be used for?'

'Uh, it can be mixed with beeswax to coat the canvas, so it doesn't get soaked from the water vapour in the clouds.'

'Quite right. We store the proleyne in tanks below the burners. A hose runs down to the bottom of each one to draw the liquid out. When the liquid rises it runs around a heating coil and then is lit by the burner . . . And as a result of all *that* the air sacs are filled with more hot air than Synvadis and his entire cabinet.'

Marcus laughed.

'Do I hear the name of our glorious prime minister being taken in vain?' asked Asperia, approaching them.

Titus bowed and smiled.

'Perish the thought, madam,' he said.

Glancing at Marcus, she drew Titus aside.

'General, I can't pretend to be happy with the turn events have taken,' she said quietly.

'I doubt anyone is, madam.'

'No, but I mean this mission in particular.'

'If there is any chance, no matter how slender, that the king may still be alive . . .'

'I understand fully the *reason* for the mission, general. What troubles me is Prince Marcus's presence on it.'

Marcus sighed. Asperia persisted in thinking that if she spoke to another adult in an undertone he wouldn't be able to catch what she was saying, when in fact he could hear and understand perfectly well. She seemed to forget that he was a lot taller and more alert to what was going on around him than he had been when she first started tutoring him. Eyes lowered, pretending to be fascinated by the toe of his sandal, he continued to listen.

'And as for everything else,' continued Asperia, 'Synvadis seems to grow more insufferable by the hour. I realise there's no evidence to suggest that he's ever been anything other than completely loyal to the king. But we both know how much he loves to exert author-ity – to feel influential. The prince's absence will only encourage him in this. It might even embolden him to do things he would not otherwise consider . . .'

'Madam,' Titus cut in, 'I agree with all that you say. But don't you see that if Synvadis really is plotting to secure permanent power, the citadel is by far the most dangerous place for the prince to be? Believe me, I appreciate that a mission across the cloudscape at this time of year has its own perils. But our aëro:cruisers are powerful, our Cloudfarers are well trained, and I will keep Marcus close by me at all times. I honestly believe that he will be safer aboard the *Noble Quest* than any-where else at present.'

Asperia nodded, but still looked worried.

'Anyway,' continued Titus, 'where is our esteemed prime minister?'

'Back in the cabinet chamber, talking to the senior ministers. I get the distinct impression he's sulking.'

'Hmm.'

A loud thud drew their attention back to the *Noble Quest*. A team of perspiring deckhands had just dropped on the deck one of the six cases that Asperia had insisted Marcus take with him. Made of dark, stained rosewood, secured with gleaming clasps, each case was large enough for a grown man to stand up inside it. Three already sat on the foredeck. Marcus was sure he could see the *Noble Quest* sinking a tiny bit closer to the surface of the landing stage each time a new case landed on it.

The Cloudfarers stood around, catching their breath and staring at the cases while rubbing the backs of their necks in a perplexed way. They also cast a few covert glances in Marcus's direction that were not exactly hostile, but not exactly warm either. He got the impression that they didn't appreciate the task of stowing away all his belongings. No doubt they would assume that he had insisted on bringing it all along, being accustomed to so pampered a lifestyle. He would like to have explained, but knew, as always, that Asperia would be outraged by the idea that someone of his status should give an explanation to anyone. He shot Titus a concerned look.

'It is reputed to get very cold out over the cloudscape,' said Asperia defensively. 'You'll need plenty of warm clothes.'

'I understand that, Asperia,' replied Marcus. 'But do you think we'll be able to take off with all that aboard?'

Smiling, Titus said, 'Madam Asperia is quite correct to take all necessary precautions. And the *Noble Quest* is a powerful vessel. We will have no trouble, I assure you.'

He nodded towards the detachment of Cloudfarers who were assembling themselves next to the gangplank.

'Would you care to say a few words to them before we set off?' he asked Marcus.

Marcus swallowed and stepped forward. These men were clearly the best the Cloudfaring Corps had to offer. Tall and broad-shouldered, they stood to attention, staring fixedly over Marcus's head, as if the only thing they could focus on was the purpose of their mission. Marcus might have imagined he had become invisible, were he not able to see his distorted reflection in the moulded breastplates of their armour. Each one was armed with a crossbolt: not the hand-held type, but a larger version with a shoulder-mounted stock; a revolving barrel and a hinged flash pan to keep the firing mechanism's powder dry.

'Uh . . . at ease,' he said.

'They *are* at ease, Your Highness,' whispered Titus.

'Oh, I see. Splendid. Well, I, uh . . . I would just like to take this opportunity to thank you all for accompanying me on so challenging a mission.'

'They don't really have a choice,' Titus pointed out. 'They would be cast over if they didn't accept the mission.'

'Right,' said Marcus, growing ever more self-conscious. 'Um . . . Well, none the less, I'm encouraged by your involvement. I feel sure that if there's even the slimmest chance my father still lives, you will be able to find him and restore him to his beloved people.'

The Cloudfarers continued to stare ahead, betraying not a flicker of response to Marcus's words.

'Um, that's all,' Marcus finished.

'Dismissed!' bellowed Titus.

The Cloudfarers spun round and marched towards their respective aëro:cruisers. While they did so, Marcus found himself pulled towards Asperia. Not trusting herself to master her emotions, she hugged him tightly and wordlessly, then pushed him up the gangplank of the *Noble Quest*.

Marcus felt dazed but excited as he stepped aboard. The gangplanks were pulled away from both aëro:cruisers. They slapped on to the landing stage. Cloudfarers strode back and forth across the *Noble Quest*'s deck, shouting instructions to one another that were rich in incomprehensible terminology. Marcus felt the bridge vibrate beneath his feet as the impellers neared full power. Peering over the aëro:cruiser's high sides – called 'gunnels' – he saw the deckhands loosening the mooring lines at prow and stern.

At first it seemed as if the *Noble Quest* was remaining stationary while the *Valorous Mission*, released slightly sooner, surged up beside it. But soon the *Noble Quest* rose as well and the two aëro:cruisers nudged forwards together. Still peering over the side, Marcus saw the landing stage slide past, severed lines coiled on it. Then the edge slipped by and there, far below, were the citadel's walls, dropping away like gigantic, curving steps.

Marcus gasped. The walls were crowded with tiny figures, all cheering as the aëro:cruisers went by overhead. Many of them waved torches, which glowed brightly in the fading light. After the dizzying plunge from one wall to the next, the fields and orchards rolled smoothly downwards until, at last, they merged with the lapping fringe of the clouds. Marcus was presented with a new, turbulent landscape of creamy peaks and shadowy troughs that passed diagonally beneath the aëro:cruiser's bows as it set a north-easterly course. Still gazing straight down, nothing below him for the first time in his life but wood braced with iron, Marcus felt instantly queasy. He stepped back and, gripping the gunnels, sought a fixed point on the horizon, as Titus had advised him to do. The experience of at last being airborne wasn't quite what he'd expected. To the people assembled on the walls it probably appeared that the

Noble Quest was moving forwards perfectly smoothly. In fact it lurched up and down every few moments, as it rode the constantly changing air currents. And all the time it rose and fell it also tilted at unpredictable angles – not enough to be alarming, but just enough to be noticeable.

Breathing deeply and evenly, Marcus glanced over at Titus. The general stood with his feet planted well apart, to steady himself. Otherwise he seemed unconcerned by all the *Noble Quest*'s perturbing movements. With Lieutenant Rhea, he held open a large chart, which flexed between them and fluttered round the edges. The two of them glanced from it to the binnacle – a low pedestal with a sloping surface that had the vessel's compass set into it. Then Titus called out figures to the pilot, Theus, who made minor adjustments to the wheel accordingly.

Not wishing to disturb them, Marcus decided to walk to the aëro:cruiser's stern. Titus had told him that it took everyone a while to find their air legs. He felt a little self-conscious about his unsteady gait. But as he crossed the aft deck, he passed crouching Cloudfarers who tended the valves clustered around the base of the burners. They glanced up at him curiously, but looked away the instant he met their eyes. He sighed as he climbed up to the aft'castle. Clearly it would be a while before they felt comfortable with his presence aboard.

Viewed from the stern, Heliopolis was already growing smaller. Marcus had never seen it in its entirety before. Even from this distance he could still make out

73

the torches – tiny, dancing points of light, stretching in bands all around it. He was mesmerised by its size and its graceful outline: the way it gradually narrowed as it rose and the contrast between the jumble of cottages encircling the immense girth of its lowest layers, the smooth inward curve of the mid-layers and the graceful blend of towers, arches and spires atop the palace. But most entrancing of all was the way the dying sunlight glanced off the palace's marble walls, turning it into a smouldering beacon. Marcus realised that Titus was right. Once you had been away from the Polis – even a few miles away – and seen it whole, it would never seem the same place again. And maybe you would never feel like the same person.

VI

Across the cloudscape

Surfing the cool, fast air currents created by the polar wind as it curved around the hemisphere, the *Noble Quest* and the *Valorous Mission* sped across the cloudscape.

Night came and the stars appeared – just a dim scattering at first, then a multitude, flickering into life. On the bridge of the *Noble Quest,* Theus stood at the wheel. Hands resting lightly on it, he shifted his weight from foot to foot as the aëro:cruiser dipped, rose, tilted, then dipped again. Lanterns hung at each corner of the bridge and cast a soft, swaying glow over it. Theus had a cloak drawn around him against the night's chill. So did the lookout, Lucis, who stood on a platform that jutted out from the rest of the bridge, a sturdy telescope fixed to its rail. Below, Cloudfarers patrolled the creaking main deck, glancing out over the silvery cloudscape and nodding as they passed one another. Marcus had lingered on the bridge for some time after nightfall. Gazing enraptured at the stars passing overhead, he'd lost any sense of the vessel around him and felt as if he were floating alone through space. But eventually he realised that he couldn't put off any longer going to his

75

cabin and dealing with his luggage – having insisted upon unpacking for himself.

His cabin lay at the stern of the *Noble Quest*, beneath the aft'castle. By the standards of accommodation aboard an aëro:cruiser it was quite spacious. Or rather it *would* have been were it not for the pile of cases that filled the floor and nearly touched the ceiling. The deckhands had chosen to arrange them in a pyramid: four on the bottom layer, two in the middle and one on top. Staring at them, Marcus wondered where he was going to put the topmost cases if he wanted to get at the contents of the ones below. After he had managed to find fresh clothes for the next day, he clambered over the cases and fell into his bed. It was shaped in a wide semicircle to fit the curve of the hull. Lulled by the constant thrum of the impellers, and exhausted by the events of the day, he quickly drifted off to sleep.

He woke early the next morning. Reaching up, he fumbled with the catch of the small casement window above his bed then swung it open. Icy air poured in. It was dawn on the sea of cloud: the streaked surface was pink-tinged and the valleys shaded from turquoise into deepest lapis lazuli.

'Breakfast, Your Highness,' said a voice from the other side of the luggage.

He glanced round from the window. The whole cabin was flooded with light and the walls danced with the shadows of the twisting impeller blades at the stern.

'Who's there?'

'It's Amik, Your Highness, from the galley.'

'Oh right. Can you climb up the cases? I'll meet you at the top.'

'Uh . . . certainly.'

Marcus scaled his side of the pyramid. When he reached the top Amik was still climbing the last few cases on the other side one-handed. In his free hand he held a wobbling tray. Taking the tray from him, Marcus sat cross-legged on the topmost case, head brushing the cabin's ceiling. The tray contained bread, figs, honey and a bowl of spiced black tea. While Marcus ate, Amik surveyed the cases shelving away below them in every direction. Marcus followed his gaze. He felt acutely embarrassed, sitting atop such a heap of possessions. In the relatively cramped surroundings of an aëro:cruiser they seemed to bulk even larger than they had before. They conveyed exactly the kind of impression he wanted to avoid: that of a pampered brat.

'You'd think I was going on a year-long state visit, wouldn't you?' he said, in as light a tone as possible. 'Instead of a rescue mission.'

'I'm sure someone as important as yourself needs many more changes of clothing than an ordinary Cloudfarer,' replied Amik.

'It was my tutor who insisted upon all of this. I'd have been happy to take no more than anyone else. I mean, like anyone else I'd like to change my clothes less often if I could get away with it.'

Amik smiled politely, but Marcus could tell that he wasn't convinced. As not only a Heliopolitan, but a member of the Corps also – raised in the rigid structure of both – he clearly treated the friendliness of superiors with caution, in case he was being tested to see if he might be lured into over-familiarity, for which he would then be upbraided.

'Perhaps we should put some of it in the hold,' suggested Marcus. 'Apart from anything else it would save us both a lot of climbing every morning.'

'Certainly, Your Highness. I shall speak to the quartermaster,' replied Amik, edging back down the luggage with the tray.

After Amik had left, Marcus got dressed and headed up to the foredeck.

By the time he got there the sun had risen fully. The cloud tops gleamed with an unreal whiteness. The *Noble Quest* swayed and tilted more than ever, but Marcus, having grown a little more accustomed to the strange motions of cloudfaring, noticed it less. Once again Cloudfarers crouched around the burners, while others scaled the rigging, checking its knots and testing the air sacs for any leaks, no matter how small. A couple also inspected the furled rope ladders, fixed at intervals along the gunnels, to make sure that they were still secure. Glancing to port, he saw the *Valorous Mission* cruising alongside about a hundred yards away, slightly above and ahead.

Climbing to the bridge he joined Rhea, Theus and Lucis. After the very public launch the Cloudfarers had discarded their armour. They now wore boots with trousers tucked into them and long-sleeved tunics over collarless shirts that laced at the front. They also had scarves tied round their necks and cloaks drawn over their shoulders.

Rhea and Lucis were standing, slightly stooped with concentration, over a device that was mounted in a similar way to the binnacle compass. The main part of it was a circular mirror, deeply etched with straight and curving lines. It had a metal frame and a pointer clipped to the side of it. The whole assembly sat on a swivelling pedestal.

'What's that?' Marcus asked.

Rhea straightened up and saluted.

'It's a nephoscope,' she explained. 'It measures the speed and direction of cloud motion.'

'How does it do that?' he asked, peering at it.

'Movements of clouds are coded with respect to the compass direction towards which they are moving,' Lucis explained gravely. 'This is usually coded as tens of degrees in any measurement system. For example, a southward-moving cloud is moving to 180 degrees and thus coded as 18 in a numerical report.'

'Uh . . . right,' said Marcus, none the wiser.

There was an awkward silence.

'Cold morning,' he said.

'I'm sorry,' replied Rhea. 'I could arrange for a shelter to be constructed on deck to protect you from the worst of the airstream. It would be quite makeshift, but . . .'

'No, no, I didn't mean that. It was just an observation. I'm quite happy as I am . . . *really.*'

He thought he noticed Theus smiling down at the wheel, looking amused – though not unkindly.

'I trust you slept well?' asked Rhea, after another pause.

'Yes, after a while.'

She nodded.

'First night in the air is always strange, even for experienced Cloudfarers. It takes a while to get used to the feeling of constant movement. Isn't that right, Theus?'

Theus glanced over. He looked somewhat older than the rest of the Cloudfarers – closer to Titus's age, in fact. He had hooded eyes and quizzically arching eyebrows, which, along with his drooping grey moustache, lent him an air of doleful humour.

'Indeed,' he said. 'The thing is, though, after a long voyage you get so used to it that it feels strange to be back in the Polis again, sleeping in a bed that doesn't move at all. Mind you, it's not so much fun if you're asleep when your aëro:cruiser hits a pocket of clear air turbulence. You can drop fifteen, twenty feet without warning and be thrown clear out of bed. But if you slept well on your first night, Your Highness, you must be a born Cloudfarer.'

'Thank you, Theus,' said Marcus, flattered.

'Yes, it's a great advantage when passengers are comfortable in the air,' added Rhea. 'Nothing is more embarrassing than arriving at a foreign citadel with a head of state who's all clammy, pale and unsteady on his feet. Doesn't convey the correct impression at all. I heard a story once about the Pro-Consul of Scythium visiting Heliopolis for a peace conference immediately after the Hemispheric Wars. It was his first time over the cloudscape. Apparently, when his aëro:cruiser landed he staggered down the gangplank, bowed to Synvadis instead of King Antior and then was sick all over his shoes.'

She paused, perhaps embarrassed by how garrulous she had become. But Marcus, prone to doing the same himself, laughed appreciatively. And Titus, who had just arrived, unnoticed, on deck, looked amused.

'Yes,' he said, 'I remember it well. One of the few occasions, I think, when Synvadis *didn't* wish he were king.'

'If you'll excuse me, sir,' said Rhea, 'I need to supervise the calibration of the blades on the starboard impeller.'

Titus nodded.

'Carry on, lieutenant,' he said.

Rhea saluted and left the bridge.

'So,' said Titus to Marcus, 'how are you getting on with the crew?'

'Well, Rhea seems very easy to talk to.'

'And the others?'

Marcus sensed Theus listening discreetly, though his gaze remained fixed on the horizon. No doubt any comment he made would be transmitted to the rest of the crew within a few hours, so he didn't want to say anything that might make his dealings with them even more awkward. Lowering his voice, he replied, 'All right. Though I'm not sure how happy they are to have me along.'

'Hmm ...Well, do bear in mind that they're on a difficult mission in far from ideal weather conditions. And in addition to that they are responsible for your safety. In private many of them probably feel that it would have been easier to do this without you aboard. Also the crew of an aëro:cruiser ... well, it's a pretty rough and ready world. With you aboard they have to mind their manners a bit more.'

'I wish they didn't feel that way.'

'No, no, it's important that they should. We may not be in Heliopolis, but the hierarchy must be preserved. The Corps is like the citadel but even more so: everyone has their level, everyone knows their place.'

Marcus was about to reply when the *Noble Quest* juddered sharply. Everyone on the bridge staggered forward. Theus braced himself against the wheel. Titus gripped the rail with one hand and reached out to steady Marcus with the other.

'What was that?' asked Marcus.

'It's the Impellerators,' explained Titus. 'The night shift is coming off duty. The impellers will be idle for ten minutes and we'll drift until the forenoon shift cranks them up. The same thing is happening aboard the *Valorous Mission*, look.'

Marcus looked to port. Sure enough, the other aëro:cruiser's impeller blades, jutting out at right angles to the stern, were revolving more and more slowly, as it fell behind the *Noble Quest*.

Soon, muffled thuds from below heralded the arrival on the mid deck of the night shift. They clambered out of the hatch that led up from the engine room. At first they all stood around stretching and groaning and squinting in the unaccustomed sunlight. But then they caught sight of Marcus watching them from the bridge, fascinated. Some paused in mid-stretch and hugged themselves self-consciously. Others coughed and stared at the deck.

As Marcus looked on, a trestle table was set up with two long benches placed along either side, so that the night shift could eat in the open air. Kitchen stewards – Amik included – appeared and loaded the table with cured meat, eggs, warm loaves and tureens of steaming vegetable soup. Still stiff from many hours of being confined to their stations, the night crew shuffled over to the food. A minor commotion ensued as they fought for a place on the side of the table closest to Marcus, so they could keep their backs to his discom-fiting presence while they ate. Between mouthfuls they chatted and some of their comments drifted across the deck to him: 'My back's killing me' . . . 'Mine too' . . . 'Still, good to be in the open air, isn't it?' . . . 'It's so cold' . . . 'I know, I can hardly move my fingers, look' . . . 'It'll get a lot colder yet' . . .

Two crew members in particular caught Marcus's attention. The others ate quickly, but this pair's spoons were just a blur between their bowls and mouths. One loaf of bread lay between them. Each tore at his end of it as if worried that the other might advance towards the middle too quickly. While doing all this they also bickered ceaselessly, undeterred by the fact that their mouths were full most of the time.

83

'I'm telling you, we were all doing seventy revolutions per minute on the starboard impeller,' one said.

'You couldn't have been,' retorted the other.

'Why not?'

'Because no one on the port impeller was doing more than fifty. If you lot had been doing seventy we'd have been flying in circles.'

'Well, you're so feeble it's a wonder we were moving at all.'

Marcus couldn't help smiling as he watched them – a spark of liveliness amongst all the other Impellerators, most of whom seemed to have been rendered mute by fatigue.

'Who are those two?' he asked Titus.

The general glanced over at them.

'Hmm? . . . Oh, Jarrid and Denihr. Just ordinary Cloudfarers. They came up to the Corps from the Farmers' layer. Childhood friends, I believe. Very close, but very competitive – argue all the time.'

Marcus smiled at them. Catching his eye, they frowned and looked down at their plates. He sighed.

A series of clanks and groans announced that the forenoon shift had started work and impellers were grinding into action once again. With another judder the aëro:cruiser picked up speed. The familiar vibration of labouring machinery spread through the hull. It made the whole of Marcus's slender frame tremble.

Several days passed and he slowly grew accustomed to the normal routine of life out over the cloudscape – as well as the symphony of creaks and groans and lurches that accompanied every moment. Each morning he saved Amik the trouble of scaling the luggage by persuading him to leave the breakfast tray just inside the door. Amik seemed to appreciate this and grew a little more relaxed in his presence. When they met at the door on the third morning he said, 'I'm afraid I have to report, Your Highness, that your belongings must stay where they are: there's no room for them in the hold, no matter how much we move everything else around. I am very sorry about this.'

Marcus waved aside his apology.

'No, it's fine. Don't worry. It's my fault for letting my tutor insist that I take so much with me. Anyway, climbing the cases is good exercise for me first thing in the morning – gets the heart rate up.'

Amik chuckled at this as he left.

After breakfast each day Marcus took some time to explore the vessel. This consisted of edging along a series of narrow corridors that smelled strongly of resinous wood, going up or down the occasional companionway, peering through open doors and slowly but unerringly getting lost. Now and then he encountered a couple of Cloudfarers, who immediately flattened themselves against a bulkhead, eyes lowered, to allow him to pass. When he asked for directions they were impeccably helpful, but never ceased to look abashed at being forced to speak directly to him.

Once, while he was trying to retrace his steps, he encountered Lucis with another Cloudfarer, whose name was Lon. He heard them before he saw them. Their voices rounded the corner several seconds before they did.

'I've told the Lieutenant that the rigging will get covered in rime if it isn't scraped regularly,' said Lucis.

'Well, it wouldn't need to be scraped at all, would it, if the prince hadn't made us fly so late in the season,' replied Lucis.

'Remember what the general said: if there's any chance of rescuing the king it has to be tried.'

'Yes . . . I know. But I still don't believe this stuff about another world. If you ask me, Naulix was injured when he jettisoned from the *Regulus* and was seeing things.'

'Well, maybe. Anyway, I don't think the prince is as pampered as everyone believes. Seems to me he just wants to be treated like the rest of us.'

'But have you heard Amik talking about all his stuff? Apparently it's . . . oh.'

Confronted with Marcus, they stopped.

'Uh, good morning,' said Lucis.

'Good morning,' said Marcus, smiling broadly. 'I was wondering if you could show me the nearest way to the deck.'

'Of course,' replied Lucis. Lon had been struck dumb.

They led him, by a series of twists and turns, to the foot of a companionway. As they set off, Marcus asked, 'What's rime?'

Looking horribly embarrassed, Lucis replied, 'It's frost formed when the water vapour in the clouds freezes.'

'I see.'

They walked a little more in silence.

'Are you, uh . . . are you both going on to a shift?' he asked.

'Uh, no, coming off one,' replied Lucis.

'It must have been a long night for you,' observed Marcus.

'No longer than we're used to on any other mission. Here we are.'

They arrived at the companionway then stood back to let Marcus climb it.

'Thank you,' he said. Pausing on the first step, which drew him up to their height, he leaned towards them conspiratorially. 'And by the way, I don't blame you at all for not wanting to be here. I'd feel just the same if I were you.'

They both saluted and hastened away. As they vanished, he faintly heard Lucis say, 'See? I *told* you he wasn't so stuck up,' to which Lon replied, 'Well . . . maybe.'

Smiling to himself, Marcus headed for the main deck.

When he reached the bridge he found Theus at the wheel. His impeccably straight posture and the way his hands were stretched wide to rest on either side of the wheel conveyed a sense of quiet confidence that Marcus found comforting. On the jutting lookout's platform another Cloudfarer, Tafril, had replaced Lucis.

'How are you, Theus?' Marcus asked.

Theus glanced round with his usual wry half-smile.

'Very well,' he replied. 'Soon we shall reach the half-way point between Heliopolis and Selenopolis.'

Marcus nodded.

'You've served under General Titus before, have you, Theus?'

'Oh yes. I was in the Hemispheric Wars: fought in aerial battles all across the cloudscape. I was actually due to retire from the Corps in the next few days. But the general asked me to stay on for this last mission.'

'I'm sorry. You could have been home – safe and warm – if it wasn't for me.'

'No, no, I was honoured to be asked to pilot such an important mission, especially given my . . . seniority.'

'Well, I'm very glad you're here.'

Though he kept his eyes ahead, Theus nodded in acknowledgement of this. They lapsed into silence for a while, the deck trembling beneath them. Then Marcus said, 'I . . . I don't want you to think I'm criticising any-one, Theus. But I must admit I find you a lot easier to talk to than some of the others.'

Theus pursed his lips.

'Well . . . as I said, they're younger than me. They're maybe a bit more self-conscious in your presence and nervous about the mission. Just give them time.'

'All right. I like Lucis, though.'

'Yes, a good man. Comes from the Artisans' layer. Very straightforward: no side to him. And utterly loyal.'

Some time later, Titus joined them on deck and said to Marcus, 'Soon we will be near the Sorianna Abyssal.'

Marcus nodded. An abyssal was a chasm in the cloud-scape that changed size and shape but was more or less a permanent feature, lasting decades, sometimes centuries.

'Is that where the search will begin?' he asked.

'Yes,' replied Titus.

He nodded to the *Noble Quest*'s navigator, Nestor, who stepped forward, holding a large, rolled-up navigational map that drooped slightly at either end. Marcus couldn't help noticing that Nestor not only wore thick glasses but had a pronounced squint, neither of which seemed a very promising sign.

'Yes,' said Nestor, smiling nervously at a spot three inches to the left of Marcus's ear. 'I have been working on these calculations since our journey began. They will give us an idea of where we should be looking.'

He unrolled the chart over the binnacle. The corners kept flapping up in the airstream, until Titus, sighing, stepped forwards to help hold them down.

Marcus scrutinised the chart. It wasn't very illuminating. At the bottom left-hand corner lay Heliopolis. Towards the top right-hand corner lay Selenopolis. Shown from above, each citadel looked like a series of circles contained inside one another, the outermost circle drawn ragged to indicate the enfolding clouds. But the area of the chart *between* the two citadels was densely covered with overlapping lines, some straight, some curved. Wherever one line crossed another a calculation was written.

Pointing at a circle drawn heavily near the centre of the chart, Nestor said, 'We're entering the edge of the search area now. Assuming that the *Regulus* plotted the shortest possible course from Selenopolis to Heliopolis, and was travelling at standard aeronautical speed – with a margin of error of five knots either way – it must have gone down somewhere within the circumference of this circle. I suggest we make for the exact centre and gradually move our search outwards from there.'

He pushed his glasses up his nose.

'Assuming of course that there is anything down there to search, rather than just an endless, freezing void, or –'

'Yes, thank you, Nestor,' said Titus. 'We shan't detain you any further.'

Looking pale and somewhat overcome by his own speculations, Nestor hastened away below deck. Titus shook his head. Leaning closer to Marcus, he said, 'Nestor may not have the calm head or air legs one would normally expect in a Cloudfarer, but he's a very skilful cartographer. His abilities are invaluable on a mission like this.'

'I think I'd be the last person to criticise Nestor for not being wholly at ease over the cloudscape,' Marcus replied. 'I –'

But Titus wasn't listening. He stepped closer to the railing and, narrowing his eyes, said, 'You know, I could swear I just saw –'

'Vessel ahoy!' yelled the lookout.

VII

The cloud depths

On the horizon, to starboard, a black dot was intermittently visible, slipping between the wind-sculpted cloud peaks. Slowly it drew closer and resolved itself into a vessel that bore the distinctive bulky outline of a Mercanteer —a trading ship. It was the same length as both aëro:cruisers, but much broader amidships, as if swollen with all the goods it contained. Out on his platform, Lucis put his eye to the telescope fixed to the rail. Training it on the approaching vessel, he reported that it bore the crest of Selenopolis.

Titus, usually so calm, looked distinctly alarmed.

'Evasive action!' he shouted to Theus. 'Get us out of range. Haul off to port. Now!'

Theus grabbed the wheel. Two other Cloudfarers darted up the steps to the bridge to help him wrench it all the way round. Grabbing the hollow coil of pipe that was clipped to the binnacle, Titus shouted down to the engine room, 'More power, starboard impeller!' The Impellerators who had been eating rushed below to help. On his platform, Tafril turned to the *Valorous Mission* and, waving two brightly coloured flags – the quickest way of communicating in such circumstances – ordered its pilot in semaphore to bear hard to port as well.

There were a few tense moments when the *Noble Quest* sheared left but the *Valorous Mission* didn't flinch from its course and it looked as if the two vessels would collide. On the *Noble Quest*'s main deck the abandoned breakfast slid straight off the table, plates and bowls smashing. At the last moment the *Valorous Mission* nudged just a little to port and the *Noble Quest*, with a surge of power from its throbbing impellers was able to cut across the other vessel's bows.

The Mercanteer gradually shrank astern, bleached by the haze of the far distance. Once the aëro:cruisers had returned to level flight, Marcus asked, 'Wasn't that a little excessive? I mean, it was quite a long way away.'

'We can take no chances. If Selenopolis or any other citadel knows that our king is missing, they may see us as vulnerable to conquest,' Titus replied curtly.

'But isn't Selenopolis supposed to be our ally? And aren't we at peace now with the northern citadels? I thought my father's diplomatic visits had ensured that.'

'Peace can only be achieved through impressing one's strength upon others, as the Cloudfaring Corps did by defending our air space and trading currents. King Antior's diplomacy, as . . . *expedient* as it may have been, merely set the seal upon the security they had achieved.'

Titus said this so emphatically that Marcus thought it best not to quibble. He did, however, notice that the general behaved differently towards him now that they were away from Heliopolis. In spite of his military bearing and clipped tones there had always been a hint of indulgence before – like a smile lightening an otherwise unvarying frown. Now he seemed . . . not cold exactly, but more formal. Then again he had a far greater responsibility to deal with. Realising this, Marcus berated himself, yet again, for being too naïve and inexperienced to appreciate such things.

Having deviated from their course to avoid the Mercanteer, the aëro:cruisers took longer than planned to reach the search area. Determined to avoid any further contact with foreign vessels, Titus ordered both vessels to partially vent a couple of their air sacs and drop among the cloud tops, using them for concealment. He explained to Marcus that this was a common aeronautical strategy, called 'cloud-hopping.'

The *Noble Quest* pulled ahead of the *Valorous Mission* and for many miles they travelled in single file along the canyons that twisted between the steep, brawny cumulus clouds. You would scarcely have believed that they were made up of nothing more than condensed water vapour. Marcus was so absorbed in watching the white walls rearing up on either side that he lost all sense of time. But towards the middle of the afternoon, Nestor reappeared on the bridge with his chart and unrolled it again. He raised a quivering hand, eyes fixed on the chart, and held it there for some time before shouting, 'Heave to!'

The message was relayed below and – by semaphore again – to the *Valorous Mission*. The Impellerators in the engine rooms of both vessels gripped the circumvolvers with tensed arms to slow them, then with great effort turned them in the opposite direction. The impeller blades began to work in reverse: drawing air in at the stern and expelling it from the prow. With a now familiar shudder, the *Noble Quest* slowed down. Prepared for it this time, Marcus kept a firm grip on the bridge's rail. Aft of the *Noble Quest*, pulling back to starboard, the *Valorous Mission* slowed too. The aëro:cruisers now hung about fifty feet above the main cloud layer. Smaller fragments of cloud, torn free by the wind, drifted past them – cloudbergs.

The main hatch burst open and several Cloudfarers hauled themselves on to the deck. Kneeling round the edge of the hatch, they grabbed hold of lengths of cable that were carefully fed up to them. For one surreal moment it seemed to Marcus as if the *Noble Quest* were a beast whose entrails were being pulled out and coiled in a heap.

Then other objects emerged from the hold: two thick posts, several joists and pulleys, a cumbersome lever-operated pump, four lengths of piping and, last of all, a wooden cage. Under Rhea's supervision they were all dragged to the edge of the deck, where the Cloudfarers started to assemble them.

At Marcus's side, Titus explained what was going on.

'Part of the mechanism you can see,' he said, 'has been improvised from a system we've used in the past to tow home crippled aëro:cruisers. The posts, called stanchions, will be bolted to the deck and braced by joists. A long handle will be slotted between them like a crossbar and attached to a pulley on either side to create a winch. A corresponding mechanism is being set up over on the *Valorous Mission.*'

He gestured to the other aëro:cruiser, where Cloudfarers crouched at the gunnels, wielding similar objects.

'Cables will then be thrown from one vessel to the other and lashed to the winches,' he continued. 'A cage, with its own cable and pulley, will be attached to the others. With our explorers in it, the cage can be winched half-way between the two vessels, then gradually lowered into the clouds.'

'How far?'

'Well, we have nearly a thousand fathoms of cable to play out – that's more than a mile. Whether or not it will be enough there's no way of knowing. But our explorers have been supplied with everything we can think of to help keep them alive during the descent and let them search: air pipes, protective clothing, flares, telescopes. And the pump, bolted to the deck, will be used to feed air down to them.'

Marcus nodded. As he continued to watch, preparations were made exactly as Titus had described them. But then, while the cage was being loaded with equipment, the general drew on his gloves and saluted.

'Well, I must go,' he said.

'Go where?' asked Marcus, looking around in confusion.

'To the *Valorous Mission.* I shall direct operations from there.'

'Why can't you direct them from here?'

'It is dictated by the way the mechanism works. The winch that moves the cage into position is aboard this vessel, but the one that lowers it is aboard the other.'

'Oh, I see. Well . . . good luck.'

'Thank you, Marcus. Good luck to *you*.'

Saluting again, he rattled down the steps to the main deck and hastened over to where the winch had been set up. Passing Rhea on his way, he drew her aside and said a few words to her that Marcus didn't catch. She nodded gravely and climbed up to the bridge to replace him.

With the help of two Cloudfarers, Titus shrugged on what looked to Marcus like a not very substantial harness. He fastened it over his chest, then the Cloudfarers clipped it to a hook that hung from the winch. Titus lifted one leg then the other over the gunnels. A powerful shove from the Cloudfarers sent him out into thin air, dangling from the sagging cables that stretched between the two vessels. Buffeted by the airstream, he slid towards the *Valorous Mission*. His face betrayed not a flicker of anxiety. But Marcus also noticed that he was careful not to look down into the abyssal that lay below him. Cloudfarers leaned over the side of the *Valorous Mission* to pull him in. Eventually, after a somewhat undignified scramble over the gunnels, he was safely aboard.

Unfastening the harness, he shrugged it off then turned towards the *Noble Quest* and raised an arm to signal that the search mission could begin. Rhea waved in acknowledgement, then shouted to the Cloudfarers, 'Continue!'

Preparations were made to attach the cage to the winch and haul it over the side of the *Noble Quest*. The cage had a circular base and a domed roof.

'This is the first difficulty,' Rhea told Marcus. 'Once the cage is prepared, the search party have to climb over the gunnels – without harnesses – and swing themselves into it. Once inside, they have to spread their weight around carefully until the last one gets in, so that the cage doesn't overbalance with the hatch still open.'

'Who are the search party?'

'Here they come now.'

Four men – easily the shortest Cloudfarers Marcus had ever seen – emerged from a door in the aft'castle. They wore thick, shapeless, one-piece garments, fastened tightly at the waist, ankles and wrists and tucked into heavy boots and gloves. Their collars were wide, but encircled by a thick cuff that nearly obscured their chins. They held bulbous helmets under their arms. Their heads and faces were also swathed tightly in strips of black material, which left only their eyes and mouths uncovered. In spite of their short stature, they strode across the deck with an indomitable swagger, clearly proud of the task for which they had been selected.

'They are called aëro:mechs,' explained Rhea. 'Every aëro:cruiser has them. They are not particularly senior crew members. But they perform a very important role. If any aëro:cruiser is damaged in some way, the aëro:mechs are winched down over the side to inspect the damage, and even repair it. The rest of the time they work in the engine room, greasing the circumvolvers between shifts and making sure the rest of the machinery works properly. They're very skilful engineers. Because of how light and agile they are, we thought they would be perfect for this mission. And they're desperate to prove that they're superior to any larger Cloudfarer, so they're extremely well motivated.'

The aëro:mechs stepped towards the bridge, where Marcus and Rhea stood and saluted. Then they slipped the bulbous helmets over their heads. The other Cloudfarers fastened them at the neck. Time was moving on. Soon it would be early afternoon, when the sun was highest and penetrated as far as it ever could into the depths of the cloudscape. The aëro:mechs slipped over the gunnels and, one by one, swung through the open hatch into the cage. There was an alarming moment when the last one lost his grip and nearly fell. He clung to the tilting floor, legs dangling in mid-air for nearly a minute, until his comrades, gripping the bars of the cage to avoid falling out of it themselves, reached down and hauled him in. When they were all at last inside, the Cloudfarers fed the flexing air pipes to them. Each attached a pipe to the crown of his helmet.

A group of Impellerators aboard the *Noble Quest* – led by Lon – grasped the gleaming handle of the winch. When the mechanism was unlocked, they immediately felt the full weight of the cage and let out an effortful grunt. Crammed together, shoulder to shoulder, between the stanchions, they allowed the handle to turn very, very slowly.

'Don't let it get away from you,' Lon warned the others. 'Turn it as slowly and smoothly as possible.'

'Slowly as possible,' Jarrid repeated to Denihr. 'Should suit you perfectly.'

'Just make sure your hands don't slip,' retorted Denihr through clenched teeth.

'What are you talking about?'

'Well, you know how your palms sweat when you start to worry about everyone realising how feeble you really are.'

'Listen, I could work this winch on my own with one hand and still knock you cold with the other.'

'Quiet, you two!' ordered Lon. 'Concentrate.'

Slowly, they winched the cage towards the mid-point between the two vessels.

Harnessed to the bars of the cage, the aëro:mechs all stared at the grid-like floor. Marcus could scarcely imagine what they must be thinking, preparing to descend into a region that had remained an impenetrable mystery to every generation of their ancestors. The cage shuddered to a halt at the mid-point. The winch aboard the *Noble Quest* was locked. The air pipes hung, sagging, between it and the cage. Now it was the turn of the *Valorous Mission*'s crew to lower the cage into the clouds as smoothly as they were able. Looking on, Marcus wondered if he were the only person to whom the cage and its occupants looked horribly vulnerable.

Titus, stepping up to the side of the *Valorous Mission*'s deck, cloak flapping, saluted the aëro:mechs in the cage. Marcus found this acknowledgement of their courage moving, but also slightly ominous. It was as if Titus were offering them a final tribute in case they should fail to return alive. As desperate as Marcus felt to know whether or not his father had survived, the idea of so frail a contraption gradually sinking into the swirling vapour below was almost unbearable. Yet he kept his eyes fixed upon it, while Titus barked orders to the *Valorous Mission*'s crew. Such was the strength of the wind now that Marcus could only catch isolated words: 'Lower . . . steady . . . strain . . . hundred fathoms first . . .'

Swaying slightly more with every few yards it descended, the cage brushed the cloud tops after about a minute. Tendrils of vapour curled like fingers between its bars. As the cloud thickened around it, it began to look less solid and the aëro:mechs even more slender. Within a few more minutes it had vanished completely. Only the cable and the four air pipes could be seen – one straight black line and a few curved ones plunging into nothingness.

Aboard both aëro:cruisers, Cloudfarers crowded together and peered over the sides to watch the cage begin its journey. One of the Cloudfarers on the *Valorous Mission* called out to the others every time five fathoms of cable had been played out. The continued gusting of the wind meant that Marcus could hear him only occasionally.

'Twenty-five . . . thirty . . .'

Strictly speaking, there was nothing more to see. But everyone continued to stare down, rapt, into the clouds. Now that the aero:mechs were deeper, other Cloudfarers began to operate the air pump, forcing the handle up and down. It began working with a series of asthmatic wheezes.

'Fifty . . . fifty-five . . . sixty . . .'

Marcus glanced up at the *Valorous Mission* and noticed something odd. Amongst all the downturned heads ranged along its gunnels and rails, Titus was staring straight across at the *Noble Quest*. His features had gathered and stiffened into a look of fierce resolve.

'Seventy-five . . . eighty . . .'

As if in a dream, Marcus saw Titus raise his arm. The general, still staring at him, shouted something. A gust of wind carried his words away. Then, a few seconds later, it seemed to return them. By the time Marcus heard them, Titus was already turning his broad back.

They were, 'Open fire!'

VIII

The world below

A shell burst from one of the *Valorous Mission*'s cannons in a shower of sparks. The force of the blast was so strong that the barrel of the cannon recoiled all the way back into the hull. Fiercely hot, the shell streaked towards the *Noble Quest* wreathed in smoke. A few seconds later there was an explosion amidships. Marcus struggled to regain his balance as the bridge tilted beneath him. The planking on the foredeck buckled and smoke poured out of the open hatch. Cries of surprise, alarm and outrage came from all around. Many of the Cloudfarers plunged into the scorched hatch to help their comrades below.

'What's happening? Why are they doing this?' asked Rhea, gripping the bridge's rail.

'I don't know,' said Nestor. 'The cannon must have gone off by accident. It must be some mistake!'

Marcus frowned. Having seen the expression on Titus's face while everyone else was gazing down, he had few doubts about the real reason for the cannon fire.

'Well, you'd better hold on,' he said, reaching out for the binnacle to steady himself. 'In case they make the same mistake again.'

Sure enough, another cannon aboard the *Valorous Mission* fired, its barrel tilted slightly higher. This time, instead of smashing against the side of the *Noble Quest*'s hull, the shell soared over its gunnels and plunged into the deck, blowing a ragged hole in it. The aëro:cruiser's hull swayed beneath its air sacs. Marcus wondered if the aëro:mechs – trapped in their cage far below – were aware yet that something above had gone terribly wrong. No sooner had this thought crossed his mind, than he noticed Cloudfarers aboard the *Valorous Mission* crouched around their winch, hacking at the stanchions with axes. In a matter of seconds, the cable that supported the cage was severed. It spun loose and shot into the void. Everyone on the *Noble Quest* gasped with horror as, a few moments later, the air pipes uncoiled in a blur on its deck. Wrenched free from the pump, they vanished over the side. The other cables that still connected the *Noble Quest* to the *Valorous Mission* thrashed.

'Comrades or no comrades,' said Rhea, scowling, 'I'm returning fire.'

'Load the cannons!' she shouted to the Cloudfarers, who stood in disarray on the main deck.

They all hesitated. Some glanced doubtfully at the spot where Titus – only moments before their unquestioned leader – had stood aboard the *Valorous Mission*.

'Do it!' she bellowed, louder than Marcus could have believed possible. 'Unless you want us all to die together.'

The Cloudfarers leaped into action. Turning to Marcus, Rhea said, 'I must ask you to retire to your quarters.'

'But . . .'

'Please, I can't defend us and be responsible for your safety as well when you're so exposed on the bridge.'

Marcus was about to protest further. But just then the *Noble Quest* shuddered as one of its own cannons fired. A shell hurtled low towards the *Valorous Mission* and blew a chunk out of the underside of its hull. As Marcus and Rhea watched in horror, three writhing bodies fell from the gaping hole. Accompanied by a shower of smouldering wood and other debris, they quickly vanished into the clouds.

'You must go now,' said Rhea, eyes still on the terrible spectacle they had witnessed. 'Magnis will escort you.'

Marcus became aware of an exceptionally tall, bearded Cloudfarer looming beside him.

'But it'll look as if I'm hiding from danger. I don't want the Cloudfarers to think . . .'

Before he could finish Magnis – at a curt nod from Rhea – took him by the arm and practically hauled him off the bridge.

Marcus continued to protest all the way. When they reached his quarters, Magnis ushered him firmly inside and said, 'I'm needed on deck. I'll return for you as soon as it's safe. Don't worry – we won't let you down.'

With that, he closed and locked the door. Still trembling from shock, Marcus kicked the door in frustration then stood for a few moments, trying to breathe more evenly and absorb what had just happened. But it was too shocking, too brutal.

He turned from the door and clambered across the luggage – some of which had toppled over – to get to the casement window. He hoped that if he opened it and leaned out far enough he might be able to keep track of the battle between the aëro:cruisers.

Hopping on to the bed, he heard a muffled voice shouting, 'Vessel ahoy!'

He fumbled with the stiff catch of the window. Eventually it freed and he stuck his head through the gap, craning his neck to look up.

An immense shadow fell across his face. It was cast by the hull of the Mercanteer, which was swinging in a tight arc around the two locked-together aëro:cruisers. In spite of Titus's best efforts, it must have followed them at a discreet distance, likewise dodging between the cloud tops. Abruptly the exchange of fire ceased. Marcus could well imagine the opposing Cloudfarers standing motionless on their decks, dumbfounded by this new development. On Rhea's instructions, Lucis semaphored the Mercanteer that the *Noble Quest* was the victim of an unprovoked attack. The *Valorous Mission* also semaphored, warning the circling Mercanteer not to become involved.

The pause in hostilities didn't last long. Desperate to secure their victory before the Mercanteer attacked, the crew of the *Valorous Mission* redoubled their efforts. A salvo of shells burst from its cannons, the barrels recoiling in rapid succession. Most struck the *Noble Quest*'s hull. Fragments of burning wood spun through the air then fell as embers into the clouds, trailing twisted plumes of smoke. But the last shell, aimed higher than any before, tore through two of the air sacs. There was an outrush of superheated gas, which caused the holes rent in the canvas to flutter round the edges. This was accompanied by an eerily human sound, like a desolated moan. Instantly the *Noble Quest* dropped ten feet closer to the main cloudscape.

Marcus saw none of this, but the downwards jolt hurled him off the bed and on to the floor. As he landed he smacked his head against one of the cases. He lay propped against them for a few moments, dazed and winded. Just when he was reaching up to feel for a bump, the *Noble Quest* tilted sharply towards the prow. The cases against which he had been propped slid across the room, slamming against the door, and he struck his head again, this time on the floor.

He lay on the floor for a while, utterly dazed, but also overwhelmed by guilt at being so isolated from the Cloudfarers who were fighting for their – and his – survival. He sat up, scrambled back on to the bed, then gazed around the room, blinking rapidly. At first he thought that hitting his head twice in rapid succession had blurred his vision. Then he saw smoke pouring up through the narrow spaces between the floorboards. The cabin below his had been hit.

It didn't take long for him to reach a decision. He might be no safer on deck than in his quarters, but he had no desire to die alone. The door was completely blocked. There was only one other option. Head throbbing, he lunged towards the open window. Sitting on the ledge, he leaned back through the open casement until his head, arms and chest were outside it and his legs and torso were still inside. Then he reached up to grasp the top of the frame and began to pull himself all the way out. The gap was so narrow that he could scarcely fit even his slender body through it. But, inch by inch, he began to wriggle out. Above him stretched the tower of the aft'castle, with several more rows of windows set in it. Below lay the twisted impeller blades – motionless, but sharp enough to slice him in two were he to slip and fall on to them. Trying not to look down, Marcus continued in his efforts. If he could just get all the way out on to the ledge and reach up to the next window . . .

Events began to gather pace. Its torn air sacs wrinkling and sagging, the *Noble Quest* dropped a bit closer to the cloudscape. The cables connecting the two vessels grew taut. A cluster of Cloudfarers aboard the *Valorous Mission* worked at severing them while the rest concentrated on trying to fight off the Mercanteer. Rhea ordered the *Noble Quest's* impellers to be started up, in the hope that it might be able to break free from its preoccupied enemy and limp out of range.

So, as Marcus finally struggled out of his quarters and crouched on the ledge, still clinging to the top part of the window frame, he heard the ominous sound of labouring machinery and the frame trembled beneath his fingertips. He glanced down, horror-struck. The blades began to ease into life, quickly picking up speed. Soon he felt the updraft they conjured rustling his hair.

In no time Marcus was standing upright on the

ledge, arms wide, pressed flat against the stern, the impeller blades a blur of movement below him. But Rhea's attempts to free the *Noble Quest* weren't working. Still bound together, one higher than the other, the two aëro:cruisers began to circle one another – as if in a parody of a stately dance – both propelled by the *Noble Quest*'s engines.

Then the decisive stroke: another smouldering shell from one of the *Valorous Mission*'s cannons tore through more of the *Noble Quest*'s air sacs. Only one now remained intact. The *Noble Quest* began to sink much faster, dragging the other vessel down with it. Meanwhile, the Mercanteer backed off, its crew clearly unwilling to be embroiled in the imminent catastrophe. Cloudfarers aboard the *Valorous Mission* rushed below to start up *its* impellers and push back in the opposite direction. All the time, slowly revolving, the aëro:cruisers descended nearer and nearer to the clouds.

At the *Noble Quest*'s stern Marcus reached up in vain with one hand for the window ledge above. Standing on tiptoe, he stretched himself as far as he could. But the ledge remained at least a foot beyond his quivering fingertips. And every few seconds, when the vessel shuddered and dropped a bit further, he had to throw both arms out wide again to steady himself. Hugging the stern, eyes closed, he was rapidly losing hope.

He felt something strike him on the side of the head. He looked up, startled. A baggy trouser leg dangled out of the window above, enclosing a thick, hairy ankle and calf. It was swiftly withdrawn and replaced by a frowning, bearded face – Magnis. Reaching out of the window, he called, 'It's all right! Grab my hand if you can.'

Ignoring all instincts to the contrary, Marcus raised both his hands and Magnis, with some grimacing, pulled him up into a sparse but neat cabin, which turned out to be Rhea's. Marcus flopped down on the bed, wheezing.

'I'm so sorry,' said Magnis. 'When we realised that the stern had been hit I came down to get you but the door wouldn't move.'

'No wonder. All my luggage had slid against it,' said Marcus. He smiled at Magnis. 'That's absolutely the last time I over-pack.'

'I was about to climb down to help you when I saw you trying to get out of the window,' continued Magnis. 'That was a brave thing to do, but terribly dangerous.'

'I didn't have much choice,' Marcus pointed out.

They were interrupted by another bone-shaking crash from the stern and a sound of shearing metal. Marcus peered out of the window.

'I think the port impeller has been hit,' he said. 'Come on, we'd better get on deck and see what's happening.'

But by the time they got up on deck it was impossible to see anything. Cloud had enveloped the *Noble Quest*. Below, it shaded into forbidding grey; above, it was pierced by shafts of sunlight. The *Valorous Mission* had vanished, but the cable that still connected the two vessels curved upwards into the glowing whiteness. All around there was nothing but a cold, white void, thick with moisture. With nothing around to mark their fall, Marcus wouldn't have realised it was happening at all, were it not for the plunging sensation in his stomach and the growing pressure in his ears. Within seconds his hair and clothes were soaked. One of the cables that curved up into the glowing whiteness, still connecting the two aëro:cruisers, snapped. It brought with it a clutch of crew members from the *Valorous Mission*, who must have been trying to sever it. They tumbled down through the hazy air and slammed into the *Noble Quest*'s deck, knocked out instantly. Occasionally there was a muffled explosion and a flash of brighter light above as the *Valorous Mission* fought off the Mercanteer.

The *Noble Quest* sank further and the cloud continued to thicken. Soon it was difficult to see from one side of the deck to the other. Edging up the steps to the bridge, Marcus bumped into Rhea. Shaken, but still resolute, with strands of damp hair plastered over her forehead, she looked genuinely relieved to see him.

'I thought you'd be safe below!' she exclaimed. 'You must believe me, I had no idea . . .'

'It's okay. After all, if you just wanted rid of me why would you still be aboard? You'd have left already like . . .'

'Titus.'

They stared at one another, unable to believe it, though it was now beyond doubt. The roar of the gas escaping from the air sacs grew louder, until it was accompanied by a hideous ripping sound. Marcus and Rhea both looked up. The holes rent in the canvas had grown much larger.

The *Noble Quest* sank faster still. The bridge dropped away from beneath Marcus's feet so abruptly that he seemed to be suspended in mid-air for several seconds before slamming back on to the wet, hard surface. When it tilted to starboard he slid across it and collided with the railing. As he lay huddled there, the breath knocked out of him, he felt a sharp pain in his eardrums. But he didn't feel as if he were going to black out, as he had expected once he was deeper into the clouds. Perhaps the fact that the *Noble Quest*'s fall wasn't as fast as it might otherwise have been made the change in air pressure more bearable.

Prevented from dropping like a stone only by still being tethered to the *Valorous Mission*, the *Noble Quest* none the less continued downwards. The collapsed air sacs now settled over the whole deck. Everyone scrambled around in the darkness under the heavy, soaking canvas. Trying to find the edge of it, they skidded helplessly across the deck. At one point Marcus collided with Rhea.

'Oof!'

'Sorry.'

'I can't see a thing!'

'Neither can I.'

'I can!' shouted Theus, from somewhere to starboard, sounding as if he wished he couldn't.

Marcus tried to do a controlled slide across the deck to where Theus's voice seemed to be coming from. He thudded to a halt a few feet away from the pilot and shuffled over to his side. Theus lifted the edge of the canvas. Looking up, Marcus gasped.

The cloudscape now lay above them. For more than a minute Marcus stared at its swollen underbelly, trying to absorb this fact. No matter how much he stared at it, he found the reality of their situation almost impossible to comprehend. So suddenly and violently had his perspective on everything changed that he actually felt tears of shock springing to his eyes.

Nestor, who had joined him at the gunnels, wailed, 'It's not possible, it's not possible . . .' over and over.

The other Cloudfarers continued to blunder around beneath the canvas, though a few managed to find their way out and cling to the gunnels or lash themselves to the deck with the lanyards and the collapsed rigging.

Marcus was still staring up in wonder when a pale Theus nudged him and pointed downwards. Fearfully, he peered over the gunnels. Only a thousand feet below, stretching as far as he could see in every direction, lay a grey mass of water. It surged and thrashed like a living creature. And there, hurled from the crest of one wave to the next, was the aëro:mech's cage – empty, pointlessly trailing its severed cables and air pipes, like so many umbilical cords.

'Those poor souls,' whispered Rhea, shuffling to Marcus's side to peer down with him.

Marcus found it hard to tear his eyes away from this new world – even when several of the Cloudfarers shouted, 'Look out!' and there was a sound like a gigantic whip being cracked against the *Noble Quest*'s hull. Forcing himself to look round, he saw that the *Valorous Mission* had also emerged from the clouds, about thirty feet above. Heeled over at a sharp angle, it was being dragged remorselessly down by the dead weight of the *Noble Quest*. The sound he'd heard was another cable snapping between the two vessels. Very soon – when they were only a hundred feet above the water – the last one was sundered and the *Valorous Mission*, suddenly freed, sped upwards into the clouds, vanishing within moments. Unsupported, the *Noble Quest* hurtled in the other direction. It fell the last stretch in moments and plunged on to the heaving waves.

IX

The lowest point

Marcus and Rhea grabbed hold of the gunnels. A wall of water crashed over the deck. The *Noble Quest* surged downwards. Marcus was convinced that it was going to plunge into the depths of the heaving waters. But the curved shape of its hull proved to be its salvation. Its prow lifted and it was borne up on the shoulders of the next wave. It sat poised there for what seemed like an eternity, then pitched down into the next trough of water.

This went on for nearly an hour. Though the *Noble Quest* remained afloat, it took on more and more water through the holes the cannon fire had punched in its hull. Its crew could do nothing but cling to their foundering vessel. Many of them, who hadn't managed to get a firm grip on the gunnels, or lash themselves down, tired and were swept over the side. Once, as the *Noble Quest* clambered to the peak of an especially large wave, Marcus thought he saw something more substantial on the horizon. Anxious not to lose his grip, he rubbed his stinging eyes with one hand and looked again. Yes – there ahead of them, hazy in the salt spray and gathering darkness, was the rocky shore with gently swollen peaks rising behind it. From their serrated out-line he guessed that they were covered in pine trees, similar to the ones that fringed the fields of Heliopolis. As they drew slightly closer, he saw fingers of rock spreading out into the turbid water, as if beckoning to them.

His relief that they may not drown after all was so intense that it took him a while to comprehend what was really happening. Watching wave after wave race towards the shore and dash themselves upon the rocks, he realised that the *Noble Quest* would soon do exactly the same.

Tugging at Rhea's sleeve, he pointed towards the shore and shouted, 'Look!'

Seeing with alarm the rocky shore that lay beyond the lines of surf, Rhea frowned and nodded.

'We have to abandon the *Noble Quest*!' he hissed. 'If we get overboard just before it breaks up maybe we can swim safely ashore.'

'And if we get as much as possible up from the hold we could stuff it into the canvas of the air sacs and salvage it. They're waterproof, so it should stay pretty dry,' she suggested.

'Brilliant!'

Taking a deep breath, she rose unsteadily to her feet. With one hand still gripping the gunnels, she turned to the depleted crew of sprawled and huddled Cloudfarers, and bellowed, 'Right! Go below and bring up every-thing you can that might be useful.' She glanced towards the shore. 'We have very little time.'

Several of the Cloudfarers – led by Lucis and Magnis – cautiously stirred. Still using the rigging for handholds, they dragged themselves across the drenched foredeck on their stomachs then dived into the main hatch.

'Jarrid, Denihr, help us get ready!' Rhea shouted.

Using pocket knives, Jarrid and Denihr severed one of the thick lanyards. Then, with Lon's help, they punched holes around the gap rent in one of the deflated air sacs and looped the lanyard through them. As they were finishing, the other Cloudfarers re-emerged from below laden with an eccentric jumble of objects: weapons, extra clothes, blankets, a couple of sturdy proleyne stoves from the galley and an assortment of victuals. Encouraged by strategic bursts of yelling from Rhea, they stuffed these items inside the gaping air sac. All the time the *Noble Quest's* deck rolled beneath their feet and the shore drew nearer and nearer. When everything that could be salvaged had been brought up, the Cloudfarers grabbed hold of each end of the lanyard and pulled with all their strength until the canvas was bound shut and bulging with supplies.

No sooner had they finished than, with a decisive crunch and sound of splintering beams, the *Noble Quest* barged on to the rocks. For the first time since the *Valorous Mission* had opened fire on it, it didn't tilt, plummet, heave or shudder. Its deck felt surreally still. Marcus peered over the side. With a mixture of joy and astonishment, he saw that its prow had wedged into the gap between two of the fingers of rock. But the waves that had lodged it there were rushing out as quickly as they had rolled in. Soon, he realised, it would be plucked from its resting-place and hurled back again until it disintegrated. There was no time to lose.

'Go! Now! Move!' shouted Rhea to the Cloudfarers.

More limber now that their vessel had stopped moving, Jarrid, Denihr, Lucis and Theus grabbed the canvas and dragged it by the lanyard to the edge of the deck. Then they unfurled one of the rope ladders attached to the gunnels. Jarrid and Theus clambered down it and took up positions on the glossy rocks. The others, with a collective grunt, hauled the canvas over the side. Gripping the wet rope with raw hands, they lowered it slowly until Jarrid and Theus had a firm grip on it.

Once it was safely down, Rhea said, 'Magnis, Amik! Escort Marcus ashore.'

'I don't need an escort!' Marcus protested.

But before he could go any further they all staggered as the *Noble Quest*'s deck convulsed beneath them. Silenced by this, Marcus accompanied them down the flexing ladder then allowed them to hook one arm through each of his and lead him across the rocks.

In spite of his protests he was soon grateful to be anchored to them in this way as an especially brawny wave pounded their backs and shoulders then clawed at them as it rushed out again. Eventually they made it ashore. Marcus flopped on to the sand while Magnis and Amik ran back into the water to help their comrades. Coughing, knees drawn up to his chest, hands clasped around them, Marcus watched the Cloudfarers struggling to drag the laden canvas over the rocks. One moment they were straining forwards, cables slung over their shoulders; the next, a huge wave overtook them and they vanished beneath its foaming crest. When the waters drew back again, the men, instead of pulling the cables, were clinging to them to avoid being swept out to sea. Luckily the weight of the drenched canvas kept them anchored to the rocks.

At last the supplies were brought safely ashore and the Cloudfarers flopped down around Marcus, wet, frozen and utterly exhausted. Flashes of lightning on the far horizon showed the narrow gap between the clouds and the water, which were just as grey as each other. In both directions the shore reared up into limestone cliffs that quickly faded amid mist and spray. Though it was still only early afternoon, the world into which they had plunged looked as gloomy as twilight in Heliopolis.

Scanning the slumped, dejected figures, Marcus recognised Rhea, Theus, Nestor, Magnis, Amik, Lucis, Jarrid, Denihr and Tafril. But that was all.

'Where's Lon?' he asked Rhea, his voice hoarse from the salt water he had swallowed.

She shook her head. He felt his stomach churn. In all, only nine Cloudfarers had survived from a crew of fifty.

'This is a nightmare . . . it must be,' mumbled Nestor.

'How could he have done this?' Lucis asked Magnis.

Magnis shrugged, struck dumb like Rhea.

As they all sat and watched, the *Noble Quest* was pummelled against the rocks time after time, until it smashed to pieces. Splinters of wood began to fetch up amid the discoloured froth that marked the water's edge. Then, further out, beyond the brimming surf, something else appeared: a series of dark, bobbing shapes.

In disorderly procession Marcus's luggage floated towards the shore. A figure clung to one of the cases. It was one of the crew members who had fallen from the *Valorous Mission*. Standing up, Marcus frowned. He thought all of them had been swept from the deck of the *Noble Quest*, still unconscious.

Once the case had reached shallow enough water, Jarrid and Denihr struggled towards it, breasting the larger waves and vaulting the smaller ones, to drag the man off. They dropped him at the water's edge and began kicking his prone form.

'Stop that!' shouted Rhea. 'It won't solve anything. Bring him here.'

They hoisted the man to his feet again and marched him over to her. Forgetting what she'd just said, Rhea promptly punched him. Being exhausted, she didn't punch him hard. But the man, being even more exhausted, went down as if struck by a cannon shell.

'No,' said Marcus, placing a restraining hand on Rhea's arm and kneeling down beside the man.

'What's your name?' he asked.

The man met his eye. His gaze had a lot less fear in it than Marcus had expected – or rather, the fear was eclipsed by an exhausted resignation which, he guessed, went back a lot further than the events of the past hour.

'Persis.'

'Why? Why have you done this?'

'I had no choice. None of us ordinary crew members did. We were told by the officers just after we set off that if we didn't carry out his orders our families would be killed.'

'Whose orders?' asked Marcus. He knew the answer, but he dreaded hearing it none the less.

'General Titus. He's responsible for all of this.'

'A truly loyal citizen, especially in the Cloudfaring Corps, would put duty to the king beyond personal ties,' snarled Rhea.

Persis shot her a look that, in spite of his vulnerable situation, was tinged with pitying contempt.

'I come from the Farmers' layer originally. My family has no more power to defend itself against the general than an insect under the heel of his boot. He could kill them all and no one in the palace would ever know about it. This is how he has gained power.'

'But *why*?' asked Marcus. 'Why has he done this?'

Sighing, Persis squared his shoulders, as if gathering strength for the awfulness of what he had to explain.

'I only picked these things up from my fellow crew members once I was aboard the *Valorous Mission*. I don't know how correct all of them are. But what I've heard is this: when he was a younger man, General Titus was a member of the Cloudfaring Corps and accompanied King Antior on many state visits to other citadels.'

'That's right. He told me.'

'Well, when he saw how other societies were organised he began to believe that military dictatorships – like Scythium or néo-Sirus – were stronger, with control of better trading currents and a greater area of the cloudscape around them than Heliopolis had. He brooded on these things for years and discussed them with his fellow officers, first in the Cloudfaring Corps, later in the Praesidion Guard, to see who agreed with him. But he never considered acting upon it. Then came the Hemispheric Wars. When the northern citadels tried to take control of *our* trading currents too, we fought them off, as you know. But Titus and his allies, all of whom were now senior officers, were incensed by the fact that the king made peace with them. They thought he should have taken advantage of the opportunity to occupy the enemy citadels and push for control of the whole hemisphere.'

'I didn't know that,' said Marcus.

Persis shrugged and continued, 'It was then that they started to hatch their plan to take over the citadel. Over a number of years they put together the Kabal: an alliance of like-minded Cloudfarers and Praesidion Guards. They met and discussed their plans in secret. When the king announced a long tour of all the neighbouring citadels – including Scythium and néo-Sirus – Titus decided it was time to act. I suppose he thought that if the king were away for such an unusually long time the citizenry would grow accustomed to his absence. So . . . he arranged for confederates of his on Selenopolis to plant a bomb aboard the *Regulus*.'

'And was Synvadis part of his Kabal?'

'No. But he was very useful all the same.'

'What do you mean?'

'The Kabal knew that Synvadis would offend many in the palace by finding it hard to conceal his pleasure at his new status – even though he *was* genuinely appalled by the loss of the king. And Titus guessed that this would help to distract any suspicion from him. His plan, as far as I can tell, was first to lead this fake rescue mission. And he knew he'd instilled so many notions of courage and daring in you that you'd insist on being part of it. He would dispose of the *Noble Quest* with you aboard. Then he would return to Heliopolis, insisting that any damage to the *Valorous Mission* had been caused by an attack from a foreign aëro:cruiser, which had also destroyed the *Noble Quest*. In this way he'd make the whole populace – Synvadis and his Ministers included – so frightened of some terrifying phantom enemy that they wouldn't enquire too closely into what had really happened. He would make every-one feel so vulnerable to attack from without that they would allow him to do whatever he proposed to keep them safe – they wouldn't question his new, harsher rule.'

Persis trailed off. Numbed by all he'd heard, Marcus knelt in the soft wet sand, water lapping around him.

'So my father really is dead,' he said eventually.

'I fear so,' replied Persis. 'Not having anything to slow its fall, as the *Noble Quest* did by being attached to the *Valorous Mission*, the *Regulus* must have been destroyed. It may have landed on the water and sunk, but I think it's more likely that it broke apart on the way down. As for the ornithopters, well, I can't imagine how they could have survived so long a descent either.'

Rhea took Marcus's hand, which hung limp in the water, and squeezed it. He felt numb. There was a difference, he thought, between the shock of a sudden tragedy and something you've long dreaded being confirmed. A small flame of hope that was growing more and more feeble within him had been snuffed out.

Sighing, he stood up and gazed at the devastation around him. It had grown even murkier. Night was falling. But the clouds that rolled overhead displayed none of the burnished red and gold hues that he was accustomed to seeing from the palace balconies. They simply grew darker and more oppressive while, inland, shadows deepened amongst the peaks.

'We'd better get started building some kind of shelter or we won't even last the night,' said Rhea.

He nodded.

Galvanised by the onset of darkness, the Cloudfarers discussed how best to carry out Rhea's orders. Or at least she, Theus, Magnis and Lucis did. Others, like Nestor and Amik, appeared to have sunk so deeply into shock or despondency that they failed to react to anything going on around them, but simply squatted on the sand, heads hanging.

'We need to use what we can from the *Noble Quest*,' said Rhea. 'Any ideas?'

'If we untie the canvas and empty it of all its contents

we can prop it up in some places with spars of wood from the aft bulkhead,' suggested Magnis.

Rhea nodded.

'Good. Carry on.'

They set to work immediately. Marcus insisted on helping. He got the impression, from the fleeting looks they exchanged, that they would have preferred to get on with the task on their own. But no one objected and he tried to make himself as useful as possible.

About half an hour later they stepped back and contemplated their work. As well as propping up the canvas, they had also placed Marcus's cases around the edge to stop it flapping. As they stood around their makeshift structure, Amik roused himself and approached from the water line. Joining them, he said, in a voice that was still somewhat muted, 'We could use the convection pipe from one of the burners.'

They all looked at him, puzzled.

'If we put it in the middle and cut a hole in the canvas above, we could use it as a funnel. That way we could light a fire at its base to warm and dry ourselves,' he explained.

Impressed by this suggestion, Theus and Magnis clapped him encouragingly on the shoulder then carried it out. They took one of the sturdy proleyne stoves salvaged from the galley and, after a few failed attempts, managed to get a fire lit.

There was a brief, ill-tempered discussion about what to do with Persis, who had sat apart while the shelter was being prepared. Most were for leaving him to freeze outside. But Marcus managed to persuade them otherwise.

'Well,' said Marcus to Rhea with a melancholy smile, as they lifted a corner of the canvas and crawled inside, 'I suppose you can't live in abject luxury all your life.'

No one could sleep at first – though exhausted, they were still too agitated by the abiding strangeness of this new world. Each person lay on his cloak, an arm crooked under his head, and listened to the wind growing stronger outside. The shelter's dim interior was filled with the musty aroma of damp clothes and hair.

'Never in all my life did I imagine that such a world could exist,' said Rhea.

Denihr nodded, gazing up at the rippling canvas.

'It's like a giant roof,' he observed.

'It *is* a roof, you idiot,' replied Jarrid.

'No, I mean the cloudscape – it's like a great roof, spanning everything, pressing down on us.'

Hearing both their commander and one of their comrades express such wonder seemed to relax the other Cloudfarers a little and loosen their tongues.

'All this land . . . could any creature need so much? How large must they be?' commented Theus.

'But what creatures could survive in so gloomy a world, cut off from sunlight and clear skies – all the things that make life worth living?' added Amik. 'How could they bear it?'

Everyone shook their heads and made vague, bewildered noises.

'I wonder how big that mass of water is,' said Magnis.

'You mean how deep?' asked Rhea.

'Well, yes. But also, how far might it stretch?'

'Maybe . . . maybe it surrounds the land,' suggested Theus. 'Maybe the land in it is like . . .'

He faltered, struggling to describe a concept for which his whole experience of life had given him no adequate words.

'Like Heliopolis and our land in the cloudscape?' suggested Marcus.

'Yes.'

'But between Heliopolis and this world,' said Lucis, 'apart from the clouds . . . is there anything?'

'You mean are they connected?' put in Theus. 'Does the land *we* live in stretch all the way down here, like some of our geologists believe?'

'Yes,' replied Lucis.

'It seems a lot more likely now, doesn't it?' said Denihr.

'But if they aren't, well . . .' Lucis's voice took on a hushed tone, as if even he seemed reluctant to hear what he was going to say next. 'How are we going to get back?'

Marcus remained awake for many hours after the others had fallen asleep. He lay on a cloak near the edge of the shelter, listening to the mutters of the fretfully dreaming Cloudfarers. At last he was able to let the reality of all that had happened overwhelm him. He had kept going over the past few hours purely in the interests of survival. Helping to build the shelter, he had moved forwards only because he felt as if he were falling forwards. His sense of shock at the nature of the world they had plunged into had kept all other thoughts at bay. Now they swarmed around him.

Above all he thought about his father. Never again – not even once – would he feel the roughness of his beard when they embraced, or the touch of those hands, whose strong yet gentle grip made him feel that there was nothing in the world this man could not put right. He squeezed his eyes shut, desperate to keep the image of his father indulgently smiling at him as clear as possible; to prevent it from fading even one little bit – though he knew all too well that in time it would.

He thought too about this world into which they had been plunged. Its low, grey roof and wan light seemed a perfect expression of how he felt – as if his own sense of overmastering dread had conjured it into existence. What greater terrors lurked in the folds and creases of its peaks and the unknowable terrain beyond? Would they have any chance at all of crossing it, of finding a way home?

His thoughts then turned to Titus. How could he have betrayed them all like this? What would happen to the people of Heliopolis under his dictatorship? Was Persis right: had the ignorance of those in the palace about the lives of those below allowed him to seize power?

Fears besieged him. And yet . . . huddled together with these Cloudfarers, he also felt part of something in a way he never had before. He had been brought as low as they had. And in a strange way he couldn't quite explain – even to himself – he was grateful for it.

Consoled a little by this thought, he at last drifted into a fitful sleep.

He woke early. Closest to the edge of the tent, he was able to slip out without disturbing anyone else.

In the open air he discovered, to his amazement, that yet another change had been wrought in the world around him. It had snowed during the night. Indeed, it was still snowing. Back home, high, wispy cirrus clouds occasionally favoured the mountaintop of Heliopolis with a sparse flurry. But he'd never seen anything like this. Fat, moist flakes fluttered down all around him. When he raised his head they settled on his face – looking like a black swarm against the low white cloud base.

The long stalks of grass that covered the dunes looked brittle in the cold morning air. Further inland, also covered in snow, the peaks bulked even larger than before.

Marcus walked a little way down the sand. In spite of all the snow it was almost as murky as it had been the previous day, with a strange, flat light that cast no shadows. The water was calm and had acquired a pearly sheen. A thick line of debris had fetched up at the slushy tidemark. It stretched as far as he could see. Most of it was recognisable as splintered wood. But in amongst it there were larger, hunched shapes. He looked closer and realised what they were – the corpses of drowned Cloudfarers.

His stomach closed and heaved. Blanching, he turned away. When he opened them again he saw Rhea approaching, her boots crunching in the snow. Back along the shore the other survivors were emerging, bleary-eyed, from the tent and gawping at the change that had taken place.

Something nudged against Marcus's foot. A fragment of the *Noble Quest*'s hull, bearing the Heliopolitan crest, was bobbing at the slushy water's edge. He picked it up. The splintered wood that surrounded the crest testified to violence and treachery. He felt the numbness of despair that had filled him since Persis's confession expelled by a surge of pure anger. His whole body glowed with it, in spite of the cold. Soon Titus would be back in Heliopolis and in control.

'We have to go back,' he said. 'We have to try at least.'

She frowned.

'It's almost a thousand miles,' she replied. 'Over terrain we can't even begin to imagine.'

'I know. But if we don't at least try . . . what was the point of surviving at all?'

Rhea glanced at the bedraggled Cloudfarers, who were standing around their pitiful shelter, watching her and Marcus, wondering what they were talking about. Then she gazed back down at the water.

'All right,' she said at last, nodding slowly. 'We go back.'

X

The expanse

Before they could think about how to accomplish this, Marcus and Rhea agreed that the *Noble Quest*'s drowned crew members mustn't be left where they lay. Rhea signalled to the Cloudfarers still watching curiously from the shelter. They padded down the beach, waded into the shallow water and, with her and Marcus helping, hauled their fallen comrades out from amongst the flotsam. The skin of the corpses was not yet bloated or discoloured. Indeed, most looked almost serene, as if they had been exquisitely consoled at the moment of death by the realisation that they wouldn't have to face a much slower and more painful death in this forbidding new world. As Marcus worked he also came across the *Noble Quest*'s compass. It had been torn free of the binnacle, but it still seemed to work. He handed it to Nestor, saying, 'Here, this might yet turn out to be useful.'

Nestor didn't look convinced, but took it anyway, wedging it under his arm. As he turned away Marcus thought he heard him mutter, 'Useful for finding our way to our graves.'

Though absorbed in their grim task, the surviving

Cloudfarers kept on glancing uncomfortably up at the low cloud base. Marcus could sense that they felt the same as he: accustomed to plentiful sunlight and limitless vistas, they were deeply unsettled by this dim, oppressive new world which, everywhere you looked, faded swiftly into impenetrable grey.

Once all the corpses had been dragged up on to the beach the survivors had to decide what to do with them. On Heliopolis all but the most eminent citizens had been cast over into the clouds. Here there was plenty of room for burial. The only question was where best to do it. Eventually they chose to dig one large, deep grave at the rear of the beach, where the soft sand formed into hillocks covered in tall, brittle stems of grass. To do this they used spades improvised from pieces of broken planking. Again Marcus insisted on helping. It was awkward, back-breaking work. But gradually they sank deeper into the ground while the pile of sand strewn around the edges of the grave grew more substantial. Though no one said a word during this process, Marcus, straightening up at one point to ease the ache in his back, noticed tears glistening on the impassive faces of several Cloudfarers.

When they had finished and smoothed over the sand Marcus looked at Rhea.

'Do you want to say anything?' he asked.

Rhea stepped forwards and surveyed the Cloudfarers who stood around the grave. Some looked at her with despondency, some with fatigue. Others, like Theus and Nestor, looked at her with lingering scepticism. After rubbing her brow for a few moments, she said, 'These comrades have ended their lives far from everything familiar to them, far from the embrace of their families. Their resting place is unworthy of them – that much is certain. But as they lie here, in the years to come, they will form the first true bond between our world and this new-discovered one. In that way their journey is not over: they are pioneers. And we should honour them as such.'

She spoke these words in a calm, measured tone. But because of that Marcus felt more rather than less affected by them. He wiped fresh tears from his eyes and saw many Cloudfarers doing the same.

Before long, however, their stomachs began to rumble – a duet that soon turned into a quintet then a full chorus – and they all realised, with a vague sense of shame, that they were ravenous. Sitting on a large, curving section of the *Noble Quest*'s gunnels that had been swept up on to the shore during the night, Marcus and Rhea watched the Cloudfarers prepare breakfast. Being a galley steward, Amik took charge and the others helped. Scooping up fresh snow, they melted it in pots over the fire to make spiced black tea.

After a while Amik approached Marcus and Rhea, bearing steaming tin mugs and chipped bowls. Each bowl had one egg – hard-boiled in the galley the previous morning – rolling around inside it. The eggs were accompanied by chunks of roughly torn, slightly soggy bread. Marcus was worried that Amik might start apologising for the presentation of the food. But, thankfully, such niceties seemed to have been forgotten already. The kitchen steward wordlessly rejoined his comrades on the other side of the fire and ate his own rations. Marcus sipped his tea. It was a little gritty from the stray grains of sand that had found their way into the pot, but blissfully warming. Setting his mug aside, he started to peel the shell off his egg. In spite of the hard edge of the gunnels digging into his thighs and the scouring wind blowing off the water, there was some guilty pleasure to be derived from not having to eat with proper cutlery or observe a bewildering array of table manners.

Everyone ate in glum silence for a while. Then Jarrid and Denihr's banter started up again, albeit milder than it had been before.

'Move over.'

'Why?'

'You keep digging your elbow into me. Your arms flap so much when you eat it's like you're about to take off.'

'If I could take off, do you really think I'd still be stuck here next to you? *You* move over.'

Instead of telling them to be quiet, Lucis, who sat beside them, listened with a faint, indulgent smile – grateful, like everyone else, to be distracted from painful thoughts.

Then Theus, still gazing down into his bowl, mopping it with a chunk of bread, said, 'So what happens after we eat, lieutenant?'

Marcus felt Rhea tense beside him, but she kept her manner relaxed, almost airy.

'We digest, Theus. Didn't anyone ever teach you biology?'

Jarrid and Denihr chortled and Theus smiled along with them. But the look in his eyes remained pensive.

'I mean, what do we do next?' he persisted.

'We try to get home,' she said firmly. 'We travel to the place in this world below where Heliopolis lies and find out if the two really are connected, if there's any route back up.'

'And then what?'

'Well . . . I have the notes on longitude and latitude I took when we stopped to begin our search. And we have charts and a working compass, don't we, Nestor?'

Nestor nodded unhappily.

'So,' continued Rhea, 'we can at least calculate the direction we should be heading with a fair amount of accuracy, regardless of whether we're above or below the uh . . . cloud layer.'

She frowned fleetingly, still finding it difficult, like the others, to come to terms with this concept.

'And what happens if we do reach the right place?' asked Theus.

'We'll find out when we get there.'

'But do you really think it's possible to make our way back up through the clouds? I mean, we must have fallen for miles and miles.'

'I'll be perfectly honest with you, Theus – I don't know if it's possible. But I know it's worth trying. We have lost our commission and been the victims of a perfidious attack, but we're still Cloudfarers. We still have a noble tradition to uphold, however much . . . Titus may have tried to pervert it. It's a tradition of courage, resourcefulness, persistence and, above all, loyalty.'

'Please, lieutenant, don't lecture us about loyalty,' Theus replied wearily. 'Some of us were loyal to Titus for many more years than you've been in the Corps. And look where that's got us.'

Marcus ached to retort. But he sensed this was a debate that had to be resolved between the Cloudfarers alone. After all, why should they listen to his opinion, given how little experience he had of cloudfaring? They would defer to him, of course – but only because that's what protocol demanded. He had yet to win respect from any of them, except perhaps Magnis.

Just then Nestor threw aside his bowl with a sob. Everyone looked at him, astonished.

'It's hopeless!' he exclaimed. 'We're nearly a thousand miles from home. We've got victuals to last us for four or five days at the most. We've got no faster way of travelling than on foot. We'll die before we even get half-way!'

'You're forgetting, Nestor, there may be animals along the way that we can hunt for food,' Rhea replied calmly.

'Or there may be animals along the way that can hunt *us* for food,' countered Theus.

'*And*,' persisted Rhea, ignoring this last comment, 'we still have quite a few crossbolts and swords – which reminds me, Magnis . . .'

'Yes?'

'I'm promoting you to the position of armaments

officer. Congratulations. I want you to gather together all our weapons. Try to find a way of drying the powder in the tips of the crossbolt bolts and repair any others that you can.'

Magnis coloured with pride.

'Yes, ma'am. Thank you.'

Rhea nodded, then surveyed the others.

'Now listen to me, all of you,' she said, her eyes fixing on Theus rather than Nestor. 'What lies before us is by far the most difficult task any of us has ever faced. It will require every drop of endurance that we possess. I have no interest in leading men who are not wholeheartedly committed to accomplishing it, who will give any less than their all . . . So this is what will happen: if you don't believe in me, you can take your portion of food and water and a weapon of your choice and go wherever you wish. But if you do believe in me and therefore decide to stay, I will not tolerate so much as a *whisper* of discontent from any of you . . . Understand?'

Marcus sat up straighter beside Rhea. He wanted everything about his body language to show how much he, for one, believed in her. The Cloudfarers began to look up, hesitantly meeting her eye.

'Follow me and I swear I will keep you alive . . . I *will* keep you alive!' she continued, pressing home her point.

Eventually Theus said, 'Forgive me, lieutenant. This was my final commission. I felt so proud that it was such an important one. So you'll understand, I'm sure, if I'm a little . . . disheartened at the way things have ended up.'

'This isn't the way things have ended up,' replied

Rhea. 'Nothing has ended yet . . . I feel the same way as you, Theus. And I'm going to make sure we get back to Heliopolis so we can both show Titus just how "disheartened" we are – show him *forcefully*, if you get my meaning.'

Theus smiled.

'Very well, lieutenant,' he said. 'I'm with you.'

The rest of the Cloudfarers nodded in agreement, some more readily than others.

'So am I,' added Nestor, in a quavering voice. 'I'm sorry for my grumbling, lieutenant. It's just that I find this world somewhat –' He glanced up at the cloud base, '– *disconcerting*.'

'That's all right, Nestor,' replied Rhea. 'Just try not to condemn us to death before we even get started, eh? Now, when you've all finished your rations you can pack up the shelter and we'll break camp.'

The Cloudfarers delved into their bowls and gradually their murmuring started again – much less sullen than before and even punctuated by the odd dry chuckle.

Rhea's serene expression remained unchanged. But when she bent her head to eat, Marcus heard her take in a deep, shuddering breath and let it out very slowly through pursed lips.

'Well done,' he told her in an undertone.

'Thank you, Your Highness.'

'Please, just call me Marcus. That whole business of "high" and "low" suddenly seems so foolish now. I don't expect special treatment from anyone. All I want to do is help as much as I can and . . .'

Rhea sighed.

'What?' asked Marcus.

'Come on,' she said, 'let's take a walk.'

Clutching their mugs to warm their hands, they wandered along the hard sand near the water's edge. Here the surf had frozen and left a residue of slushy grey ice. Marcus glanced sideways at Rhea's angular, resolute profile, waiting for her to begin. She was frowning. She seemed to be considering her words very carefully.

'I . . . I understand what you're saying,' she told him. 'And I'm sure the men will appreciate your being willing to help. But please bear in mind that they have no experience of being commanded by me – still less of being commanded by a woman. This was my first mission as a First Officer. Titus told me that he had chosen me for so important a task over several better-qualified candidates because he wanted to give a female officer a chance to prove herself. In fact, I think he chose me because he thought I would be a less experienced and difficult adversary when he attacked the *Noble Quest*.'

A look of bitterness clouded her features for a moment.

'Anyway, the point is that Nestor is quite right, in his way. We're in an almost hopeless situation. And I've had no chance yet to prove to these men that they can trust me as they would an officer they had served under many times before. Right now, well, as you saw for yourself, they're bewildered, frightened, unsure of me. They want a commander who gives the impression that she knows exactly what she is doing and believes that

138

we have every chance of making it home alive. And they will be looking to you as well. Though you may not want any special treatment from them, you're still a symbol of the place they yearn to return to. If they see that you have faith in me it will make my task ten times easier. So please . . .'

'I understand,' he interrupted. 'I understand what you mean. And don't worry, I *do* have faith in you – complete faith.'

Rhea smiled. For a fleeting moment she looked much younger.

They walked a little further along the sand. Then, giving him a sidelong glance, she asked, 'How, um . . . how are you holding up anyway?'

He frowned, far from clear what the answer to this question was.

'It's hard to put into words,' he began. 'I mean . . . I loved my father. And the idea that he's gone is too much to bear. But the thing is . . .' He faltered. 'The thing *is* . . . that for as long as I can remember I've been used to him not being around. There were always so many other things he had to do, so many other things he had to think about, even when he was at home. And though I loved the times we did spend together – especially if he used to spar with me or let me stay up late on clear nights to watch the stars from the observatory with him – I could tell when he looked at me that he was always a bit distracted, a bit worried that he wasn't giving me enough of his time, that I might not be shaping up right to be his heir. So what I always tried to do was show him how self-reliant I was, how well I was getting along on my own. When he got back to the palace from state visits to other citadels I'd always make sure I walked up to him instead of running, so he wouldn't see how much I'd missed him and feel guilty . . . I suppose what I'm trying to say is that part of me feels as if he's just gone off on a long trip, even though I know he hasn't.'

Rhea nodded sympathetically.

'And anyway . . .' he continued. 'He wouldn't want me to fall apart. He would be so incensed by what Titus has done that he would want all of us to make every effort we can to survive in this world and get back to Heliopolis. So the best way I can honour his memory is by doing just that. But if . . .'

'But if we do succeed . . . *then* you can mourn him, then you can let yourself cry.'

'Yes.'

Rhea placed her hand on his shoulder.

'I understand,' she said.

'Thank you.'

'It's okay. Listen – while the others are finishing their food, why don't we climb up and see exactly what lies ahead of us?'

'Good idea.'

They struggled across the hillocks of sand. The brittle stalks of the long grass snapped beneath their feet. Then they threaded their way up a steeper incline, between the pine trees.

The incline was covered in thick snow that clung tenaciously to their boots. But when he was about half-way up Marcus noticed that he was still breathing slowly and evenly. His calves weren't aching as much as he would have expected either.

'Is it my imagination or should we be a lot more out of breath by now?' he asked Rhea.

'I was just thinking the same thing,' she said, striding onwards. 'The air in this world must be thicker than we're used to above the cloudscape. Hopefully that'll give us all more strength and stamina . . . We'll certainly need it.'

They climbed on, then reached the top at last. Though neither of them was short of breath, both gasped. The inland side plunged down even more steeply and the pines that clung to it were sparser. They looked as if they were leaning back in a vain attempt to avoid toppling downwards. At the bottom, stretching into the opaque grey distance, lay a vast, flat expanse of ice. It was enclosed on all sides by a mountain range. The mountains' foothills were covered with pines. But further up, above the tree line, there was nothing but scree and fissured ridges.

'This isn't going to work,' said Rhea. 'We can't cross this landscape. Those peaks are too sheer and too deep under snow.'

'But surely we'd move faster if we crossed the expanse,' replied Marcus.

'It looks like ice. It might not be able to support our weight. Even if it did we would probably run out of victuals before we'd even trekked half-way across.'

Marcus frowned.

'There *must* be some other way.'

They stood for a long time, gazing down the hillside, tossing ideas back and forth in an increasingly half-hearted way. Some of the Cloudfarers climbed up to join them. They too were appalled by what they saw, and though they offered some new ideas none seemed any more practical than Marcus's or Rhea's. Eventually they lapsed into a morose silence. Everyone stood perfectly still, as if the awful reality of what lay before them had stunned them into immobility. Then, stirring, Rhea said, 'Wait. I think I've got an idea.'

The ice:cruiser

An hour later Marcus and the Cloudfarers were kneeling on the beach. A large piece of canvas was spread out before them and all the Cloudfarers were gathered round it. Rhea was drawing on the canvas with the blackened tip of a stick she had pulled from the fire.

'You see?' she said. 'We take two of the longest thwart planks we can find from *Noble Quest*'s stern. We lay them parallel on the sand ... I'd say about eight feet apart. Then we lay some of the shorter, straighter planks between them, as crossbeams. We nail all this together – there must be lots of nails left in the wood. Then we put the cases on top, two abreast. We lash them together and nail them down on to the crossbeams as well. We can stand inside them to protect us from the cold.

'Some of the rigging is still in one piece – I saw it lying out on the rocks. We can use the trunk of one of the smaller pines as a mast and a piece of deck planking as a boom. We cut the rigging to fit and stretch it between them. Then we drape the canvas over the rigging and tie it into place.'

She looked up at Marcus and the others. They all stared back at her, nonplussed.

'It's like a yacht,' she explained. 'Only one made to go on ice.'

'An ice:cruiser,' said Magnis, nodding slowly.

'Exactly,' Rhea replied.

'I've sailed yachts before,' observed Theus.

'Really? Where?' asked Marcus.

'On a stopover at the Meridiana chain,' explained Theus. 'The citizens there sail yachts on the calderas.' He hesitated, peering at the design. 'Then again . . . their yachts were slightly different from this one.'

'If we do manage to build this thing,' Magnis began cautiously, 'how do we get it on to the expanse?'

'We drag it up to the top of the hill, then set it off down the other side. By the time we reach the bottom we'll have built up enough momentum to carry us on to the expanse. Then, once we're out of the lee of the hill, the wind blowing off the water should fill the sail and keep us going at a pretty good speed – maybe up to fifteen knots.'

'And how do we drag it up the hill?' asked Lucis.

'We put logs under it and roll it over them. Take the ones at the back out and keep on slotting them into the front.'

This prospect prompted a groan from Jarrid and Denihr.

'I know this all sounds impossible. But we already seem to have greater strength in this world,' Rhea added quickly. 'That at least will make building the, uh . . . ice:cruiser less tiring.'

'Theus, do you think you could pilot a vessel like this?' asked Marcus.

Theus hesitated. Marcus sensed that he was torn between the pessimism recent events had plunged him into and pride in his own abilities.

'I don't see why not,' he said. 'Like I said, the design is a bit different from a normal yacht, but it's the same basic idea. We'll need to put a rudder at the stern with a heavy tiller for steering – we could use one of the impeller blades, if it still has its pivot attached. And we should step the mast forwards to get the centre of sail balance right. If it's too far aft the whole thing will run away and be impossible to steer. A flat-headed sprit would probably be the best type of sail for power and control. We should be able to fashion something reasonably like it.'

'Okay, I have no idea what some of that means, but you clearly do, so I'll trust you,' said Marcus, smiling. 'Nestor, what about you? Do you think we can navigate to the place in this world below Heliopolis?'

In the bright but ever so slightly shrill tones of someone trying to conceal his nerves, Nestor said, 'Uh, yes . . . I think so. As you said, we have calculations to show where we are and charts and a working compass. It's just that they won't show us if there are any features in the landscape that are impossible to cross, or if the ice on the expanse is too thin in some places to support us, or if an avalanche might . . .'

'Yes, thank you, Nestor,' interrupted Rhea, before he could indulge in yet another litany of possible calamities.

She looked at the others. 'We need someone to go a little way on to the ice and test how thick it is . . . Jarrid, can you do that?'

Jarrid seemed a little startled to be volunteered in this way. All the other Cloudfarers gazed solemnly at him.

'Oh, right,' he said. 'Uh, how will I do that exactly?'

'There are bits from the drive shaft of one of the impellers washed up at the water's edge. They're kind of corkscrew-shaped. You could drill down into the ice with one of them.'

'Okay,' replied Jarrid. 'And, um, how will you know if it's too thin?'

'Well, if you don't come back we'll assume the worst,' Denihr told him.

'Oh, right,' said Jarrid, looking more perturbed all the time. 'Well, in that case I'll just –'

The other Cloudfarers could control themselves no longer. Their peals of laughter sounded brittle and slightly eerie in the cold, clear air. Marcus wondered if laughter had ever been heard in this world before.

'Come on, Lucis and I will go with you,' said Denihr. 'I can stay on the bank and we'll tie a rope between us in case anything happens to you.'

He, Jarrid and Lucis went off to fetch their equipment. As they departed Jarrid could be heard saying, 'You really embarrassed me there.'

'I know, I know,' replied Denihr. 'But you were a great help.'

Marcus glanced again at the design of the ice:cruiser.

'Do you really think this will work?' he asked Rhea quietly.

'When I was training to become an officer,' replied Rhea, 'I was told that if you're in a, uh . . . *challenging* situation and have no other ideas, the one you do have may generally be considered a good one. Come on, let's get started.'

Some time later Jarrid, Denihr and Lucis reappeared to report that the ice was at least three feet thick. Everyone set to work. They continued, uninterrupted, for two days. During the first night they noticed that, although the blackness of the overarching cloud layer was absolute, the snow retained a strange luminescence that supplemented the light of their proleyne-soaked torches. Meanwhile Amik kept the fire burning and served thin but warming soup. During rare pauses in work they heard the steady pulse of the waves collapsing and trawling at the sand again and again. To them it was an alien, unsettling sound.

Marcus helped with everything. At first each time he lifted any object a Cloudfarer darted forwards to take it from him. But eventually he prevailed upon them to let him do his bit. In particular he helped the newly promoted Magnis collect up all the intact weapons. The shoulder-mounted crossbolts were much heavier than he expected. He dragged yet another one up the sand and handed it to Magnis. Taking it from him, Magnis explained how its firing mechanism worked.

'See here,' he said, proffering it and turning it over in his hands. 'The hammer is tipped with flint and powered by a mainspring attached to the trigger. When the flint strikes this piece of metal – called the frizzen – it creates a spark, which in turn ignites the powder in the flash pan.'

Marcus nodded, then, after hesitating for a few moments, said, 'I hope you don't mind me mentioning this, Magnis, but I'm surprised you weren't promoted sooner. I mean, you seem so capable.'

Magnis shrugged, colouring slightly.

'I . . . it's not so easy when you're from a farming family.'

'You mean that would stop you from getting promoted? But that's . . .'

'No, no. I don't mean that. It's more like . . . if you're brought up in the lowest layer, everyone around you has done the same thing for generations, right? So you're taught to keep your eyes on the ground, work the soil, not think too much of yourself. But then, if you're strong and smart, you maybe get called up to the Corps. Suddenly you're training among people whose families have always been Cloudfarers. They've learned lots of important stuff while you were still running around barefoot in the fields. So they're way ahead of you already. And they haven't been taught from when they were children not to get above themselves. They've been taught that they're the best there is. So even if they're not any smarter or more able, they usually become officers because they've got much more confidence.'

'Yes, I see what you mean,' said Marcus, reflecting on this. 'Well, if it's any consolation I grew up in the palace, above everyone else, but I certainly wasn't made to believe that I was best at everything – quite the opposite, in fact.'

'Don't get me wrong, I love being in the Corps,' continued Magnis. 'The feeling of freedom out over the cloudscape, seeing other citadels. It was more than anyone in my family had ever dreamed of. And I didn't mind taking orders from officers less experienced than me – not too much, anyway, as long as the orders made sense. 'Course, the best officer of all was the general and now he's . . .' He trailed off, frowning. 'It's sort of confusing.'

'I know, Magnis,' said Marcus. 'It's confusing for me too.'

Sighing, they both set to work again.

Persis helped too. While the other Cloudfarers' loathing of him had in no way diminished, they realised they needed every pair of hands available. So they gave him all the most tedious tasks, like planing down a felled pine trunk with a sword to create the ice:cruiser's mast.

Construction of the sail proved to be the hardest part of all. The mast had to be sharpened to a point and balanced in exactly the right place on the centre runner plank, with four cases packed round it, so that it would remain upright but could pivot smoothly.

Just before dawn on the third day Rhea pronounced the ice:cruiser complete. Sturdy, if not very elegant, with its blunt prow and squat outline, it looked more or less the way it had in Rhea's plan, albeit with Theus's suggestions incorporated. Marcus had nailed to its stern the shattered portion of the aëro:cruiser's hull that bore its name and the crest of Heliopolis. After the words *Noble Quest* he had, using an iron bar heated in the fire, engraved two vertical stripes: *II*.

Bleary-eyed, the Cloudfarers chopped down more pines to clear a path for their vessel up one side of the hill and down the other. Then they planed down the pine trunks, arranged them beneath the prow and began to drag it upwards. In spite of the extra strength the thicker air poured into their lungs, they still had to stop frequently. Each time they did so, they twisted round to face their burden and leaned back against the snowy incline, heels dug into it, hands still gripping the rope. They were exhausted by the time they reached the top. Sitting to rest alongside the others, Marcus looked eastwards and saw light beginning to seep up through the mist that shrouded the distant shore of the expanse. Once they had recovered, the Cloudfarers manoeuvred the ice:cruiser into position, so that it was ready to plunge down the other side of the hill. All that prevented it from doing so were the mooring ropes lashed to the trunks of pine trees on either side.

Theus, Denihr and Lucis hurried back down to the sand, to collect the supplies that had been left there so the ice:cruiser could be hauled up unladen. When they returned they dropped everything on the snowy ground to sort through it. Marcus crouched down beside Magnis, who was checking the weapons. In front of him lay an assortment of swords and daggers, as well as some cross-bolts: both the hand-held, T-shaped type and the larger, shoulder-mounted ones with the revolving barrels. Scattered across the pristine backdrop they looked slenderer than usual and pitifully insufficient.

'Do you think they'll be any use?' Marcus asked.

'Hard to say,' replied Magnis. 'Depends on what attacks us.'

Sighing, Marcus stood up and felt a cold gust of wind rake his hair. There was a distant burst of thunder that roved all round the horizon, as if compressed by the narrow gap between the land and the clouds. He hugged himself and looked at Rhea.

'Well, I suppose this is it.'

She nodded.

'Are you all right?' she asked.

'I suppose so. Just a bit apprehensive. All the rest of you have been in the Corps for years. You're used to this sort of thing.'

'None of us is used to this world, Marcus,' she pointed out. 'Every time I look up and can't see the sky I feel my guts curdling.'

'No, I realise that,' he replied. 'It's just that . . . you've all been trained to face danger.'

'Don't worry. You're doing well.'

'Thanks.'

'There's just one more thing.'

'What's that?'

'What do we do with Persis?'

They looked over at him. His involvement in building the ice:cruiser completed, he had retired glumly from the others once more, slouching against the trunk of a pine, trying to draw as little attention to himself as possible.

'He comes too,' said Marcus.

'You do realise that if we leave him here there will be more victuals for the rest of us.'

'We can't leave him here. He's as much a victim of Titus as we are.'

'So he says.'

'Well, I choose to believe him . . . for the moment. Something tells me we might still be grateful for his help.'

'Very well,' she replied unhappily.

Seeing how steep the inland side of the hill really looked – and how vast and forbidding the frozen expanse – Marcus was assailed by all sorts of misgivings.

'Do you think this can possibly work?'

She sighed.

'I don't know. But I doubt anything else possibly can.'

The supplies were packed with care into the cases at the ice:cruiser's stern. Marcus looked around.

'Where's Magnis?' he asked.

Before Marcus could answer, Magnis reappeared from amongst the trees, tucking a folded piece of cloth into his tunic and looking vaguely furtive.

'Ready, corporal?' asked Rhea.

'Yes, ma'am,' he replied stoutly.

The rest of the Cloudfarers looked expectantly towards Marcus and Rhea.

'Do you want to say anything to them?' Rhea asked him.

Marcus remembered his last, floundering attempt at addressing the Cloudfarers when they left Heliopolis. He now suspected that Titus had gained no small amusement from watching it. Could it really have been less than a week ago?

'Not right now,' he said. 'Let's just get going.'

Everyone clambered aboard, the vessel rocking from side to side as they did so. All the cases, except the one containing supplies, had their lids propped open. Rechristened 'compartments', they could accommodate the Cloudfarers in only mild discomfort. The centre compartment, nearest the prow, contained Marcus, Rhea and Theus. Persis was told to climb into a compartment at the stern on his own. He did so and slumped down miserably inside it. At Rhea's command, Jarrid and Denihr – standing at port and starboard quarters – swung axes at the mooring ropes. It took three strokes before the last straining fibres of each rope snapped. With a lurch that threw the occupants of each compartment against one another, the *Noble Quest II* accelerated rapidly down the snow-covered incline.

Marcus gasped, startled by the rawness of the slipstream. The ice:cruiser creaked all around him, sounding worryingly elderly, even though it was newly built. He closed his eyes, convinced that at any moment their improvised vessel would break apart and tumble downwards in a flurry of broken planks, cases and flailing limbs.

But, remarkably, the whole thing held together. And when he next peered over the lip of the compartment, he saw that they were nearing the bottom of the hill.

The expanse was fringed by a thick bank of compacted snow. Already travelling at more than fifteen knots, the ice:cruiser hit the bank square on and exploded through it in a dense white flurry. Everyone ducked down with their cloaks drawn over their heads. It then sailed through the air, slammed into the ice and slewed wildly before regaining its forward course. One by one, its occupants' dazed faces – framed by the darkness – emerged from the compartments and gazed cautiously out at the featureless terrain that now stretched all around them.

Soon the *Noble Quest II* lost much of the momentum it had gained careering down the hillside and began to slow. But just when Marcus thought they were going to come to a humiliating stop, a gust of wind sent the sail spinning. Lucis and Amik – in the compartment closest to it – ducked as the boom swept over their heads. After several failed attempts, they managed to reach up and grab the ropes that trailed from it. Held at the correct angle, the sail billowed and the ice:cruiser began to pick up speed again. Soon it was travelling faster than ever. In the compartment behind Marcus and Rhea, Nestor clasped the compass in both hands, tilting it towards him. His fingers, curled round it, were already white from the cold.

'Twelve – no, eleven – degrees south-south-west,' he said. 'We need to turn further to port.'

Magnis and Tafril wrenched at the boom and relayed Nestor's orders to Jarrid and Denihr, who gripped the tiller. They lowered the pivoting impeller blade on to the ice, where it spewed up glinting shards.

'Slightly more,' said Nestor. 'Good. That's it. That's our course.'

With its sail and tiller angled the right way and held steady, the *Noble Quest II* fled on across the ice.

Crouched in their compartments, the Cloudfarers gazed in undiminished wonder at the world unfolding around them. Amik and Lucis pointed out to one another the complex, often beautiful tracery of pressure ridges in the ice as it flashed by. Meanwhile Magnis and Tafril stared at the fringes of the expanse on either side, mesmerised by the way the mountain crags punctured the grey, overarching canopy. It started to snow again – not the plump flakes that had feathered the shore, but stinging pellets. Even without them the hurtling air around the ice:cruiser was so cold that no one could survive exposure to it for long. In each compartment two people kept watch while the third crouched down for shelter. The lookouts had their heads swathed in thick scarves, with narrow gaps for eyes and mouths.

Marcus took the first watch in his compartment. He soon discovered that it was surprisingly hard to stay alert while on watch – not because of the cold but because the sheer featurelessness of the terrain tended to lull you into a trance. The way to avoid this was to keep on moving your head and looking in different directions, even if you did end up feeling a bit like one of the birds perched on a branch in the Hortoreum, restlessly searching the undergrowth for insects.

He shivered. Thinking of the vibrant fertility of the gardens only made him feel colder and this new world seem even more grey and louring.

'I don't think I've ever felt this cold before,' said Theus, who had taken the first shift in the compartment beside Marcus's. 'Not even out over the cloudscape, flying to Scythium in midwinter.'

'Well, think of me,' replied Marcus. 'I've scarcely ever set foot on a floor that didn't have central heating running under it.'

Theus smiled, then winced as his lips cracked. They stood in silence for a while, swaying and twitching with the motion of their vessel as it bumped over the ridges.

'I'm sorry this had to happen on your last mission,' Marcus said. Theus shook his head.

'It can't be helped,' he replied. 'I had two weeks to go in the Corps – didn't really expect to be called up again. I was winding down to retirement, spending most of my time teaching trainee Cloudfarers. But Titus told me he wanted his most experienced pilot aboard the *Noble Quest*, given what an important mission this was. Now I think he wanted me at the wheel because he thought someone, well . . . senior and out of practice would have less chance of saving the vessel.'

Marcus opened his mouth to reply then hesitated. It was perhaps better not to mention that Titus had manipulated Rhea in almost exactly the same way. But resentment at the general's contempt for all three of them flared in his chest. He welcomed the sensation, cradling it to him. It obliterated his fears and the ache of grief – for a while, at any rate.

'Did you serve often under Titus?' he asked.

'More times than I can remember . . . More times than I'd care to now.'

'You . . . you must have known him quite well,' suggested Marcus hesitantly, wondering just how much admiration Theus still felt for his old commander, in spite of what he had done.

'You don't really get to know a man like Titus,' Theus replied firmly. 'Discipline was everything to him. "Observe the chain of command or you'll soon be in chains yourself" – that was his style. But he was a fine tactician . . . I have to admit that. Never seemed beset by many doubts.'

'So he must have commanded a lot of loyalty.'

'Well, yes. But it was more that we were all terrified of him and what punishment he might visit on us if we stepped out of line. It's a strange thing – sometimes the crueller you are to people the more devoted to you they become. They sense just how far you're willing to go to achieve what you want, so they think you must be strong. And that in turn gives them faith in you, makes them feel safe under your command.'

'I had no idea things were so bad in the Corps.'

Theus smiled.

'How could you?' he said.

'Do you still admire him?' Marcus asked.

'I find it hard to admire someone who tries to kill me,' he said dryly. Thinking it over some more, he added, 'In the past I feared Titus, but sort of respected him, same as all the other Cloudfarers here ... Now I just loathe him. I will tell you this, though: his will is unbending. There is nothing he won't do, no one he won't sacrifice to win a victory. He gives no quarter. If we do make it home and fight him, we'll have to be just as ruthless.'

Marcus considered this. Then, with a despairing laugh, he said, 'I liked him – I really did. I thought he liked me too.' He shook his head. 'I'm such a fool. I had so few friends in the palace that I know nothing about understanding people.'

'Don't be too hard on yourself,' replied Theus. 'I'm afraid I would suggest that he was cultivating you.'

'What do you mean?'

'Well, he was so arrogant he might originally have thought that once he'd disposed of the king he could manipulate you into being a mere façade for his power. You would be a figurehead for the citizenry to look to while he carved out a Heliopolitan empire stretching far across the cloudscape – all in your name of course ... and all for your greater glory.'

Marcus glowered. Not only had he lost his father, but the man he had looked to for guidance and support during his father's many long absences had been manipulating him all along; he'd had no regard for him at all. It was too much to bear.

'If we do get back, I'll ... I'll ...' He slammed his fist against the edge of the compartment.

'I'm sorry, I didn't mean to upset you,' said Theus, placing a hand on his shoulder. 'You've already suffered a great loss.'

'No, it's okay,' replied Marcus, taking a deep breath. 'It helps me block out the pain. You know, in a strange way, I'm almost grateful that we have such an impossible task before us. It gives me so many other things to think about to stop dwelling on my father. I know that might make me sound cold, but for the moment I just need to . . .'

'I understand,' replied Theus. 'And I certainly don't think you're cold. Or at least –' He looked around at the other Cloudfarers, hunched at their stations, beads of ice sparkling on their clothes and hair, '– no colder than the rest of us.'

They travelled on for many hours. Marcus took two more turns as lookout. During the second he saw mountains at the far end of the expanse looming out of the mist. He watched them growing more and more solid with a sense of inescapable doom. They were at least as high as the ranges that enclosed it on either side. How could he and the others possibly continue their journey in the ice:cruiser with such an obstacle ahead of them? His heart sank. Already he noticed a greying and thickening of the air that heralded the onset of night.

Still gazing up at the mountains, he thought he saw two tiny dots, almost lost against the shadowy under-belly of the clouds. He frowned and continued to watch them for a few moments. Then he reached down and tapped Rhea on the shoulder. Struggling to her feet, she squinted in the direction he was now pointing.

'Birds,' she said. 'Big ones too. Maybe we could shoot one down for food?'

'Are you *sure* they're birds?'

'Well, they have wings. It's usually a bit of a giveaway.'

'I don't know. They look more like ...'

The realisation of what they were dawned on both of them at the same moment. They stared incredulously at one another, then Rhea turned and yelled to the others:

'Ornithopters!'

XII

The Nullmaurs

There was an immediate commotion aboard the *Noble Quest II*. All the Cloudfarers who weren't already on watch staggered to their feet and looked wildly around them.

'Where? Where?' asked Nestor.

Lucis snatched up a telescope and trained it on the ornithopters – with difficulty, owing to the bumpy progress of the ice:cruiser.

'Do the pilots look like Cloudfarers?' asked Rhea.

'They don't even look like Heliopolitans,' replied Lucis. 'They're shorter, stockier.'

The ornithopters drew closer, wings beating steadily. Marcus strained forward, trying to get a better view of the pilots.

'They must be native to this world,' said Marcus. 'Could they have invented the same kind of flying machines as we have?'

Rhea shook her head.

'It's too much of a coincidence. They can only have salvaged them. I mean, how many aëro:cruisers must have crashed in the Hemispheric Wars alone?'

'But that means someone from the crews might have survived,' said Theus. 'It might even mean that the king . . .'

Rhea shot him an admonitory look and he trailed off. Marcus shook his head. Though he tried with all his might to suppress it, telling himself he was being foolish, hope sprang up within him that his father might be alive.

'What do you think they want with us?' asked Amik.

'They're probably a little curious about who we are,' replied Lucis with heavy irony.

'And why we've blundered into their world,' added Denihr. 'Let's hope they're not territorial.'

'Surely no intelligent creature could bear to live in a world like this, cut off from the sun . . . from light and warmth,' observed Lucis, shaking his head wonderingly.

'Do we raise cross-bolts?' asked Magnis.

'No,' said Rhea, eyes still following the ornithopters. 'I don't want our first act when we meet beings from this world to be pointing weapons at them.'

'Should we furl the sail and stop?' asked Theus.

'No. Let's keep moving.'

The ornithopters came closer and closer in ever tighter circles. As they swooped overhead Marcus felt the rhythmic downdraught from their wings. And when they made their closest pass yet, he saw what looked like two clay pots tumbling from them and skittering across the expanse's frozen surface. Each pot had a pinched neck with a sputtering wick protruding from it. There was a few seconds' silence then a lurid flash tore through the gloom. It was accompanied by an eruption of shattered ice. Freezing water drenched the *Noble Quest II* and its crew.

'Evasive action!' spluttered Rhea. 'They may just be trying to scare us off their territory.'

Amik wrenched at the boom, twisting it round to set a new course. Lucis did the same with the tiller. Jarrid and Denihr clambered out of their compartments and stood on the port-side runner, leaning perilously far out to help pull the ice:cruiser in that direction. The starboard runner lifted clear off the ice and the vessel slewed to the left.

It soon became clear, however, that none of this would do any good. The ornithopters swooped lower and lower over the ice:cruiser, grazing its mast with their wingtips. And their pilots hurled down yet more bombs. One of these landed in the aft starboard compartment. Persis ducked down, scrabbling around for it. Just in time he managed to scoop it up and hurl it clear of the ice:cruiser. It exploded in mid-air. Like the ones before, it created a starburst of bleaching light.

The next bomb exploded just as it hit the sail. The frame splintered and the canvas burst into a sheet of flame. Within a few minutes it had been reduced to a few blackened shreds fluttering uselessly in the wind.

'Incendiary bombs,' muttered Magnis grimly.

Deprived of any means of propulsion, the *Noble Quest II* soon slewed to a halt.

'If we can't outrun them we have no choice but to fight back,' said Rhea. 'Shoulder weapons!'

Crouching down in their compartments to shield themselves as best they could, the Cloudfarers raised their crossbolts and trained them on the circling ornithopters.

'Fire at will!' Rhea shouted as they swooped over the ice:cruiser once again.

Instead of a fusillade of shots there was a series of fruitless clicks. Not one of the barrels revolved and not one of the bolts fired. The Cloudfarers stared in bafflement at their weapons, then at Rhea and Marcus.

Rhea groaned.

'The powder must still be too damp to fire,' she said.

'Look out!' shouted Marcus.

They all ducked as the ornithopters skimmed over them with only a few feet to spare. Marcus saw that the pilots' faces were bearded and scowling. Their dark hair had a reddish tint to it.

Yet more bombs struck the expanse. There were explosions all round the *Noble Quest II*. Cracks in the ice raced away in every direction and water brimmed up between them. The ice:cruiser tilted sharply.

'Abandon ship!' yelled Rhea – adding, in a resigned tone, 'Again.'

Without time to grab even a few supplies, they all leaped from their sinking vessel. The ice they landed on had been broken apart and they had to scramble from one wide, bobbing chunk to another until they reached a firmer surface. Arms full of his precious charts, Nestor fell into the water and the chunk he'd toppled off closed instantly over his head, as if on a hinge. Already safe himself, Persis grabbed a crossbolt from Magnis. He leaped back to where Nestor had vanished, slammed the stock into the ice to shatter it into smaller pieces and, reaching into the churning water, hauled the navigator out.

As soon as he was safe, Magnis and Lucis dragged the shivering, retching Nestor further away from the shattered ice. They shot looks at Persis that were still hostile, but tinged with grudging respect.

Slumped on the frozen surface of the expanse, everyone watched their vessel founder for a second time in nearly as many days. It heeled over and sank in an eruption of bubbles. Soon there was nothing left on the surface of the water to mark its presence, save for a few blackened shreds of canvas.

Marcus scowled up at the ornithopters. Having sunk the ice:cruiser, they had gained altitude, but were still circling. Lowering his eyes, he spotted something approaching from the fringes of the expanse. At first it looked like a low black cloud. Then it split into six different shapes, though each still had a strange, pulsating outline. Due to some trick of this world's spectral light they looked as if they were floating above the expanse's white surface. As they drew closer their outlines became clearer. Each one appeared to be some kind of transport, slung between two galloping beasts. Marcus took the telescope and trained it on the leftmost one. It had a blunt, wedge-shaped prow, which swept upwards to a height of five feet. Its sides then sloped down more gradually to a low, tapered stern. An unusual-looking gun was mounted there, on a swivelling pedestal. A stocky, bearded figure – similar to the ones who piloted the ornithopters – stood behind it, gripping the handles that protruded from it.

The transport's sides also curved inwards to rest more easily against the shoulders and flanks of the beasts that supported it. It was bound to them by a thick harness lashed around their torsos. The beasts themselves were even more extraordinary to behold. At least three times as large as the largest Cloudfarer, each one was covered in short, coarse fur. This was mostly pure white, except for where it bristled in a dark grey ridge along the spine. The beast had not one but two pairs of powerful rear legs. Its haunches rippled with muscles while its paws boasted long sharp claws with which to grip the ice. Its hooded, slit-like eyes were set far back on either side of the head. A faceplate, with blinkers, ran down its nose.

Reins stretched from the beasts' necks to a pair of slots in the vehicle's prow. Another figure stood there, gripping them on the other side and peering over the top.

As they drew closer Marcus could see that these transports, though stubby and inelegant, were formidably adaptable. The surefootedness of the beasts meant that they could probably manage any terrain, no matter how steep or irregular.

'This is it, we're doomed,' said Nestor. 'We may as well just jump into the water and get it over with.'

Perhaps thinking that this was a churlish remark from the navigator, considering he had been rescued from just such a fate, Theus said, 'Don't let us detain you, Nestor.'

The transports drew even closer. Everyone started to back away instinctively across the ice.

'I don't want to sound like the miserable coward of this group,' said Theus. 'But shouldn't we be trying to get away?'

It was as if a spell had been broken.

'Yes, run!' shouted Rhea. 'And spread out – it'll make it harder for them to catch us.'

The Cloudfarers needed no second bidding. They set off as fast as they could. In spite of this it proved difficult for them to make progress. The quicker they tried to move the more they were prone to slipping. Twice Denihr went sprawling over the ice, only to be helped up by Theus. Others fell just as often. In spite of Rhea's orders to spread out everyone tended to remain in pairs, so they could clutch at one another whenever one of them lost his footing. For her part, Rhea kept Marcus close to her, though he had to help her up as often as she helped him.

As he struggled onwards Marcus glanced round and saw that the transports were overtaking the Cloudfarers in a wide arc on either side. The pilots steered them with near-suicidal recklessness. When they wished to turn they yanked viciously on the reins, causing the beasts to bellow and lunge in a new direction, claws scrabbling on the ice. Each time the beasts did so the transports lurched sharply, throwing their occupants from side to side. It looked terrifying, but the pilots let out exultant whoops. Suddenly Marcus understood: this was sport to them.

In this way, they manoeuvred between the Cloudfarers. Each pilot focused on a different pair, bearing down on them no matter how many times they changed direction. Lucis and Magnis – the most closely pursued – slowed down deliberately until the beasts' slavering jaws were within inches of them, then rolled in opposite directions. They avoided having stray limbs trampled and won a few moments' liberation. But the beasts quickly spun round and bore down upon them again.

The figure at the stern of the transport pursuing them hooked one arm through the handle of the gun to steady himself. He then reached down and picked up a long piece of rope coiled on the floor. It had a loop at one end. He spun it above his head several times then hurled it, with scarcely believable accuracy, towards the fleeing pair. The first few times the looped end slapped on to the ice. The gunner swiftly pulled it in for the next attempt.

Still trying to run from his own pursuers, Marcus glanced round and saw Lucis wincing and reaching his hands to his throat as the loop of rope finally closed around it. The creature at the stern wrenched at it. Lucis's head snapped backwards and his feet shot out from under him. Marcus cursed at the sight, but kept on running, Rhea still at his side.

One by one, all the Cloudfarers were felled in the same way. Those already captured staggered, or in some cases skidded, along behind a transport as its pilot pursued others who were still free. When Marcus felt the gentle but ominous touch of a rope flopping over his shoulders he yelled out, 'No!' But it was too late. Within a second there was a searing tightness around his throat, constricting his windpipe, and he was slammed to the ground. The same happened to Rhea moments later.

At first everyone lay thrashing on the ice. Then, gradually, they struggled to their feet. The transports began to circle them, some clockwise, some anticlockwise. The ropes wound themselves around the bewildered Cloudfarers, pulling them closer and closer together, until they were huddled in a tightly bound clump with their arms pinned at their sides.

The transports lurched to a halt. The beasts that carried them stood panting from their exertions. Their breath steaming in the air, they pawed fretfully at the ice. One of the pilots leaped down from the stern of his transport. He was dressed in matted animal skins, coarsely stitched together and dyed muted shades of brown and green.

Though clearly mature, he was only about two-thirds the size of the Cloudfarers – Marcus's height. The few parts of his face not covered in hair were daubed in some kind of black tar. He paused to survey the Cloudfarers for a few moments then walked unhurriedly towards them. He unsheathed a stubby sword: it had two blades that intersected at right angles, each edge deeply serrated.

The Cloudfarers all scowled down at him. Returning their gaze, he betrayed no sense of intimidation at the difference between his height and theirs. Indeed, he seemed to be amused by how tall they were. Silently, assuredly, he wandered round the clump of fidgeting bodies then stopped in front of Marcus.

He studied Marcus's features for more than a minute, leaning forwards until their faces were only inches apart. His eyes were striking. The pupils – fully dilated – glittered black but the corneas were a vivid yellow. His breath was equally striking – hot and rank. With a callused, dirt-encrusted hand, he prodded the skin on Marcus's face.

Eventually, in a much lower voice than Marcus had expected, the creature unleashed a stream of guttural sounds in a piercing brogue. Marcus flinched as warm spittle flecked his face. He understood nothing of the words, but the rising intonation at the end suggested that they formed a question.

'I . . . I don't understand,' he replied.

The creature's intrigued yet complacent look was replaced by one of utter astonishment.

'You . . . speak . . . M'num?' he asked haltingly.

'I, uh . . . I suppose I must,' replied Marcus.

'What . . . name . . .' the creature began.

'What is my name?'

'Yes . . . what is . . . your name?'

'Marcus.'

The creature frowned again and looked away for a moment. Marcus got the impression he was trying to re-master a language that he knew quite well, but rarely used.

'Where . . . come you from?' he asked.

'I come from Heliopolis.'

The creature's frown only deepened.

'What is . . . Hel'plis?'

'It is a citadel.'

This word was clearly unfamiliar to the creature, but he ignored it.

'Where lies it? I have not heard from it.'

'I'm not surprised you haven't heard *of* it,' said Rhea. She gazed down at the creature with a look which, in spite of the captives' plight, was unmistakably condescending. 'It lies above the clouds.'

'*Above* the clouds?' exclaimed the creature. 'There is no above the clouds. Our land is made from them. They go on . . .'

He held his hand flat and raised it in stages above his head. Marcus guessed that he was trying to convey the idea of the clouds stretching up for ever.

'We used to believe the same, only the other way round,' he said. 'But I assure you they don't.'

The creature continued to study Marcus's face. Some faint instinct told Marcus that he wasn't quite as amazed to hear about their origins as he pretended.

'And why are you here?'

'We fell through the clouds.'

'How?'

'Our king . . .'

'What?'

'The leader of our citadel – he was lost among the clouds. We were flying over them, searching for him.

But we . . . we got into trouble. We were trying to return home when you attacked us.'

'Daldriadh is ours! You will *not* take it from us!'

'Oh, don't worry,' said Denihr, facing away from the creature, but craning round to look at him. 'We wouldn't be interested in a land as gloomy and miserable as this one. You're most welcome to it.'

Marcus winced. Something told him that their captors wouldn't appreciate such flippancy.

Sure enough, the creature sauntered round the perimeter of fidgeting bodies to where Denihr stood. Denihr smiled down at him, his expression defying him to reach up high enough to punch him with any real force in the face. Instead the creature drove his fist into his stomach. Denihr crumpled, retching. He was prevented from sinking on to the ice only by being so tightly bound to his fellow Cloudfarers.

Returning to Marcus, the creature asked, '*Why* did you fall through the clouds?'

'It's . . . it's a long story.'

The creature surveyed the Cloudfarers again. They returned his gaze with undisguised hostility. He turned and signalled to the other pilots of the transports. Drawing swords, they leaped down and approached. Some unsheathed swords. Others wielded an even uglier-looking weapon: some kind of flail. It had a seared wooden handle and a chain hanging from it with a spiked iron ball attached. The spiked ball swung like a pendulum as they crossed the ice.

'I am Kroy,' the creature said. 'We are Nullmaurs.

We will take you to Gorloch, our chief. He likes long stories.'

Kroy raised his sword and held it against Marcus's throat.

'Just pray he does not wish to cut it short.'

With scant regard for whether or not they might lacerate the prisoners' arms, the other Nullmaurs sawed at the ropes that bound them together then herded them towards the transports. In spite of what had just happened to Denihr, several of the Cloudfarers – especially Jarrid and Tafril – looked as if they still found their captors somewhat difficult to take seriously, given the size difference.

'You know if we tried to take them on they'd be too short to get a good lunge at the head or neck,' Marcus overheard Tafril say to Rhea.

'No, but they could easily take your legs off below the knee,' replied Rhea. 'I think you'd find it slightly difficult to escape then.'

'I suppose so,' Tafril said, disconsolately.

Half an hour later Marcus, Magnis and Rhea were huddled inside Kroy's shuddering transport, heading south across the expanse at high speed. There were no seats so they had to prop themselves against the sloping sides. Every time the beasts heaved their shoulders with more than usual vigour they ended up sprawled across the hard floor. The Nullmaur at the stern of the transport – who had swung his gun round and angled it down at them – watched impassively as they fell this way and

173

that. In spite of the difficulty he was having trying to stay upright, Marcus noticed that the gun looked very like a larger version of a crossbolt. It was loaded with only one hefty bolt, which had a serrated iron tip and was attached to a length of cable.

The other transports contained the rest of the Cloudfarers. The ornithopters were still swooping and circling. Sometimes, when they passed overhead, a Nullmaur in one of the transports raised his sword and let out an exultant holler. The ornithopters' pilots responded likewise. Trying to ignore the growing evidence that their captors were not only belligerent but deranged, Marcus said, 'There was me thinking an ice:cruiser was an uncomfortable way to travel.'

'It *was* an uncomfortable way to travel,' said Rhea. 'But this is worse.'

'Do you think we're going to find a chance to get away from these creatures?' Magnis asked her.

'I don't know, Magnis. But out on the ice, with no weapons, we didn't stand a chance.'

'You never know,' said Marcus hopefully. 'Once they've realised we're not a threat they might let us go.'

Rhea looked sceptical.

'Well, maybe,' she said. 'But let's not count on it.'

'How do you think it is that they speak our language?' asked Magnis.

'It seems impossible, doesn't it?' replied Marcus. 'Maybe we share a common ancestor.'

'Surely not!' exclaimed Magnis, with a look of distaste.

'But even if we did, how would we have ended up above the clouds while they stayed down here?' said Rhea.

Marcus sighed.

'I don't know. Of course we're assuming they all speak our language. I mean, Kroy was the only one who spoke to us before. And even he seemed to struggle a bit at first. Maybe it's a language only some of them use . . . and even then only at special times.'

'Maybe,' said Rhea.

After more painful falling around, Marcus decided to test his theory. He glanced towards the Nullmaur at the stern and offered a nervous smile.

'I suppose it must be strange living under the cloud-scape, having so little sunlight,' he suggested.

The Nullmaur said nothing, merely stared straight ahead.

'Although I suppose you might not notice it because it's all you've ever been used to,' Marcus added.

Still the Nullmaur said nothing.

'In fact, I suppose you might actually like it because the sun is never too strong. No chance of getting burnt, eh?'

The Nullmaur favoured him with a brief, baleful glance then looked away again.

Meanwhile Rhea, who had hauled herself off the floor to see where they were going, nudged Marcus with her foot.

'Look,' she hissed.

He stood up beside her. Along the fringe of the expanse, which was now very close, he saw a row of bobbing lights. Others were descending the lowest slopes of the mountainside, emerging from amongst the thickly planted pines in clusters of three or four. Looking closer, he realised that they were torches wielded by more Nullmaurs. Then he raised his eyes and noticed that the underbelly of the clouds, where the mountainside vanished into them, was suffused with a pulsating orange glow. Silhouetted against it, the ornithopters peeled off and vanished.

'Maybe they're just here to greet us?' suggested Marcus hopefully.

'With what, though?' asked Rhea.

Marcus glanced back at the still silent Nullmaur gripping the gun.

'With few words, I'd imagine,' he observed.

The transports stopped at the expanse's edge. Wheezing amid the occasional mutinous growl, the beasts bent their forelegs then both pairs of hind legs before settling on their haunches. As a result, each transport tilted forward then backwards as it sank to the ground. The torch-bearing Nullmaurs, who had by now reached the bottom of the mountainside, froze, gazing in astonishment at the prisoners. But then, after a gruff exchange with Kroy, they helped to lead them up through the trees. The overloaded branches of the pines, disturbed by the footfall of captors and prisoners alike, shed snow over both at random. Shaking it off, they all toiled onwards.

Eventually they emerged into a clearing. A hole

gaped at its centre. Marcus and Rhea approached and peered into it. In spite of the glow from the Nullmaurs' torches, it looked impenetrable. Marcus felt a strong urge to grab one of the torches and drop it down to see more, but something told him this wouldn't be appreciated.

'What happens next?' Rhea asked in an undertone.

Marcus shrugged. But the answer was instantly and shockingly provided. He felt Kroy's palms slam against his back and he pitched headlong into the hole. As the darkness engulfed him, he heard Rhea's voice quickly fading above:

'Marcus, are you all right . . . ?'

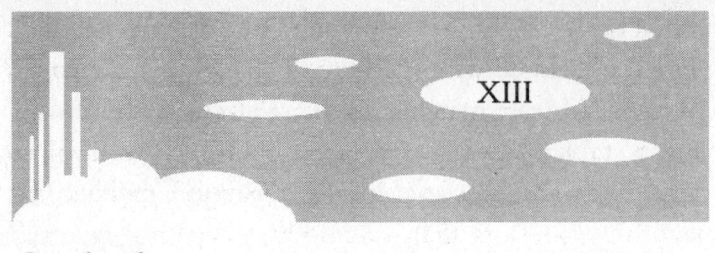

Gorloch

For a few seconds he was too shocked to fathom what was happening. Then he realised that the hole, instead of plummeting vertically – as he'd expected – curved to the left. It was smooth-sided and he was sliding down it at great speed. Gasping, he tried to recover the breath that had been knocked out of him by Kroy's blow. The air whistling past his face smelt faintly smoky and was surprisingly warm. Each time the tunnel twisted in a new direction he felt himself zooming up one side of its curving walls. For a while he travelled head first, then was spun round and continued feet first. With no visible markings around him he had no way of telling how far he had fallen. Then he noticed a faint glow reflected in the tunnel's glassy walls. He spun wildly as the tunnel twisted one last time then shot backwards out of the end like a shell from a cannon. He'd already grown so accustomed to the darkness that when light burst upon him it felt blinding. Eyes screwed shut, he slid on before finally slowing to a halt.

He lay motionless on his back for a few moments then opened his eyes and looked around. He was inside a cavern. It was immensely wide but not especially tall. The roof bristled with stalactites. They looked like icicles of rock and were matched in many places by the equally sharp stalagmites that stretched up from the floor to meet them. He felt as if he were trapped inside a vast jaw, full of incisors, that was about to clench shut at any moment.

Struggling into a sitting position, he saw that he was at the far end of a shallow channel that stretched from the opening of the tunnel all the way across the floor of the cavern. The portion of the roof above it had been cleared of stalactites. Small bridges spanned it. The Nullmaurs who had been crossing them when Marcus burst out of the tunnel froze and stared at him, amazed. They weren't daubed in tar, like their comrades, but otherwise they looked the same. He stared back at them, wondering what the appropriate greeting was when you've just slid backwards into someone's dwelling place. Before he could think of one, he felt two rough hands encircle his upper arm. Looking up, he saw a florid-faced Nullmaur scowling down at him. The guard hauled Marcus out of the channel and deposited him on the floor beside it.

A few seconds later shouts of protest issued from the mouth of the tunnel and grew swiftly louder, heralding the arrival of the Cloudfarers. Sure enough, a few seconds later they burst into the cavern in a disordered heap. They hurtled along the channel, slammed into the wall with a loud, collective 'Oof!' and then, after a few moments of silence, began the painful task of untangling themselves from one another. Hurrying over to them, Marcus reached down to help Rhea out of the channel.

'Thank you,' she said breathlessly.

'Are you all right?'

She straightened up, placing her hands against the small of her back.

'I think only my dignity's been hurt. How about you?'

'Same.'

'Good.'

While the rest of the Cloudfarers scrambled out of the channel, Marcus and Rhea looked around. The floor on either side of it was littered with abandoned tools, animal skins and what looked like the remains of numerous partially gnawed bones. The stale air was filled with a mixture of different aromas, each one striving to be the most unpleasant. Marcus could now see that in the farthest recesses of the cavern the space between the floor and the ceiling was filled with wooden scaffolding. Indeed, it was so enmeshed with the stalactites and stalagmites that they seemed to form part of its structure. A couple of ornithopters, in various states of disrepair, were sitting amid the scaffolding while Nullmaurs worked on them from above and below.

As they continued to watch, Nullmaurs abandoned their work, swarmed down the scaffolding to the floor of the cavern and wandered towards the channel. They all looked like minor variations on the same person:

squat, swaggering and muscular, with reddish beards and yellow eyes. Hammers, chisels and other implements hung from their thick belts.

'Where are all the females?' asked Rhea.

'Maybe some of these *are* females,' said Theus. 'You never know.'

Marcus smiled in spite of himself. Just then the Nullmaurs who had captured them – Kroy included – emerged from the tunnel's mouth in single file. Their arrival was very different from Marcus's or the Cloudfarers'. They crouched on short skis, keeping their centre of gravity even lower than it already was. Once they had emerged into the cavern they shook their fists triumphantly at the onlookers. The Nullmaurs gathered on the bridges stamping their feet in response.

As Kroy and his comrades neared the end of the channel, each one squatted even lower then leaped over its curving sides and crunched to a sure-footed halt on the cavern's floor. Kicking off his skis, Kroy immediately strode on to the nearest bridge. He surveyed the assembled Nullmaurs then unleashed another stream of guttural sounds, accompanied by a wide range of gestures, none of which looked particularly friendly. Soon the Nullmaurs were muttering to one another and casting venomous glances towards the Cloudfarers. Kroy grew louder and more vociferous as he went on, ending his speech with an exultant bellow. It was repeated by all the other Nullmaurs and echoed round the cavern. They shook their hammers at the bewildered Cloudfarers.

'Maybe he's just describing how he caught us,' said Marcus.

'Maybe he's describing how he's going to *cook* us,' countered Nestor.

Before they could speculate any further Kroy stomped over to them. Pushing his face to within inches of Marcus's once again, he said, 'We will take you to Gorloch.'

Soon Marcus and the Cloudfarers were dodging stalactites and stalagmites as their Nullmaur guards – some now wielding swords, others ugly looking coshes wrapped in leather – herded them in pairs across the cavern and into one of the many tunnels that led off it.

Unlike the tunnel by which they had arrived, this one was square, with roughly hewn walls. Brackets containing guttering torches were fixed to the walls at regular intervals. These torches filled the tunnel with weird leaping shadows that made the walls themselves seem as if they were flexing in and out. Marcus was the only one among the captives who could move with ease beneath the low ceiling. Glancing behind him, he saw Rhea, Theus and the others following in an awkward crouch.

'My back's aching,' said Jarrid.

'Just our luck to get captured by a bunch of murderous dwarves,' remarked Amik.

Their guard prodded them repeatedly with his sword, but did little to silence their grumbling.

Soon, however, they were offered a break from their

ordeal. Led by Kroy, they emerged into a much larger space. It was another cavern – not nearly as wide as the one they had come from but with a higher roof. At its centre stood a raised dais with a chair on it. Though far from ornate, the chair was solidly made and the dyed animal skins draped over it were not some muted shade of brown or green, but purple and scarlet. Marcus also noticed that the cavern was lit in a very unusual way. Circular holes all around the edge of the floor threw up a purulent orange glow. He nudged Rhea and pointed this out.

She nodded.

'It's like there's a crucible of fire underneath,' she said.

A figure appeared from another entrance at the far side of the cave and strode towards the dais. Another Nullmaur trailed behind him, whispering in his ear, clearly informing him who the prisoners were and where they had been captured. He nodded impatiently, strode up the steps of the dais and settled himself into the chair. He was taller than the other Nullmaurs and older, with silver hair and beard. He stared at the captives for a few moments then barked an order to the guards while pointing at Marcus.

Marcus braced himself for whatever was about to happen to him. But instead the guards, with a vicious swipe, slammed their coshes into the back of the Cloudfarers' knees. The Cloudfarers buckled, howling, and sank to the floor. Gorloch grunted with satisfaction.

'You,' he said to Marcus. 'Come.'

Marcus stepped towards the dais. Like Kroy before

him, Gorloch seemed more comfortable speaking to someone closer to Nullmaur height.

'You are a youth?' asked Gorloch.

'Yes.'

'You will grow as far as these?'

He indicated the Cloudfarers.

'I hope so,' replied Marcus.

'Why would a *youth* be with these?'

'I'm . . . I'm a cabin boy.'

'What?'

'A young servant.'

Gorloch grunted his understanding.

'And you fell through the clouds. Why?'

'We were flying across the clouds in our . . . vessel. There was an accident.'

'What accident?'

Marcus hesitated fractionally.

'A storm. Bad weather.'

Even as he said this he realised how lame and implausible it sounded. A look of utmost loathing crossed Gorloch's features. Rising, he strode down the dais. He drew a dagger, wrenched Marcus's head back by the hair and pressed the tip of the blade under his chin.

'You lie!' Gorloch bellowed. 'You are spies. You will bring an army down upon us to take our land!'

'No! No, please. We're not spies.' Marcus's mind raced. 'If we were spies would we have been travelling the way we were when your people found us? Would we have been in a vessel patched together from wreckage?'

Gorloch narrowed his eyes. His anger subsided a little.

'So again, *why* did you fall?' he asked.

The last thing Marcus wanted was to admit the truth to Gorloch. But he also realised that he had underestimated the Nullmaur chief; he was so shrewd, so acute that he would be able to detect any lie, no matter how fleeting. Resigned, Marcus admitted everything: about Heliopolis and its society; about the disappearance of the *Regulus*; about the journey across the cloudscape in search of it; about Titus's attack on the *Noble Quest* and its fall through the clouds.

'So we were trying to find our way to the place in your world above which Heliopolis lies,' he finished.

'And then?' asked Gorloch.

'And then get back home.'

'How?'

'We don't know. But we have to try.'

Gorloch said something to Kroy. Kroy bowed and disappeared into the recesses of the chamber for a few moments, reappearing with Nestor's charts. They studied them. Then, sharing a look of dawning comprehension, they had another conversation, which Marcus couldn't understand. The one word he could make out, because it was repeated several times, was 'Ins'lberg'.

'Can I ask you something?' said Marcus, as diffidently as possible.

Gorloch glanced over at him, surprised.

'Go on,' he replied.

'We speak the same way. But I get the feeling that it isn't your native language. How did you learn it?

Gorloch stared at Marcus for a while. Then he whispered something to Kroy, who vanished again and returned, arms piled high with what looked like the tattered, rain-damaged remnants of several books. He handed them reverently to Gorloch, as if they were priceless artefacts. Taking them with equal care, Gorloch gestured to Marcus, Rhea and Theus to come forward. Marcus approached and took the first of the proffered volumes, Rhea and Theus the second.

Marcus's was an anthology of Heliopolitan myths. He had seen many such before. Most were sagas, chronicling, mainly in blank verse, the deeds of magical beings during the prehistory of his world. He stood staring at it, nearly rocked back on his heels by the sudden force of comprehension. Every aero:cruiser contained a well-stocked library: journeys across the cloudscape were long and there was little else to do between shifts but read. He thumbed through it. On one torn page near the beginning he read fragments of words he had known by heart since childhood: 'And so Omn . . . moulded the face of . . . with purifying sanctity . . . and reached through the depths of the void . . .'

At last he understood: these myths, which had evolved in his world over generations, were about magical creatures roaming a cloudy, formless region that stretched down for ever. The people in this world, finding them in their incomplete state, had imagined them to be about magical creatures roaming a cloudy, formless region that stretched *up* for ever.

Rhea nudged him and showed him her volume. It was

a textbook. This too made sense: one of the main princi-
ples of the Cloudfaring Corps was that its members
should be as highly trained, both physically *and* mentally,
as possible. The libraries were stocked not only with
anthologies of myths, but also with dictionaries – called
'lexikons' – and other language guides.

'The tongue is different,' said Gorloch. 'But most of
the letters are close to ours.'

Marcus nodded. No one reading these books would
be able to fully understand what they were about. But
they would be able to piece together a basic grasp of
the language in which they were written. He recalled
Kroy calling their shared language 'M'num.' This had
to be a corruption of 'Omnium' – the word that
appeared most often in the pages of the books, though
often partly erased. He continued to gaze at them,
stunned, for several minutes.

'It still doesn't explain how they would know how to
pronounce the words,' said Rhea, in an undertone.
'Even if they learned the lexis.'

Marcus shook his head, still astonished.

'Maybe we *do* share a common ancestor after all,'
Theus said. 'Maybe the land we live on was once the
same land as this one – or closer to it, at any rate. Maybe
our land was thrust up in some ancient eruption.'

Marcus looked again at Gorloch.

'Wh . . . where did you find these?' he asked at last.

'Some were found a long way back, before us,'
explained Gorloch, gesturing to himself and Kroy. 'One
was found when I was a . . . youth, like you. Only the

leaders among us see them and learn them.'

Marcus shook his head slowly, still trying to comprehend this.

'Only once in many, many seasons do we find . . . pieces fallen from the clouds,' continued Gorloch. 'Even less we *see* them falling, on fire. We find tools, weapons, the wooden birds. Most are broken. We fix them . . . They give us power.'

'Power over whom?'

Certain movements at the centre of his beard suggested that, somewhere beneath it, Gorloch was pursing his lips thoughtfully. He began to pace back and forth, staring at the floor of the cavern. The other Nullmaurs stepped discreetly out of his way as he passed.

'This land is called Daldriadh . . . in our tongue. It stretches from the great waters in the west to the Ins'lberg in the east.'

Marcus frowned – *that word again*. But he thought it best not to interrupt.

'It is our land . . . ours by might,' continued Gorloch. 'We have used the weapons we have found to help us cleanse it: to drive out all other people and make it pure for our own race . . . Only the Eihlans still resist.'

'Eihlans?'

'They raise food from the earth.'

Gorloch said this as if it were a foolishly misguided, almost comical activity.

'So do our people above the clouds,' replied Marcus. 'Don't you?'

'We do not raise. We *take*! We raid their fields, steal their

188

food. But still they will not go. They say this land is –' He paused, struggling for the right word, '– *holy* to them.'

'In what way?'

Gorloch sighed.

'The Eihlans have found things also – things fallen from the clouds. They too have learned from the books. This is how we speak to them: we share the words. But when *they* see fire in the sky, they fear. They think these things come from magical beings far above. They worship them. They look up and ask for things, like this . . .'

He raised his eyes to the ceiling, arms outstretched, a beseeching expression on his face, in parody of a praying Eihlan. The other Nullmaurs snorted appreciatively.

'You're saying that if the Eihlans saw us they would think we were . . . *gods*?' asked Marcus, hardly able to believe it.

'Gods . . . yes.'

'But if you and the Eihlans have both found the same books, the same objects . . . why don't *you* believe in gods in the clouds?'

'When we have seen things fall from the sky we have gone abroad soon after to search for them. Among the pieces we have found tools and weapons. And once, just once, we found bodies of beings like you before beasts had taken them. They were burnt, not whole – so we knew they were . . . *mortal*. But the Eihlans . . . they are not bold. They do not go abroad as much as us, or as far, for fear we will attack them. So they have never seen bodies or found weapons.' He smirked. 'They think the broken pieces they do find are gifts from the gods.'

Marcus struggled to absorb everything Gorloch had told him. More than anything else, it obliterated the small glimmer of renewed hope that his father might still be alive – lit within him by the first sight of the ornithopters. His sense of loss and desolation returned, as keen as when he had first felt it, kneeling at the water's edge after Persis's confession. His heart pounding, tears glazing his eyes, he looked at Gorloch and said, 'Please . . . let us go. Let us try to get back to our home. I promise you that if we do we won't tell anyone about your people. No one will come back to this world or try to take it from you.'

'No one will try to . . . colonise you,' added Theus hesitantly, as if uncertain whether or not Gorloch would understand this word.

Whether Gorloch understood or not it was impossible to tell. He simply shook his head.

'You cannot be allowed to leave . . . ever.'

'But our people are suffering!' exclaimed Rhea.

'To my ears this . . . Titus is the only one amongst you all with any real strength,' retorted Gorloch. 'Your people will do better under him. And if you do not go back we will know for sure that they will not know of us; that this . . . Titus will not know of us.'

'But don't you want to learn from us? Don't you want to learn more about our culture or society?' asked Marcus, improvising desperately.

'Why should we care? We will never see your world – we have no way to reach it. We do not need to know of it. All that matters is that your world does not know of us. *That* will keep us safe.'

'But . . .'

'We will take you to the Eihlans. We will show them their 'gods'. You will tell them it is your 'divine wish' that they leave this land to the Nullmaurs. If you do not, we will kill you all.'

He climbed the steps of the dais again. Facing the Nullmaurs he uttered yet more guttural words. Marcus guessed that he was repeating the plan in his own language. This prompted yet more exultant hollering from his audience. They raised their swords and clashed the blades together. After this had subsided, Marcus and the Cloudfarers were herded out of the cavern and along another series of cramped tunnels lit by guttering torches. Kroy led the way. As he trudged along, Marcus noticed that all the tunnels were curving downwards to differing extents. It grew much, much warmer. The air also grew more rank.

'I know that smell from Meridiana,' Theus muttered to Marcus. 'It comes from the rocks on the shore around the lake. They call it sulphur.'

The last tunnel widened abruptly and he emerged into the most incredible space he had yet seen. He was standing on a wide ledge of rock, more than half-way up a vast chasm. It wasn't narrow, but its great height made it seem so. A quarter of a mile below lay a luminous, churning pit of lava, source of the stifling heat. It was clad in a rippling orange skin that blistered and burst in different places to reveal oozing, incandescent yellow beneath.

The chasm's walls were disfigured with other outcrops

of rock. All the shadows cast by these outcrops flared upwards, as the lava provided the only illumination. When its skin split in several places a blast of even hotter air surged up the chasm. It brightened and the shadows grew more sharply defined.

Nearly as far above was the roof, again covered in stalactites, though these were much longer and thicker than the ones in the main cavern. Stretching up the centre of the chasm was an octagonal tower of basalt, with lower, narrower columns clustered round it. The top of it, which had been hewn flat, reached only slightly higher than the ledge where Marcus stood, but the space that gaped between them was more than fifty feet wide.

Marcus gawped at this for a few moments, only to be racked by a dry cough. If you breathed the hot, pungent air through your mouth it rapidly grew parched and you soon started gagging. The only solution seemed to be to strain it through slightly parted lips.

On the ledge to their left was a narrow wooden drawbridge with a crude but sturdy winch at its base. Two Nullmaurs shouldered past the Cloudfarers and grasped the crank handle of the winch. Leaning into it, feet braced against the wall of the chasm, they hefted it into motion. The bridge began to descend in a jolting, spasmodic way towards the top of the basalt tower.

Kroy said, 'Better than a cage. The chasm is too wide to jump across, even for beings like you. And if you move around too much you'll soon be dying of thirst in this heat.'

With a final lurch the end of the bridge thudded against the edge of the tower. Shoved forwards by the Nullmaurs, the Cloudfarers stepped on to it, Marcus and Rhea leading the way. It flexed and creaked beneath them. Preoccupied by this, Marcus kept his eyes down as he crossed the chasm. When he stepped on to the tower, he saw, to his surprise, that it wasn't empty. Two small figures were huddled at the opposite side.

The Eihlans

The two people were simply dressed in plain, loosely belted, one-piece garments that seemed to be woven from some kind of flax. As the Cloudfarers stepped off the bridge to join Marcus they all stopped short, astonished at the sight of these fellow captives.

The huddled figures stirred. Propping themselves on their elbows, they stared drowsily at the Cloudfarers. Though one was taller than the other, neither was any taller than the Nullmaurs. They were slender, with fair, wispy hair and large, pale-blue eyes. Stepping closer, Marcus saw that the shorter of the two was female. She had a more delicate countenance, but even the male, though clearly mature, looked like an aged child. The female shrank back, closer to the male, who put his arm around her.

Slowly the bridge rose again from the edge of the tower.

'Your gods,' Kroy shouted mockingly across the chasm. 'Fallen from the clouds.' Then, laughing, he and the other Nullmaurs vanished back into the tunnel.

Marcus and Rhea gestured to the others, telling them

to sit down so they would appear less threatening. Slipping off their cloaks, grateful to be rid of them in the heat, they folded them up and settled down on them. Marcus turned back to the huddled creatures.

'Are you . . . Eihlans?' he asked.

They said nothing, merely continued to stare at him.

'How long have you been here?'

Still they said nothing.

'We don't want to harm you.'

He reached out to them, palms upward, fingers spread, but they shrank back.

'We know you speak our language,' said Rhea. 'Just as the Nullmaurs do.'

'Are you . . . are you gods?' asked the male Eihlan, in a hoarse, barely audible voice.

Marcus hesitated then said, 'No . . . we are not. My name is Marcus. This is Rhea.'

All the other Cloudfarers introduced themselves, bowing to the Eihlan from their kneeling position. Both looked slightly overwhelmed at meeting so many of them so quickly.

'I . . . I am Aònghas,' the male said, pronouncing it 'Ang-gas'. He motioned to the female. 'This is Breah, my daughter.'

'Pleased to meet you both,' replied Marcus.

He smiled, rather self-consciously, at Breah, who frowned and looked down.

'You seem more like us,' said Aònghas, nodding at Marcus. 'But if these others are not gods, why are they so . . . so great?'

Marcus and Rhea glanced at one another. He could tell that she was thinking the same thing as he: how to be honest with Aònghas about their origins without robbing him and Breah of their most cherished beliefs?

'We come from a citadel that lies above the clouds,' said Marcus.

Aònghas frowned, struggling to comprehend this.

'You live *among* the gods?' he asked.

Marcus hesitated.

'There *may* be gods above the clouds. Spirits may roam the upper air, I don't know . . . But we are mortal beings.'

'In our world the sunlight is not filtered through cloud,' explained Magnis. 'That is why we look different from you: less pale, not so stunted.'

It occurred to Marcus that this wasn't the most tactful comparison to draw, but if Aònghas felt offended he was still too bewildered to show it.

'And how are you in this world?' he asked.

'We fell through the clouds,' said Marcus.

'Why?'

Marcus sighed. He didn't want to recount the whole dispiriting story again. But he sensed that if they were to win the trust of these frightened Eihlans it was unavoidable. He tried to keep it as clear and simple as possible. The Eihlans listened, but now that their initial fear of the strangers had ebbed slightly, their drowsiness grew again. Their heads nodded and several times they threatened to drift off to sleep until Rhea and Theus loudly cleared their throats.

When Marcus had finished Aònghas frowned and said, 'So, our sacred texts, our holy relics . . . these things all came from your people?'

'Yes . . . I'm sorry.'

'And the language we are using,' continued Aònghas, 'our priests say the liturgy in it when we worship. Many of our people do not understand it. But for them, to hear it spoken is sacred, comforting. This language is also from you?'

Marcus nodded.

Aònghas stared at the floor, devastated. In spite of the logic in what Marcus had told him he looked as if he were tempted to reject it utterly.

'It doesn't mean that there *aren't* gods in the sky,' Theus reminded him, as gently as possible.

'No . . . no, I understand,' replied Aònghas, setting his features into a stoic expression. They got the impression that, whatever his true beliefs, this was a subject he didn't want to discuss any further.

'Could you tell us, please . . . how you came to be captured?' Marcus asked instead.

But Aònghas was still preoccupied by what they had told him and didn't seem to hear. So Breah answered for him.

'Our world may seem gloomy and miserable to you.' Here she shot a resentful look at Magnis. 'But it is everything to us. Our people are farmers. We keep our fields fertile by leaving some fallow for a season and changing the crops we grow in others. The crops that follow each other should not make the same demands of the soil, or be prey to the same pests or diseases . . . In the same way we choose a council of elders at set times and no one may sit on the council twice in a row. It probably sounds a very simple way of doing things to beings like you, but it is fair. It keeps peace amongst us.'

'It sounds a good system,' said Marcus. 'Better than some I've known.'

Theus and some of the other Cloudfarers glanced at him upon hearing this, but said nothing. Breah looked slightly mollified.

'The Nullmaurs are a scourge upon us,' she continued. 'They want to drive us into the north, as they have done to all the other races who used to live in Daldriadh in harmony. They ruin our crops, they defile our graves, they kill our animals. Our people resist bravely. But they do not have such weapons as the Nullmaurs wield. And they are peaceable at heart. All they wish between attacks is to tend their fields and repair the damage the Nullmaurs have wrought.'

As he listened to Breah's plain and formal way of speaking, Marcus realised that his overwhelming impression of this world beneath the clouds was how ancient it seemed. He felt that he had travelled not just from warmth and sunlight into gloom and oppression, but from the present into the mist-shrouded past.

'Only a few of us believe that we should take the fight to the Nullmaurs,' said Aònghas, rousing himself. 'I have been trying to persuade our people that we can defeat the Nullmaurs if only we can find their weakness. I came to explore their lair to do that. I was almost here when I found that my elder daughter had followed me.'

'I was worried about him,' explained Breah stoutly.

He smiled down at her and stroked her hair.

'She is far too bold for her own good,' he said.

'It comes from you,' Breah pointed out.

'Impudent also,' he added. 'It was too dangerous to send her back alone. There are many beasts in this land other than the grashiels that might have preyed upon her.'

'Grashiels?' asked Lucis.

'The ones that bear the Nullmaurs' transports – their heavekairts,' Aònghas explained.

'We use the grashiels to pull our ploughs,' continued Breah. 'But the Nullmaurs torment them and breed them to make them more aggressive.'

Lucis nodded.

'So I had to keep her with me,' Aònghas continued. 'We were exploring the tunnels when they caught us.'

'When was that?' asked Rhea.

Aònghas blinked at her.

'I cannot remember,' he replied. 'The heat drains all your energy . . . One day merges into the next.'

'What have the Nullmaurs done with you since?' asked Marcus.

'Nothing . . . yet. Gorloch boasts that he will put us to death in front of our people, to weaken their resistance. I think he is waiting to do it after launching a great attack on them, when they are weakened already.'

'And now he has us too,' said Rhea. 'He's threatened to kill us, unless we command your people to leave this land.'

An anguished look clouded both Aònghas and Breah's features.

'*Why?*' exclaimed Breah. 'Why did you have to come into our world? You have made everything so much worse!'

Eihlans and Cloudfarers alike lapsed into a morose silence. The only sound was the churning of the lava far below. Marcus struggled to come to terms with the idea that wars fought over the cloudscape for centuries had so affected, even poisoned, the world below – a world which no one above the clouds had ever realised existed. He glanced at Breah, who was stroking her father's hand comfortingly. He would have liked to speak to her again. He would have liked to ask her more about how she and the other Eihlans lived. But her obvious anger – as well as his slender experience with people his own age – deterred him.

The Cloudfarers stared at the floor with a variety of expressions. Theus, being the oldest, looked resigned, in a melancholy way. Rhea looked angry; Nestor as anguished as the Eihlan. Jarrid and Denihr murmured quietly to one another. The others just looked despondent in varying degrees.

Eventually Rhea looked up at Aònghas.

'As Marcus said, we are mortal,' she began. 'We have no special powers, we can perform no miracles for you – or for ourselves, sadly. We can't rely on any kind of magic to help us get out of this lair. The world we live in is governed by harsh realities – just like this one. When we landed on the shore of your land, all we had were our strength, our ingenuity and a few weapons. Now we don't even have the weapons, but we are still determined to escape from the Nullmaurs and somehow find our way home. Our best chance might come when they take us to your village.'

The other Cloudfarers looked somewhat surprised to hear this, but didn't comment.

'If you escape from them, where will you go?' asked Aònghas.

'Well . . . first of all we'll try to reach the part of your world below our citadel.'

'And where is that?'

Rhea whispered to Nestor. He shrugged. Then, not displaying much faith that it would work, he picked up a loose chunk of rock and drew a crude map on the top of the tower. Peering at it as it raspingly formed, Aònghas's eyes widened. He and Breah looked at one another, intrigued.

'The Ins'lberg?' she whispered to him. He nodded.

'Gorloch used that word,' said Marcus. 'What does it mean?'

'The Ins'lberg is our greatest mountain,' explained Breah. 'It is wider at the base than any other in Daldriadh. It stretches up into the clouds. We have no idea how high it is.'

'I think *we* do,' said Rhea, voice hushed with amazement.

'So it's true: our citadel really does sit atop a . . . *mountain*?' asked Lucis.

'I believe so,' replied Aònghas.

'But that means we might be able to climb it!' said Amik eagerly. 'Climb up through the cloudscape.'

In spite of the heat, all the Cloudfarers stirred in anticipation, but Aònghas shook his head.

'No. Every race native to Daldriadh, past and present, has tried. No one has ever climbed more than a few miles. The air is too thin for us.'

'But we're used to much thinner air,' Magnis pointed out. 'We could survive.'

'Maybe . . .' said Denihr, inclining his head. 'But if Heliopolis sits atop rock that stretches all the way down to this world, why has no one who has tried to descend from it ever returned alive?'

This question tempered the Cloudfarers' enthusiasm, but failed to extinguish it completely.

'Still . . . it *has* to be worth trying,' observed Rhea.

Marcus nodded. He looked at her and the others.

'Has any of you climbed before?' he asked.

A few nodded, including Theus and Magnis.

'On the Cydonian chain, up near the North Pole,' said Magnis. 'We did it during a stopover in Cydonia itself. The . . . peaks I suppose, stretch much further and more steeply out of the cloudscape there. We practised free climbing and ice climbing: going up and down gullies and flutings of ice, trying to get from one peak to the next along ridges. Very difficult, very dangerous.'

'Okay,' said Rhea. 'So if we do get there, we have a chance, no matter how slender it might be.'

There were murmurs of agreement. Marcus turned back to Aònghas.

'If we escape the Nullmaurs, will you show us how to get to the base of your . . . Ins'lberg?' asked Marcus.

Aònghas frowned.

'Your people . . . your cloud dwellers . . . have given the Nullmaurs weapons over so many years that have allowed them to drive all other races from Daldriadh and make the lives of my race an unending struggle . . . And now you have given them a new chance to deceive us, to weaken our resolve,' he said.

'If we show you the way to the Ins'lberg you will leave us to our plight,' added Breah. 'Why should any of us help you?'

Marcus sighed, seeing the truth in this.

'I can't think of a single reason,' he said.

There was another despondent silence. During it no one noticed Persis biting his lip and glancing round at the other Cloudfarers. Eventually he rose to his feet.

'*I* will stay,' he said. 'I will stay and help these people defend themselves against the Nullmaurs.'

Everyone stared up at him in surprise. After a few moments' indecision, Jarrid also rose.

'So will I,' he said.

'And I,' said Denihr.

'And I,' said Amik.

'And I,' said Lucis.

'And I,' said Tafril.

They all smiled grudgingly at Persis.

Magnis made to stand up as well, but Rhea placed a restraining hand on his arm.

'No, Magnis,' she said. 'Some of us will still need to

make the ascent to Heliopolis – or at least try.'

Aònghas gazed around at the assembled Cloudfarers. He had a new glint of hope – not to mention wakefulness – in his eye, but he remained cautious.

'*How* will you help?' he asked.

'We are trained Cloudfarers,' replied Tafril, with renewed pride in this fact. 'We know tactics. We can drill your people: teach them to fight better. And we can show them how to make new weapons like the ones the Nullmaurs have.'

'And if the rest of us do manage to get home and defeat Titus, we will find a way to return with many more Cloudfarers like these,' added Marcus, pressing the point. 'We will help you rout the Nullmaurs once and for all – maybe even bring the exiled races back to Daldriadh, to put right the ills we have unknowingly caused.'

Aònghas sat up straighter, but Breah looked worried.

'How can we trust them?' she said to her father. 'We have only their word.'

'They say they are not gods. But perhaps, perhaps the gods have sent them to us, to help us free ourselves from the Nullmaurs at last,' he replied.

Breah still seemed uncertain. Marcus sensed that even Aònghas wasn't quite convinced by what he had just said, but found it easier to cope with the Cloudfarers' existence in such a way.

'Very well,' Aònghas continued. 'If you can help us repel the Nullmaurs and some of your comrades promise to stay behind to show faith, I will lead you to the Ins'lberg.'

Marcus bowed to him from his kneeling position and said, 'Thank you.' The Cloudfarers did likewise.

'Well,' said Rhea, 'if we're going to try to escape the Nullmaurs when they take us to your village we'd better get as much rest as we can.'

Marcus nodded. Though he had barely moved during their discussion with Aònghas and Breah, the intensity of it had caused rivulets of sweat to spring from his temples. Like the others, he lay down and tried to sleep.

Aònghas was right: time itself seemed paralysed by the heat atop the tower. The only thing that allowed its passing to be marked, Marcus discovered, was the discomfort of the floor. Every few minutes he had to shift his position to ease the ache in his hip or shoulder blade or elbows.

All over the tower Cloudfarers twisted and turned, trying to make themselves comfortable. This frequently involved limbs getting entangled or sat on, followed by a series of gruff apologies.

'You're lying on my arm!' Jarrid hissed at Denihr at one point.

'I can't help it, there's no room to move,' Denihr hissed back.

'But it's getting numb. I can't fight if I have a numb sword arm.'

'Why not? You usually fight like you do.'

'Quiet, you two,' said Rhea, eyes closed. 'Try to rest.'

'Sorry, ma'am.'

Some time later Magnis developed cramp in his left leg, which spasmed, kicking Marcus in the shoulder.

'Oh! I'm sorry,' he said.

Marcus winced and rubbed his arm.

'It's all right,' he replied ruefully. 'Woke me up a bit.'

Magnis smiled, then peering over the edge of the tower asked, 'What do you think our chances are?'

'I don't know, Magnis. I mean, we have Aònghas to guide us now. But that won't make it any easier to escape from the Nullmaurs.'

Magnis nodded.

'I don't see how we can even try it until we're out in the open again,' he said. 'We have to remember that this lair was built to suit them, not us – they can move a lot faster along the tunnels than we can.'

'That's very true,' replied Marcus.

Sighing, he rolled on to his back and gazed up at the ceiling, arm crooked under his head. Time limped by.

Some while later, noticing something out of the corner of his eye, he glanced down at his chest and saw that a spider was crawling across the folds and creases of his tunic. It must have found its way on to him some time earlier – most likely it had dropped from the branch of one of the pines during the trek up to the Nullmaurs' lair. Not fond of spiders, he brushed it away irritatedly. It vanished over the side of the tower. Then, a few seconds later, it reappeared, bobbing upwards, legs waving, borne aloft on a thermal of heated air. When the surge subsided it sank again and was deposited back on to the edge of the tower.

Marcus stared at it as it resumed its hectic journey, meandering towards his leg. The outline of a plan began to sketch itself in his mind. Sitting up, he stared at the chasm between the tower and the ledge of rock, where the bridge stood, fully drawn up. *Could it work?*

Reaching across the now slumbering Magnis, he shook Rhea's shoulder. She was lying with her back to him. She rolled over.

'Wha . . . is it?' she asked, swallowing painfully, her throat dry.

'I think I can get us out of here,' he told her.

A few minutes later he stood at the edge of the tower with Rhea, Theus, Magnis and the others, facing the ledge and the tunnel's square, roughly hewn entrance. In his arms he held one of the Cloudfarers' cloaks.

'There's no way any of us could jump across,' he said. 'It's just too far.'

'Agreed,' replied Rhea and Magnis.

'Wholeheartedly,' added Theus.

'Right, but watch this.'

He stretched his arms out over the edge of the tower. After a few moments the cloak, which had been sagging between them, billowed upwards, like a loaf of bread rising with improbable speed in an oven. It remained like this for about ten seconds then deflated again. The others frowned.

'So?' said Rhea.

'So, if I had some kind of canopy above my head to hang on to and took a running jump at the right moment and got enough lift from the hot air rising up the chasm, I might just make it over to the ledge, given that it's a bit lower. I mean there's no way I'll just sail safely across – I realise that. I'll still fall, but hopefully not nearly so fast.'

Rhea frowned and ran her hand repeatedly through her hair. Marcus could tell she was torn between astonishment at his ingenuity and reluctance to allow him to imperil himself.

'And if you do get across, then what?' asked Theus.

'We try to find a way out before the Nullmaurs realise we've freed ourselves. Aònghas has explored the tunnels before. He knows ways out of here.' He looked at Aònghas. 'You *do*, don't you?'

Aònghas nodded uncomfortably.

'You don't have to do this to prove your courage to us,' Theus said. 'We already . . .'

'It isn't about me proving my courage. Believe me, I'd rather not do this,' Marcus said. 'But I'm the smallest and the lightest. If I do get across I'll only barely make it. The rest of you could never do it.'

'What if you don't make it?' asked Rhea.

'Then you'll still have another chance to escape when they take you to the Eihlans' village. Get back to Heliopolis. Defeat Titus. If you can't do it with me promise you'll do it *for* me . . . and for my father.'

Theus and Magnis frowned then glanced at Rhea. In the past few days, amid the usual aura of tense preoccupation that surrounded her, he had seen flashes of warmth and sympathy. But now, for the first time, he saw something else: the first small stirrings of genuine belief in him. And he drew strength from this.

'I promise,' she said and hugged him.

'Thank you,' he replied. 'Okay, let's get started.'

They set to work immediately. There was some debate amongst the Cloudfarers about how best to create a canopy that would keep Marcus aloft for the longest possible time. Both Tafril and Amik unfolded their cloaks. Then they and the others stood around in a tight huddle, passing the two cloaks back and forth, kneading and stretching them in their hands.

'Seeing as they're wider at the hem than the neck, couldn't we lay them end to end and tie them together?' suggested Tafril. 'That would create the biggest area to catch the rising air.'

'But what would we tie them with?' asked Lucis.

Denihr leaned down, pulled a lace from his boots and dangled it in front of the others.

'Will this do?' he asked.

Lucis tugged at it. It stretched but didn't snap. Rhea smiled.

'Brilliant. Let's do it,' she said.

So they tore small holes in the hems and threaded bootlaces through them to bind the cloaks together. They also took the cords that dangled from the necks of both cloaks and knotted them so that Marcus would have a hand strap on either side. What they had created, with amazing speed, was a makeshift parasail that was wide in the middle but tapered on either side. With evident pride, they handed it to Marcus. He took hold of it by the makeshift hand straps and examined it. Then he jerked his arms back so that it swung over his head and sagged down his back, like a large hood.

'Okay,' he said. 'Well, I suppose the only way to test it is to use it.'

His hands felt clammy as he walked to the other side of the tower. Rhea, Theus and the rest of the Cloudfarers drew back on either side to give him space. All eyes were on him. Magnis gave him an apprehensive but encouraging smile. Nestor, constantly pushing his glasses back up his nose because he was sweating so much, looked frankly appalled. The Eihlans were still huddled just to his left. Breah gazed up at him, her previous hostility forgotten in her astonishment at what he was about to attempt. In spite of what lay before him, he allowed himself to savour this, just for a moment.

'It's okay,' he said, smiling at her. 'If there's one thing we're not afraid of, it's heights.'

Rhea, with one hand gripping Theus's, leaned as far over the edge of the tower as she dared and peered down into the chasm.

'There's a surge fading right now. Each one seems to last about ten seconds,' she reported.

Not long, thought Marcus. He waited. His vision narrowed to the gap ahead of him between the Cloudfarers; the Cloudfarers themselves were just a loitering blur on either side. This seemed to go on for ever, then . . .

'Go!' shouted Rhea.

By some miracle he persuaded his legs to work. He

raced across the tower and launched himself off it, throwing his arms wide above his head as he did so. With a snap that nearly wrenched them from their sockets the canopy was filled by an intense surge of heated air. His legs churned the void for several seconds, as if he were still running flat out.

Elation that he hadn't plummeted immediately gave way to despair. The forward momentum he had built up was moving him towards the ledge, as he'd hoped, but not nearly fast enough. On the other hand, though he was falling slowly, supported by the canopy, it wasn't slowly enough.

Helplessly, he saw the ledge, still some way ahead, draw level with his flailing body then rise above him. He was no longer moving forwards. As the far wall of the chasm slid upwards there was nothing he could do now to draw it any closer. Feeling oddly calm, he knew what was going to happen next.

Sure enough, the surge of heated air from below subsided. He seemed to hang motionless for an instant. Then he felt the canopy sag and he plummeted.

XV

The grashiels

He closed his eyes, surrendering himself to his fate. Not knowing why, he continued to cling to the slackened hand straps. He felt heat caress his ankles – a gentle but ominous touch that threatened to become excruciating at any moment.

Then his arms were wrenched upwards again, even more sharply than before. His eyes snapped open. He looked up. The canopy had snagged on a frail spine of rock that stuck out from the wall at an angle. Already the two cloaks that formed the canopy were separating from one another, the stitching of bootlaces popping open.

Unable to believe that he still had a chance to survive, Marcus let go of one of the straps and lunged for a handhold in the wall. His fingers burrowed into a shallow cavity. He was still seeking another when the last stitch popped. The separated cloaks fluttered down either side of his body and fell – pirouetting gracefully – towards the lava. The instant they landed they were consumed by flames.

Marcus dangled from the wall by his right arm. Within seconds it was clad in a tight sleeve of pain. His body seemed to grow heavier with every passing second, as if someone were attaching weights, one by one, to his feet. He twisted his head round, searching for another handhold. But he couldn't see one. His breath came harder and faster. His fingers started to lose their grip.

Summoning up all his remaining strength, he managed to switch hands in the cavity. Pain pulsed down his spine as he did so. His right arm hung limp at his side, but this was only a temporary solution. Soon his left arm was aching just as badly as the right had. He continued to scan the rock. He was so close to it that he could only see a foot or so in any direction. It was impossible . . .

Then he heard a voice, hissing as loud as it dared. It was Lucis's.

'On the left, just a bit higher than your head!' the lookout said, sharp-eyed as ever.

His right hand scrabbled across the rock in the direction Lucis had described, feeling for the handhold. When he found it he burrowed his fingers into it as deeply as he could. The ache in his left arm lessened slightly, now that both were supporting him.

With Lucis guiding him in this way, Marcus inched up the wall. His soaking fringe was plastered to his forehead and his palms were slippery with sweat. Every few moments, ignoring all instincts to the contrary, he had to remove one hand from the rock and rub it against his tunic to dry it.

From across the chasm he heard Rhea hiss, 'You can make it. You're nearly there!'

He finally drew level with the ledge and clambered on to it. He lay panting for a few moments, treasuring the solidity of the rock beneath him. Then he crawled over to the winch. Still on his knees, he grasped the crank handle and pushed. Nothing happened. The mechanism was much stiffer than he had expected. And the effort of climbing to the ledge seemed to have bled his arms of all strength – they felt hollow, weightless. He grimaced at the Cloudfarers, who peered across the chasm, anxious faces rippling in the heat haze. Bracing his feet against the wall – as the Nullmaur guards had done before – he tried again.

Slowly the handle creaked into motion and the bridge began to descend. It did so in spasms, shuddering all the way. As he had when climbing, Marcus paused frequently to rub his moist hands on his tunic. When the tip of the bridge was still about six feet above the top of the tower Jarrid and Denihr reached up to grab it and wrenched it downwards. The crank handle was jerked from Marcus's grip, straining the tendons in his wrists, but he didn't mind. Grinning, bathed in pride as well as sweat, he watched the Cloudfarers running towards him across the bridge, led by Rhea, heedless of the drop below. Aònghas and Breah followed, not quite so heedless, but just as eager to be free.

Marcus's elation was short-lived, however. Still grinning at the Cloudfarers, he saw their expressions change, one by one. Instead of looking admiringly at him, they looked past him, horror-struck. He whirled round. Kroy and several Nullmaur guards stood in the tunnel mouth. The guards gawped at the Cloudfarers, astonished to see them crowding the ledge. But Kroy – sharper and more guileful – had already mastered his surprise and was smirking.

'Thank you for lowering the bridge,' he said.

He nodded to the guards. Drawing their swords, they spread out around the fringes of the ledge and corralled Marcus and the others into the tunnel.

'You still did so well,' Rhea whispered to him, lowering her head to enter it. 'It was just bad luck.'

Though Marcus could stand upright in the tunnel, he lowered his head along with the others, bowed down by the weight of his disappointment. He said nothing.

Once again the Cloudfarers winced as they bumped their heads and chafed their elbows. Each new tunnel seemed to diverge from the one before at an unpredictable angle, some curving steeply upwards, some downwards. Marcus sensed that Kroy, out of pure spite, was deliberately leading them along a much longer, more tortuous route than the one they had followed last time. When they finally arrived back at the main cavern it was, as he had suspected, through a completely different entrance.

The cavern was filled with a low, ceaseless rumble of activity. Nullmaurs jostled around, preparing for their expedition: pulling on coarse leather boots, fastening sword belts. Some crowded round a lathe and sharpened their sword blades. Sparks flew up amongst them, illuminating their exultant features. Others squatted down with crossbolts cradled in their hands, rubbing what looked like animal fat against the mechanisms (Marcus guessed that this was how they prevented them from seizing up in the cold.) And in a far corner he saw four Nullmaurs carrying an ornithopter over to one of the tunnel mouths.

From time to time one of the Nullmaurs punched another in the shoulder. They did this with a vigour that amongst any other group of people would have been a sure sign of aggression, but here seemed to be a gesture of camaraderie.

The captives stood around disconsolately, waiting to see what would happen next. The Nullmaurs who had herded them through the tunnels stood sentry around them. Breah held her father's hand but kept her head high and her chin tilted up.

'Perhaps we should make a break for it,' observed Denihr.

'We'd still have to get out through the tunnels, though. We could never outrun them,' replied Amik.

'Patience,' said Rhea. 'Keep your nerve. We need to wait until we're in the open.'

Another Nullmaur approached them. He had a long rope looped over one shoulder. Surveying the captives, he said something.

'What?' asked Lucis.

The Nullmaur glared at them and gestured impatiently.

'I think he wants us to put our arms out,' said Denihr.

They all did so. The Nullmaur looked pleased — or, at any rate, slightly less irritable — and approached Magnis, who stood at the end of the line of captives. He bound Magnis's proffered wrists then turned to Theus, who stood beside him, and did the same. Eventually each person was bound in the same way: the rope was knotted around one wrist, stretched a short way to the other and knotted around that too, then hung in a wide loop between it and the next captive's wrists. Once all the knots were cinched the Nullmaur stood back and nodded approvingly.

Jarrid contemplated his own wrists and everyone else's with a sigh.

'Things aren't improving,' he observed dryly.

'Hmm,' replied Rhea. Even she looked dispirited.

Presently Gorloch swaggered over. Wandering up and down the line of captives, he accomplished the impressive feat of gazing condescendingly *up* into the Cloudfarers' faces. Then, reaching Aònghas, he said, 'Your time in Daldriadh is ending at last. Ours is beginning. Your "gods" will make sure of that.'

Aònghas didn't flinch from looking Gorloch straight in the eye, but said nothing. Nor did Marcus or any of the Cloudfarers. Chuckling, Gorloch turned and walked away. With more sharp tugs on the end of the rope than were strictly necessary, the Nullmaur who had tied the captives led them in the same direction. Wrists growing more chafed with each tug, they shambled along after him. Soon they were plunged into another cramped tunnel, which twisted steeply downwards, its floor littered with shale. For the already crouching Cloudfarers progress down it was almost impossible. Several times someone slipped, pulling his comrades immediately in front and behind down with him, all three crying out in alarm. More Nullmaurs followed behind, swords drawn. Marcus, Aònghas and Breah found it easier not to slip, but were often over-balanced by those who did.

Half stumbling, half slithering, the captives neared the end of the tunnel. It was exactly the opposite experience of sliding into the Nullmaurs' lair: the warmth and the rank odour receded, to be replaced by cold, sharp air. Eventually they emerged near the foot of the mountainside. It was almost dawn, but as always there were no stars. The only light came from the snow's strange pearly luminescence. The blackness above was total and pitiless. Though he was more accustomed to this fact by now, it still made Marcus shudder. He felt as if he were looking up into his own death.

Without pausing, the Nullmaur guard pulled the captives down the snowy slope between the pines. This time everyone slipped, regardless of his height. Toiling onwards, Marcus heard a muffled rumble behind him. He paused and looked round, struggling to keep his footing. Further up the slope an ornithopter burst from the clogged mouth of another tunnel. Its wings beat hard, trailing twin vortices of snow. It swept by overhead and quickly vanished again, devoured by the night.

'They must launch them down smooth-sided tunnels like the one we were pushed into ... only curved up at the end to give them speed *and* lift,' he said to Rhea, who had also stopped to watch.

Rhea nodded.

'I wonder if they'll follow us all the way to the Eihlans' village,' she said. 'It'll make things even more difficult if they do.'

Before they could speculate any further an especially vicious tug on the rope from their guard set them staggering onwards.

At last the trees thinned and they could see the fringe of the expanse below, though a different part of it this time. Here there were three wide bays carved into the foot of the slope. Two contained heavekairts, the grashiels that supported them scratching the ice and tossing their heads, eager to be on their way. Nullmaurs stood at the rear of these bays, hurling supplies into the heavekairts. Over to the right stood a high-sided wooden pen. It was very solidly made: its corner posts were the severed trunks of pines. Looking more closely, Marcus saw why it was so sturdy. Confined within it, more grashiels jostled for space. Snarling, jaws snapping, they looked as if they were constantly on the verge of attacking one another and were prevented from doing so only by being so tightly packed together.

The captives were dragged down the last twenty yards or so then bundled into one of the heavekairts. It was larger than the other, borne up by four grashiels rather than the customary two. Unlike the other it also had low benches laid breadthwise within it. Much grimacing and squirming ensued as they all tried to sit without growing too entangled in the rope that hung between them.

Marcus looked across at the other heavekairts.

'I don't see Gorloch anywhere,' he said.

'There's not quite so many Nullmaurs as I expected either,' added Theus.

'I'd guess they probably want to show the Eihlans that it didn't take too many of them to capture the "gods",' observed Rhea. 'And that they don't need their leader with them to control us.'

'There's no way we can escape like this – bound together, jammed into this contraption,' said Amik. 'Our only chance now has to be in the village.'

Rhea nodded pensively.

A Nullmaur leaped into the heavekairt as pilot, pausing only to sneer at the captives. Another took up his post at the stern. Planting his feet wide apart, he grasped the handles of the swivel gun and wrenched its barrel upright. Several more Nullmaurs clambered into one of the other heavekairts, laden with weapons.

And then they were off. The pilot yanked on the reins and they lurched forward, heading out over the expanse, rocking from side to side once again. The other heavekairts flanked them for a while then pulled slightly ahead. Though they couldn't see the ornithopter they heard the beat of its wings as it circled them in a series of predatory swoops. This inspired all the Nullmaurs to indulge in an exchange of demented whoops and hollers.

'An air escort. Just what we need,' muttered Theus.

Crammed together, neither Marcus nor any of the others could help but notice the musty aroma which seemed to have developed between them, even though they were no longer in the confined spaces of the Nullmaurs' lair. It wasn't unpleasant – yet. But it definitely spoke, louder all the time, of clothes and hair unwashed for many days.

Rhea remained silent for some time, chin tucked into the collar of her tunic, arms folded. Then, looking at the others, she said quietly, 'Okay, we desperately need some kind of plan for when we get to the village. Does anyone have a brilliant idea they'd like to share?'

They huddled even closer together and spoke in an undertone. Marcus glanced back at the gunner, who stared impassively ahead. They were far from sure that he couldn't hear them above the commotion of the galloping grashiels. It was also possible that more of the Nullmaurs were bilingual than Gorloch had admitted. But they had to take the chance.

'We can't be fast or agile the way we are right now,' said Tafril. 'I say our only chance is to *use* the fact that we're prisoners to capture them.'

'What do you mean?' asked Rhea.

'Well, we've got all the rope we need to tie them up, haven't we?' he said, raising his bound hands with an ironic flourish. 'When we get to the village and they take us out of the heavekairt we spread out as much as we can. Then, while they're shouting to the Eihlans about how they've captured the "gods", we could surround them: rush at them and use ourselves to trap them.'

They all considered this.

'I don't know, Tafril,' said Rhea. 'I mean, I understand

what you're saying, but it doesn't sound too plausible to me. We might not be able to get ourselves into the right position. If we're not fast enough they could get their swords out and run us through. And even if we succeeded, how would we untie ourselves from them? It would be an impasse.'

'Yes,' said Tafril, frowning. 'Yes, I see what you mean.'

'We might just be able to overpower the Nullmaurs in this heavekairt before we reach the village and get their crossbolts,' observed Amik. 'But even then we wouldn't have enough ammunition to fight off the others.'

Rhea nodded.

'And anyway . . .' she began.

She was about to go on when something hit both her and Marcus on the side of the head several times in rapid succession. Wincing, they looked round. The Nullmaur at the stern had angled the barrel of the gun downwards and jerked it back and forth. He grunted something. As with most brief Nullmaur statements, it sounded as if he was trying to dislodge a bone from his throat. But it didn't take a linguist to work out his meaning.

'I think he wants us to shut up,' observed Denihr.

'So why are you still talking?' muttered Jarrid.

With the Nullmaur still glaring at them they fell silent.

The sluggish dawn arrived. Their route skirted the edge of the expanse for several hours. Then it took them up the shallow slope of a frozen river, wide at first but rapidly narrowing. The heavekairts swung into single file to ascend it, the one containing the prisoners bringing up the rear. Its surface was covered in ripples and small waves. It looked as if it had frozen in spate, its hectic downward rush halted within seconds. The snowy banks were high and had been sculpted by water before it stopped flowing. They were topped by large overhanging cornices that looked as if they might collapse at any moment. It was a natural architecture of erosion more beautiful than any design Marcus had seen in the palace of Heliopolis. For a long time he was mesmerised by it.

The sure-footed grashiels were slowed by the incline as it grew steeper, but seemed in no danger of slipping back down. Clenching their claws, they punctured the ice to maintain their grip on it, splintering the crests of the wavelets. After a while trees began to overarch the river on either side. The ornithopter, which had been little more than a black dot skimming the underside of the clouds, became only fleetingly visible then vanished altogether.

Peering up, Marcus thought he saw movement among the trees: a fleeting commotion in the shadows, as if the branches themselves were agitated. He was about to dismiss it as an illusion when something erupted from one of the trees in a spray of snow and swung on to the back of the first grashiel on the right hand side of the heavekairt.

It took him a few seconds to comprehend what it was. At first it looked like an even smaller Eihlan. It had a thin, wiry body. But then he noticed that both its hands and feet ended in long, grasping talons. It was hairless and its grey, mottled skin looked puckered in various places, as if loose on the frame beneath. Most striking of all was the head: it seemed too large for the body and was almost split in half by a mouth like a wound, crammed with several rows of fangs. Conversely, its eyes were tiny and deep-set and its nose was snub – a misshapen excrescence, punctured by two large, pulsating nostrils.

Marcus heard Aònghas gasp and Breah shriek as the creature clung to the grashiel and sank its teeth into the back of its neck. The grashiel roared and tried to twist its head round. But, constricted by its harness, it could do little to repel its attacker. Marcus heard frantic rustling among the branches that kept pace with the heavekairt, even though it was travelling at considerable speed. He guessed that the other creatures were waiting to see how the first one fared before they decided whether or not to attack as well.

The pilot grunted with anger, but didn't seem especially shocked. He drew his sword, leaned diagonally across the prow and hacked at the slavering creature. It shrieked and tumbled off its victim in a spray of blood. Seconds later the heavekairt lurched up on the right as the second grashiel on that side trampled over it. The shrieking abruptly stopped. So did the commotion amongst the trees.

Marcus realised he had been holding his breath while watching all of this. He let it out then glanced at Aònghas, who was still scanning the trees.

'What was *that*?' he asked.

'An eildritch,' replied Aònghas. 'They live in the tree canopy and prey on any other creatures passing below.'

Marcus quizzed Aònghas some more about eildritches as the heavekairt lumbered on. There was no more movement amongst the trees, which continued to overarch the frozen river. Indeed, their gnarled branches grew interlaced, like arthritic fingers, creating a tunnel of snow and ice. Razor-sharp icicles dangled from them and every now and then one would fall, spearing downwards.

The first few times the icicles shattered on the river's surface. But then one landed in the captives' heavekairt, splitting into several chunks on one of the benches, between Lucis and Amik. Neither had room to leap out of the way, but they flinched and looked deeply unsettled. If the icicle had fallen just a few inches to the left it would have drilled into Lucis's thigh; a few inches to the right and it would have done the same to Amik.

'Are you all right?' Marcus hissed, as the chunks slid around the floor between their feet.

'I'm fine,' said Lucis, though he didn't seem too sure.

Rhea glanced round at Aònghas.

'Is this usual?' she asked.

Aònghas shrugged.

'It's best to avoid the rivers when they freeze and take slower routes,' he replied. 'But the Nullmaurs are impatient, incautious.'

'All right,' said Rhea, with a resigned air. 'Stay alert and keep looking up. I don't want anyone getting perforated.

It's not going to do much for our chances of escaping.'

They fell silent, all the time glancing up at the branches. The Nullmaur at the stern smirked at their consternation. He seemed unconcerned about being skewered himself. As they continued upriver, Marcus gazed at the branches as they flashed by, glinting and bristling with potential danger. For a while he watched them with an expression similar to that of the Cloudfarers and the Eihlans: wariness mingled with fear. Then, very slowly, his expression grew rapt and intrigued.

He nudged Rhea. Keeping his voice as low as possible, he said, 'I've got an idea!'

For a fraction of a second she hesitated. He sensed, with an acute pang, that their failure to escape the Nullmaurs' lair had tempered her growing faith in him.

'Go on,' she replied.

He whispered urgently to her. Her head was tilted towards him and she was staring at her lap. Slowly her expression changed too, with scepticism yielding to guarded hope.

'I know it's a long shot – *literally*,' he confessed with a faint smile. 'But what other option do we have?'

She thought for a few minutes more, chewing her lip.

'If we decide to try it,' he reminded her, 'it'll have to be soon.'

She nodded then tugged on the section of the rope that connected her to Theus. He glanced round. When she had his attention, she whispered to him. As he listened he too sat up straighter, shrugging off the weariness that had begun to settle on him during the journey. He nodded, then whispered in turn to Tafril. Meanwhile Marcus did the same with Persis. Gradually the message was passed among the captives. Marcus worried that it might get garbled through being repeated so many times, but no one looked too perplexed by what he was being told. Only Aònghas and Breah showed any real signs of consternation.

'I do not wish to sound as if I lack faith,' whispered Aònghas. 'But do you think your comrades will be able to fight in as confined a space as this river?'

'Well, if they can't we'll still have another chance when we reach the village,' replied Marcus.

After some more thought Aònghas nodded too. He still seemed worried, but offered no further objections.

'Right,' whispered Marcus, 'let's make a start.'

First of all everyone crouched down, as discreetly as possible, searching for the tip of the broken icicle as it slithered around the floor. By aiming light kicks at it, they tried to send it towards Magnis's outstretched fingers. Several times it brushed them as it spun past. But at last he got a secure grip on it and nodded to the others. There was no time to lose: the icicle would start to melt almost immediately, numbing his fingers and making them less nimble. Also the captives had no way of knowing how long the branches would continue to overarch the river. Squirming about slightly, so that they were all in as good a position as the confined space allowed, they prepared for the next part of the plan.

A few moments later Lucis and Amik, closest to the

prow, lunged forward. Tafril and Persis, next in line, lunged forwards with them, to give them as much reach as possible. Taking the section of rope that hung in a loop between their bound wrists, Lucis and Amik threw it over the pilot's head then pulled with all their might. Crying out with surprise, he toppled backwards between his assailants. His hands, still gripping the reins, yanked on them involuntarily and brought the galloping grashiels on either side scrabbling to a halt. Each one dug its claws even more firmly into the ice, and planted its two pairs of back legs wider apart. Lucis and Amik pinned the pilot's thrashing body to the floor. They drew the rope tighter and tighter round his neck until, after seemingly endless spasms of gurgling, he passed out.

At exactly the same moment as they launched their attack on the pilot, Magnis, sitting closest to the stern, twisted round. He had been quietly moulding the tip of the icicle into an even sharper point with the warmth of his fingers. Now, emitting an urgent grunt of effort, he drove it into the Nullmaur gunner's thigh. Bellowing with pain, the Nullmaur buckled. He tried to hug the pedestal of the gun to stay upright, but Theus and Denihr helped Magnis drag him down between them. They looped the rope around his neck and wrenched at it. After a struggle he too lay unconscious.

The first part of the plan had been accomplished, but it was by far the easiest; the real danger had only just begun. Hearing the pilot's initial cry of surprise, Kroy and the other Nullmaurs had brought their heavekairt to a halt, about fifty yards ahead. They glanced back and saw the commotion in the captives' heavekairt. Scowling, they leaped on to the ice and began to hasten downriver. In spite of how well balanced they normally were – with their large feet and low centre of gravity – the glassy surface, together with the steepness of the incline, meant that many went sprawling almost immediately. They struggled to their feet and made better progress with shorter strides.

In the captives' heavekairt, Magnis gripped the downward-tilted barrel of the stern gun. While he held it steady, Rhea rubbed her bound wrists desperately against its bolt's serrated tip. She kept on glancing up the river as she did so. Still the Nullmaurs drew closer, led by Kroy, faces contorted with outrage and hatred. Meanwhile Lucis and Amik struggled to remove the crossbolt still slung over the unconscious pilot's shoulder. The loop of rope they had used to throttle him kept on getting entangled with their hands and with the stock of the weapon as they worked. But eventually they managed to free it and passed it back between the other captives.

'Quickly, quickly! They're almost in range!' shouted Denihr.

'Nearly there!' Rhea shouted back, grimacing each time her wrists slipped and the tip of the bolt cut her hands.

At last she managed to saw through the rope, freeing herself. Grabbing the crossbolt, she leaped to her feet. The hollering Nullmaurs were now ten yards from the heavekairt, faltering only slightly as they reached to draw their swords. This was it – everything had built to this moment. Impassive, utterly calm, Rhea raised the crossbolt to her shoulder and fired.

But not at her advancing enemies.

XVI

Liberation

She fired instead at the overhanging branches of the trees. Six bolts streaked from her weapon in rapid succession and, within seconds, a much larger salvo of thick, needle-sharp icicles hailed down on the Nullmaurs. Suddenly they were no longer running. Instead they were thrashing around in agony, icicles protruding from limbs and necks. Already patches of blood smeared the ice, and their crossbolts, which had slipped from their shoulders, lay strewn across it.

Rhea immediately threw down her own spent weapon and leaped from the heavekairt. She edged past the restless grashiels then scrambled as fast as she could upriver and hurled herself upon the nearest of the felled Nullmaurs. They threw their arms out to defend themselves, looking, for a surreal moment, as if they were about to receive her in a tremulous embrace. Meanwhile Theus took over holding the barrel of the stern gun as steady as he could while Magnis frantically cut through his own bonds. As soon as he had freed himself he wrenched the bolt from the barrel and, gripping it tightly, sawed at the rope that tied the others' wrists. It seemed an agonisingly slow process in such desperate circumstances, but as soon as each Cloudfarer was free he leaped from the heavekairt. Before too long Jarrid, Denihr, Amik, Lucis, Tafril, Persis, Theus, Nestor and Magnis himself had all followed Rhea into the fray. Marcus, to his annoyance, was told to stay in the heavekairt with Aònghas and Breah. With their help he struggled to free his hands, glancing upriver every few seconds to see how the conflict was developing.

Though injured, the Nullmaurs fought back tenaciously. Locked in confrontation, they and the Cloudfarers rolled back and forth – punching, kicking, butting heads, even biting one another. Whenever two antagonists slammed into one of the banks the corniced snow collapsed over them, but they shook it off in an instant, barely aware of it. And as Nullmaur and Cloudfarer alike panted with exertion a rising pall of steam formed over them.

After more hand-to-hand combat a few of the Nullmaurs managed to hold the Cloudfarers off just long enough to draw their swords. Having done so, they leaped back just far enough to aim broad, wild strokes at their foes. Improvising desperately, the Cloudfarers retaliated by using the severed lengths of rope that still dangled from their wrists like whips and cracking them against the Nullmaurs' faces. Elsewhere, other Nullmaurs who weren't able to draw their swords snatched up the icicles strewn over the river and tried to stab the Cloudfarers with them. The Cloudfarers quickly fought back in the same way. Marcus saw Persis and a

Nullmaur circle one another close by, each gripping an icicle, each making wild lunges at the other.

Marcus had been trying to persuade himself that by ensuring the pilot and the gunner in his heavekairt didn't wake up he was making a real contribution to the conflict. But as he watched the writhing antagonists he felt his own limbs twitch with frustration. Eventually he could stand it no longer. He *had* to do something more.

'We'll need as many crossbolts as we can get later,' he told the others. 'Someone should collect up the ones the Nullmaurs dropped in case they get broken in all the fighting.'

Before Aònghas could dissuade him, Marcus leaped from the heavekairt. He advanced cautiously towards the pulsing mass of bodies then began to dart around the fringes, snatching up weapons and hurling them out of reach over either bank.

If Rhea, Theus or any of the others had seen him in the thick of the fray like this they would have yelled at him to get back into the heavekairt. But they were too preoccupied to notice. He had disposed of several crossbolts when he spied another one lying close by, lodged in a partially collapsed cornice. Lucis and one of the Nullmaurs were locked together just next to it. Marcus lunged forwards to grab it. His fingers had just closed round the stock when something slammed into his body, knocking the breath out of him.

He rolled over several times. When he looked up, dazed, he saw Kroy's flushed, outraged face scowling down at him. The Nullmaur had lain motionless on the

233

edge of the mêlée after being felled by the salvo of icicles, and had therefore been ignored by the Cloudfarers. Now he held Marcus down, squirming, with one hand while the other fumbled for his sword. The tip of an icicle protruded from his neck. The blood from the wound flowed faster the more infuriated he grew, but he scarcely seemed aware of it.

Seizing his sword, he raised it above his head, preparing to cleave Marcus's skull in two. Marcus squirmed with renewed effort. He managed to slide out from under Kroy's grip just as the sword lanced downwards. Its blade splintered the ice, spitting shards that stung Marcus's face. Kroy bellowed with frustration. Marcus rolled over several more times then sprang to his feet, snatching up another unattended sword. He gasped at the weight of it and had to grip it in both hands. Kroy staggered to his feet also and they began to circle one another. Gazing into Kroy's glittering pupils – aswim in jaundiced yellow – Marcus recalled, with bitter irony, what Titus had said after his last sparring session: *the day will come when you'll have to encounter a foe your own size.* Surely even the general – with all those vicious, vainglorious schemes festering inside him – could not have imagined that it would happen so soon, and in circumstances like these.

Kroy stabbed at Marcus, who twisted sideways, blocked the blow then retaliated. Both skidded slightly down the incline with each lunge, feint and parry. They continued in this way for some time, clashing every few seconds then springing apart, trying to stay upright as they staggered between the other antagonists. Though Kroy was more muscular and more experienced, he was weakened by his wound. Marcus began to feel confident that he could at least hold off the Nullmaur. But then Lucis, still locked in a violent embrace with another Nullmaur foe, slammed into his legs. He toppled backwards. Kroy leered triumphantly. Marcus tried to roll away a couple of times until he was blocked by something he couldn't see. Throwing himself upon Marcus, Kroy knelt on his chest and raised his sword with both hands to drill his victim into the ice. The sword blade plunged.

Then it stopped, quivering, its point pressing against the soft cavity above Marcus's breastbone. Kroy looked puzzled and dropped his sword. His head jerked back and forth then up and down, as if he were violently disagreeing with something, then changing his mind and agreeing with it just as vehemently. Marcus struggled to comprehend this strange performance. Then, with an appalled gasp, he understood. When he rolled over he had collided with the forelegs of one of the grashiels. Already discomfited by having to stand motionless with the weight of the heavekairt bearing down on it, it had grown even more incensed when Kroy – all his attention focused on killing Marcus – had hurled himself in front of it too. The grashiel had responded by sinking its teeth into his bare neck.

Kroy continued to jerk around for a few moments, emitting a deep gurgling sound. Then, just as Marcus scrambled clear of both him and the grashiel, he slumped on to the ice, a deep wound gaping in the nape of his neck. Marcus slumped, wheezing, against one of the cornices, grateful for its sheltering overhang as the battle raged on around him.

At last, in spite of the desperate fervour with which they had fought, the rest of the Nullmaurs were also over-come – sprawled dead over the river or huddled, moan-ing, against the banks. Everywhere you looked, blood smeared the ice. The Cloudfarers struggled to their feet. The pall of steam gradually dispersed into the freezing air. There were a few moments of sudden, crystalline silence as everyone absorbed the fact that they had freed themselves – and that they had slain so many of their captors in the process.

Theus and Magnis were the first to approach Marcus. They didn't look joyful. Joy would have seemed wrong in the midst of so much carnage. Instead they muttered a few halting words of approval about his plan then hugged him. He smiled dazedly at them. Their faces rip-pled as they had done in the chasm. This time, however, it wasn't the heat that made them do so, but the tears that swam in Marcus's vision. He clutched at Rhea, Nestor, Lucis, Tafril, Amik, Jarrid and Denihr's out-stretched hands as they too approached. Even Persis pat-ted him diffidently on the shoulder. For the first time in his life he felt no invisible barrier of status or his own shyness isolating him; no constant, inhibiting pressure to live up to some obscure tradition or other. He was one of them at last. His comrades – *yes,* his comrades –

crowded around him. Their frank affection wasn't enough to heal the wounds of grief and betrayal that he still carried with him, but it was a balm for them at last.

Wiping her eyes, Rhea stepped back and frowned.

'Was that *you* I saw fighting Kroy?' she asked Marcus. He shook his head solemnly.

'You must have imagined it,' he replied. 'It can happen, you know, in moments of stress.'

Though still unconvinced, Rhea was too relieved to pursue the matter further.

'So what do we do with the survivors?' asked Amik, surveying the Nullmaurs.

Rhea looked at Aònghas.

'This is your world,' she said. 'And your struggle. What do you think?'

'Leave them,' he replied firmly. 'Taking them with us as hostages would only slow us down and I doubt if it would deter the others from attacking us. I do not wish to have wounded, sullen Nullmaurs in the midst of our community nursing vengeance. If we leave them they will make a feast for those eildritches in the tree canopy.'

'Very well,' said Rhea. 'Let's collect up all the weapons we can then get on our way.'

Everyone set to work. Their task was enlivened by the fact that stray icicles, loosened by the crossbolt's salvo, continued to fall from the overarching branches every now and then.

Working alongside Theus and Nestor, Marcus said to the navigator in an undertone, 'You did really well.'

Nestor gave a pained smile.

'I'm not a natural fighter, I'm afraid,' he replied. 'Not like the others. I've spent most of my career in the observatory, making maps of the stars for aëro:cruisers to navigate by. Or gathering data on vectors and parabolas brought back by pilots, so they know exactly where different citadels lie in relation to one another. I was always good at doing those things. But all this . . .' He gestured around him. 'This is slightly outside my experience.'

'I think it's outside all our experiences, Nestor, mine most of all,' Marcus pointed out. 'But I understand what you mean.'

'Incidentally, how many missions over the cloudscape have you been on?' asked Theus.

Nestor hesitated then said, 'Two . . . including this one.'

Theus glanced at Marcus, raising his eyebrows in his usual quizzical way. But he refrained from commenting. Instead he placed a supportive arm around Nestor's shoulder and said, 'Well, in that case I think you should be even more proud of yourself.'

'After all,' added Marcus, 'we wouldn't even have known which direction to go in the first place if it hadn't been for you, would we?'

Nestor smiled, looking just a little consoled.

At last they were ready to set off. Since he knew the route they would be taking, Aònghas was elected pilot of the first heavekairt. Rhea, Marcus, Breah and Magnis joined him in it, while Theus took up the reins in the other heavekairt. But Aònghas had trouble coaxing his grashiels forward. No matter how hard he wrenched at the reins and how loud he shouted, they remained in a state of tranced stillness, heads lowered, ears twitching.

'Should we get out and push?' shouted Jarrid from the other heavekairt.

'Should we get out and *walk*?' added Denihr.

'Quiet,' Rhea shouted back. 'Order in the ranks.'

Aònghas's efforts continued to no avail. Then, just when everyone was losing hope, yet another icicle fell and buried itself in the rump of the harnessed grashiel on the right-hand side of his heavekairt. It bellowed with an unmistakable note of outraged ferocity and lunged forwards. The right side of the heavekairt reared up, nearly tipping out all its occupants. Rhea grabbed the pedestal of the swivel gun to steady herself. As if woken from a deep slumber, the grashiel on the other side jerked into life too and they were off, with the familiar rocking motion. Seeing the lead heavekairt moving, the grashiels behind broke into a gallop too.

The journey began again. The river continued to wind upwards in unhurried curves. After an hour or so, the gnarled, interlaced branches surrendered their grip on one another, growing sparser then parting altogether. Marcus immediately looked up, scanning the grey vault of the sky in search of the ornithopter. At first he could see nothing amid the shadowy folds and creases of the cloud base. Then he spotted it. It was circling far above, as it probably had been for some time, its pilot waiting for the heavekairts to emerge from the forest.

'Quickly!' he shouted. 'We have to bring it down.'

In the other heavekairt Magnis shouldered a crossbolt, trained it on the ornithopter and fired. Bolts hurtled upwards, but the top of their arc fell short of the target. The ornithopter banked sharply and headed back across the forest, wings beating faster.

Rhea cursed and said, 'Its pilot will be back at the lair before long, telling Gorloch what has happened.'

Marcus nodded, still gazing up at the ornithopter. There was nothing else they could do for the moment.

They travelled on. The slope became less steep and they found themselves on a snow-covered plateau. It was strewn with large boulders, stray petrified trees and scrubby bushes that looked stiff and friable, as if they would shatter when you reached out and brushed your hand over them. Marcus also noticed that some of the bushes were smothered in clusters of black flowers. He wondered if they were black to absorb as much as possible of the feeble light in this world beneath the clouds.

Marcus glanced at Breah. She sat with her eyes closed and her back resting against the shuddering side of the heavekairt, but he could tell she wasn't asleep. The outpouring of emotion he had shared with his comrades had been like the undamming of a torrent: it had carried with it all the old timidities that he felt had held him back for so long. But now, looking at Breah – her features delicate yet resolute, even in repose – he still felt the old, paralysing awkwardness when it came to talking to someone his own age. But his curiosity was such that he asked, 'What are these flowers?'

Opening her eyes, she craned her neck to see where he was pointing.

'We call them semperennials,' she said.

Stretching perilously far over the steaming flank of a grashiel, she picked one and handed it to him. Its petals were sealed in a thin film of ice and edged with frost. Almost as soon as he took it the warmth from his fingers melted the ice and a strong scent invaded his nostrils.

'They don't lose their petals,' she explained. 'They freeze in full bloom then come back to life when the warm weather returns.'

Marcus shook his head.

'This really is an amazing world.'

'To *you*. It is the only one I've known my whole life.'

'How old are you?' he asked.

'I will have fourteen years next harvest.'

'So you're thirteen?'

She looked slightly put out.

'. . . Yes,' she said. 'How old are you?'

'Fourteen.'

'Oh.'

Marcus cursed himself for sounding as if he'd been patronising her, when in fact he had been thinking that she seemed much more mature than her years and admiring her aura of confidence, which was strong but lightly worn. Trying to make amends, he said, 'It was very brave of you to follow your father to the Nullmaurs' lair.'

'Or foolish, he would say. But I was worried about him.' She paused, then gave him a sidelong glance that was both guarded and lit with fascination. 'Please, I would like to hear more about your world above the clouds.'

He smiled, relieved that he no longer had to flounder about with small talk. He described the texture of different seasons on the cloudscape: the rich colours that drenched it at dawn. He told her too some of what he had learned about other cities in the hemisphere: how the ones at Meridiana clung to the edge of their brimming lakes, or calderas; how others straddled several peaks, their citizens passing between them on swaying rope bridges. She listened avidly then shook her head.

'When you use such words as "sun", "moon" and "stars", I cannot imagine them – they form no picture in my mind. But, at the same time, the idea of a world without this –' She gestured at the overarching canopy of cloud, '–without a limit above . . . it frightens me. I would feel as if I might float away at any moment. That must seem foolish to you.'

'Not at all,' Marcus replied earnestly. 'In your world I feel the opposite: the clouds seem to press down on me and I feel imprisoned.'

She frowned and looked down at her folded hands.

'You will be glad to leave it, I think.'

'Well, in some ways. I mean, it's important for me to get back. But I find this world fascinating too. I should like to see more of it.'

She nodded, then said, 'And in your, your . . . what do you call it?'

'Citadel.'

'Citadel, yes. Your mother must be missing you there.'

'My mother died when I was born.'

'Oh, I'm sorry,' she said, the last traces of reserve and suspicion vanishing from her expression, while her speech became a little less formal. She pondered this for a while then, brightening, said, 'We have men and women in our village without children. I'm sure they would be happy to take you in.'

He smiled sadly.

'It's okay. I have to get home.'

'But you're alone.'

'Well, kind of. I mean, I have my tutor Asperia. We used to fight all the time – over my studies, over me not being "regal" enough. I suppose I never realised she pushed me so hard because she cared so much about me. But then, it was only when my father went missing that she really began to show it. And it's only since I've been in this world that I've realised how much I always relied on her to be there.'

Breah nodded sympathetically.

'And then there's Rhea and the others,' he continued, glancing back at the other heavekairts. 'I realise I've not known them for long. But we've been through so much together already. I think maybe they believe in me a little now and I'm proud of that. Maybe it sounds strange, but they've become . . . like family to me. If we do get home I want to make sure that doesn't change.'

'But they're all adults. Is there not anyone your own age in the palace?'

'There are, but I've never been allowed to have much to do with them.'

'But who did you play with?'

243

'I never really played. I was usually too busy.'

Breah looked appalled.

'Too busy to play? Doing what?'

'Well, learning mostly. I suppose it's a bit like being a grown-up, only much sooner.'

'But my father is a grown-up and he still plays.'

'Does he?'

'Yes, of course, he plays with my younger sister.'

Marcus felt his throat tighten again. He swallowed.

'My father was usually too busy with more important things to play with me. At least . . . I was told that they were more important things and I believed it.'

Breah frowned.

'I understand. But it still seems wrong.'

'A lot of things seem wrong now, Breah – more than you can imagine. Things that I never thought about before.'

Breah reflected on this some more.

'If you do get back and free your people you should learn to, well, not play – you have too many years for that now. But maybe to enjoy your life more,' she said.

'I'll try, Breah,' said Marcus. 'I promise.'

They continued talking for some time, Marcus quizzing Breah in turn about the flora and fauna in her world and life in the Eihlans' village. All the while the heavekairts lurched on over the plateau. Only when he lay down to get some rest, pulling his cloak over his head, did he realise that this was the longest conversation he'd ever had with someone his own age.

XVII

The Eihlan village

It took them more than a day to cross the plateau. As they did so they encountered many more wondrous things. Fuming geysers sprayed not steam but ice crystals into the air and were lit from deep within, so that the crystals glinted like shards of diamond. Dervishes of snow spun across the flat terrain and changed direction at random, as if in a furious hurry to get somewhere but constantly changing their minds about the route. Octagonal columns of ice thrust out of the ground — the remnants of some ancient geological event. And all the time the clouds, looking closer than ever, pressed down upon the land.

At one point Marcus glanced round to see Magnis examining the swivel gun at the stern.

'Interesting?' he asked with a smile.

'Hmm,' said Magnis. 'It's more or less the same as the swivel gun we use to tow home crippled aero:cruisers. We fire grappling hooks with cables attached across their bows, which snag on the gunnels. The bolt this one's loaded with has a cable attached too. But it's been adapted in other ways.'

'How?'

'Well, for a start it's got a wider bore.'

'A what?'

'A wider barrel to slot a larger bolt into.'

'Ah.'

'You fire it by pulling this rope attached to the trigger,' continued Magnis, twisting the rope around his fist in illustration. 'And the firing mechanism uses gunpowder. But it's a coarse-grained powder – I'd imagine that's so the bolt will be fired more smoothly. There's also a hinged door covering the flash pan to stop the powder getting damp in a world as snowy and rainy as this one. And see here –'

He pointed to the pedestal that the gun sat on.

'It's wrapped in animal hide all the way down. That's probably to absorb the shock when the bolt is fired, so it doesn't split the thighboard that the pedestal is mounted on. It's like everything else these Nullmaurs adapt or make – simple, but fiendishly ingenious.'

'Hmm.'

Marcus nodded and glanced out worriedly at the passing terrain.

At last they reached the other side of the plateau and plunged once again into the tree line. This time there was no river to follow. They descended slowly, threading their way between the pines. The grashiels had to change direction again and again as they scrambled down a succession of snow-covered shelves of rock. Each one was more than a mile long, and collapsed at a different angle on to the next.

Night began to fall – or rather to rise, with the already feeble light seeming to drain upwards into the cloud base. As they neared the end of the last shelf the trees thinned. Marcus looked to the far distance and saw a wide but shallow depression in the landscape, surrounded by gently undulating hills. Nestling in it was a large cluster of what he thought at first were even lower hills. But as the heavekairt drew closer he saw that they were the roofs of numerous Eihlan lodges. On the far side lay the fields: a patchwork of square plots, separated by dry stone walls and deeply gashed here and there, showing the signs of spoliation by the Nullmaurs that Breah had talked about before.

A high stockade, made from tree trunks sharpened at the top, surrounded the lodges, with one narrow gap in it. On either side of the gap lay bonfires, which threw out a wincingly stark white light.

'How do you get them to burn so brightly?' Marcus asked Breah, squinting at the bonfires.

'We use sophorus,' she replied, as if it were self-evident.

'Sophorus?'

'It's a mineral you can get from certain rocks. The Nullmaurs use it too. They put it in their bombs.'

'You mean that's what makes the explosions so bright?'

'Yes. They use it so that if they attack at night they won't just kill some of us but see where the others have fled ... Don't you have sophorus in your world?'

'I don't think so.'

'Well, I suppose there is not much gloom to banish there.'

Marcus nodded, still peering at the village. There was a small clump of trees on the fringes of it. The lodges themselves were squat: curved like the caps of mushrooms and moss-covered. When Marcus remarked to Breah how close to the ground they appeared to be, she said, 'Those are just the roofs. The main part of each lodge is dug into the earth and trenches run between them.'

'Why?' asked Marcus.

'We are farmers. We work the earth, so we wish to stay close to it. But also, it can help us to protect our youngest from the Nullmaurs when they attack. Some of the trenches run all the way out to the fields. It is in the fields that we are most vulnerable.'

The lodges were lit within. A thick shaft of light rising from a hole in the crown of each roof pierced the freezing mist. A softer glow also spilled from the doors of the lodges into the trenches that connected them, so they all looked as if they were enmeshed in a luminous web. The overall effect was of a cradle of warmth and security in a cold, hostile landscape.

They crossed the low hills then bumped down into a new terrain: marshland. Tussocks of long, stiff grass lay stranded amid a morass of brackish water. In spite of the extreme cold the water wasn't frozen; indeed, it bubbled in certain places, as if it were boiling. When Marcus asked Breah about this she said, 'It's oily because it's full of marsh gas, made by the plants rotting under water. The gas burns very easily. We distil it and use it to heat our homes.'

The grashiels struggled on between the tussocks and the heavekairts rocked from side to side. Gripping the pedestal of the gun, Marcus felt as if he were back aboard the *Noble Quest* when it first landed on water.

Drawing closer still to the village, Marcus saw silhouetted figures standing sentry around the bonfires. The intense glare of the fire slenderised them, making them look impossibly spindly. Ignoring the indignity of being hoisted up by Rhea so that he would be more visible above the prow of his vehicle, Aònghas shouted and waved to them. They paused, unable to see the heavekairts yet, but staring in the direction the sound had come from. When they saw them at last, the right arm of each figure grew longer, tapering to a point. Marcus guessed that they must have drawn swords.

Aònghas continued to yell to them in their language. It had more inflections in it than the Nullmaurs' and, in spite of his raised voice, sounded gentler – almost melodious. The guards stood still with swords drawn a few moments longer. Then, recognising Aònghas, they shouted greetings. They drew back and allowed the heavekairts to pass.

The grashiels lurched towards the other side of the marshland, where there was a short, steep slope leading up to the stockade. Without even slowing down, Aònghas managed to manoeuvre his heavekairt through the gap. As it passed between the tree trunks on either side, Marcus saw the stockade had a raised walkway running round the inside of it, with ladders propped against it.

The other heavekairt, still piloted by Theus, followed

close behind. As the grashiels staggered to a halt some of the Eihlans who had been milling around the compound, absorbed in various chores, approached curiously. Others hung back. Still others peered out from the top of the trenches, wide-eyed faces just visible above ground level. They were all adults, but, like Aònghas, they resembled careworn children. Also like Aònghas, most wore loosely belted flaxen smocks. But some, a little greyer than the others, wore capes made of beautifully interlaced feathers and armbands of dyed animal skin that blazoned their rank. Marcus guessed that these must be Aònghas's fellow elders.

Though they stood their ground, the Eihlans who approached the heavekairts reached out to clutch one another's hands, seeking mutual reassurance.

Before anyone could stop him, Jarrid stood up to stretch. Catching sight of his huge frame all the Eihlans gasped and hurled themselves to the ground. Kneeling, heads bowed, they began a murmurous chanting.

Denihr tugged at Jarrid.

'Sit down!' he hissed.

'Sorry!' replied Jarrid. 'I didn't mean to . . .'

Aònghas cast aside his reins and grimaced at Marcus. 'I did not wish this,' he said.

Leaping down from the heavekairt, he hastened over to his fellow Eihlans. He coaxed several of the older ones to their feet and began to speak urgently to them. He was trying, Marcus sensed, to impress upon them not only who his companions were but also who they *weren't*. He kept on pointing up at the sky, shaking his head emphatically and making all sorts of negative sounds. As he went on, the Eihlans kept on glancing over at the Cloudfarers with steadily diminishing awe. Jarrid, now sitting hunched in the heavekairt again, smiled as benignly as possible.

Aònghas was still explaining when he was interrupted by a wail of recognition from one of the trenches. A female Eihlan scrabbled up the steps carved into the side of it and rushed towards him and Breah, one hand outstretched, trembling, the other covering her mouth as she sobbed. Though her features, framed by a knotted headscarf, were almost as delicate as her daughter's, they looked worn and pinched from weeks of anguished uncertainty. She fell into a tight huddle with her husband and daughter. A few moments later an Eihlan child – smaller than Breah – also ran over and was drawn in amongst them. The four of them remained like this for several minutes. They murmured to one another, heads lowered, slender, quaking backs turned to the rest of the world. Marcus watched this with an anguished smile. He felt pride and happiness at having helped to reunite Aònghas's family. Yet, at the same time, the spectacle of them so tightly clasped together – a small, perfect unit, indifferent to anything else – gnawed at his heart. Breah's closeness to her father when they were captives had induced an ache in him. But this, though he didn't begrudge them it in any way, was much more painful. Sensing his distress, Rhea gripped his arm tightly and murmured a few comforting words.

Disentangling himself from his wife, Aònghas talked to the other Eihlans a little longer. Then he walked back over to Marcus's heavekairt. Tears had left meandering tracks down his grimy cheeks.

'I have managed to persuade them that your friends are not gods,' he said, adding, with a faint smile, 'merely very tall.'

'Did you say where we come from?' asked Marcus.

'No,' replied Aònghas, firmly. 'I . . . I do not wish them to be robbed of their beliefs. They will need all the faith they can summon if they are to fight off the next Nullmaur attack. I told them you come from the southern uplands where it is warmer and lighter. They seem to accept this, though they are still a little wary.' He glanced back at his fellow Eihlans. They were standing on tiptoe, trying to peer into the heavekairts. 'I would advise your friends to, uh, *slouch* as much as possible so they do not appear too threatening.'

'And *will* they allow our people to help them? Will they let themselves be trained?' asked Rhea.

'I believe so. When they find out that they can at last have weapons like the Nullmaurs', it will embolden them, I think.'

'Remind them also that we can manufacture more weapons like these,' Theus put in. 'We will be much better armed soon.'

Aònghas nodded.

'I shall, I shall. But first, I am sure your people must need food and plenty of rest.'

★

Marcus, Rhea and the rest of the Cloudfarers jumped down from the heavekairts, which rose and fell slowly with the laboured breathing of the exhausted grashiels. Gesturing to the beasts, Theus said, 'What should we do with them?'

'Our grashiels are stabled out near the fields,' replied Aònghas. 'But these ones would tear them to pieces.' He nodded towards the clump of trees. 'We shall tether them over there, in the copse.'

First they led the beasts over to the copse and tied them up. Then – with due respect for the grashiels' strength – they unbuckled the harnesses and eased the heavekairts to the ground. Each one sat on two stubby runners, making it easier to move. Using these, the Cloudfarers dragged the heavekairts clear of the grashiels and left them near by.

Having completed this task with what little strength they had left, most of the Cloudfarers descended into the trenches, by means of steps carved into the side of them, then headed towards the largest of the lodges. Marcus and Rhea made to follow them, but before they could do so, Breah, without a trace of self-consciousness, took Marcus by the hand and led him over to her mother.

'Her name is Morveyn,' she explained as they approached her.

She whispered in Morveyn's ear for some time, pointing to Marcus. Fresh tears sprang to Morveyn's eyes as she listened and the instant Breah finished her explanation she embraced him as tightly as she had her husband and children. This went on for some time.

Moved as he was to be encircled by Morveyn's frail arms, Marcus was trying to think of some way to extricate himself when she released him anyway. With an expression of immeasurable sympathy she said, 'I be . . .'

Frowning, Breah tugged at her arm and whispered to her again.

'Oh, I *am*,' Morveyn began again. 'Very . . .'

She looked at Breah and asked, '*Fìor thoilichté?*'

'Very . . . pleased,' supplied Breah.

'Ah! . . . Very pleased . . . to meet . . . you,' Morveyn finished haltingly.

'Thank you,' replied Marcus, still somewhat dazed by so emotional a greeting.

'Come,' said Aònghas to Marcus. 'I wish to show you something you may find interesting.'

He led Marcus and Rhea to another lodge. They walked along a series of trenches. The Eihlans they encountered on the way – mainly female, some carrying infants – flattened themselves against the cool earth walls and lowered their heads as they passed. In spite of Aònghas's assurances it seemed as though they were still uncertain about their guests' true origins and were treating them with extreme deference, just in case.

When he turned the last corner to reach the lodge, Marcus froze. The trench ahead widened, its walls growing concave. They did so to accommodate a battered section of an impeller. The tall, wide metal tube was hollow and formed the entrance of the lodge. Exchanging astonished looks, Marcus and Rhea walked through the echoing interior of the tube, then gasped.

At the far side of the lodge, elevated a few feet above the ground, stood a substantial chunk of an aëro:cruiser's prow. It was pitted and scarred in certain places, but scrupulously polished. A wooden railing ran, still intact, along the top of it and its tapered nose jutted into the room. It was an altar.

The rest of the lodge was similar in layout to a chapel in Heliopolis. The chancel – the area around the altar reserved for clergy – was surrounded by sections from an aëro:cruiser's gunnels. Steps, cut from halved sections of a pine trunk, had been added on either side. Aònghas climbed up to the altar. He spread his arms wide. In a voice laced with mournful but unembittered irony, he said, 'Where we worship . . .'

Broken deck planks, sawn to equal length, were mounted in rows and filled the nave – the main part of the church. These were the worshippers' benches. Large swathes of canvas from air sacs were fixed to the ceiling, bunched in some places, artfully sagging in others. As Marcus and Rhea gazed dazedly around them they noted all sorts of other familiar objects on display in the room: fragments of nephoscopes, compasses, telescopes, window casements – all kept gleaming, like the prow, as if they were priceless treasures. Marcus saw that there were impeller blades mounted in pairs on the wall, blades crossed in a ceremonial arrangement, an intricately carved wooden handle fixed to each. And, in several shadowed alcoves, sat polished, hinged coffers, which he guessed were reliquaries: containers for even more sacred relics.

Descending from the altar, two tattered books

wedged under his arm, Aònghas followed Marcus's gaze and said, 'We have more blades. We use them as ploughshares. The lore says that many generations ago there was a deluge during harvest time. Our ancestors could not bring the food in quickly enough. Most of it was fated to rot. But then they found these blades. They were seen as a gift from the sky gods. Before then our people had only worked with stone and wood.'

Marcus nodded. A shiver of comprehension ran through him. As incredible as it seemed, the wreckage of aëro:cruisers, many years past, had brought the Iron Age to this world.

'And there are these,' Aònghas continued, handing the books to Marcus. 'Some of our sacred texts.'

Marcus opened them. Like the volumes he had been shown by Gorloch, one was an anthology of Heliopolitan myths and the other a lexicon. Again, the pages were wrinkled and partially burnt away, much of the text faded beyond legibility. From what was left the Eihlans had gleaned all their most cherished beliefs.

He closed the book and looked around the lodge again. For some reason – perhaps because he himself still brimmed with so much grief and regret – he felt a profound sympathy for Aònghas.

'I'm so sorry,' he said.

Aònghas nodded and took the book from him. There was nothing else to say.

They left the church and he led them along the trenches once again. It was now completely dark and torches lodged in the earth walls had been lit to show them the way. As they walked Marcus whispered to Rhea, 'I can't believe we've deceived these people so much without even knowing they existed. I feel so guilty somehow.'

'They deceived themselves,' Rhea replied. 'But it's understandable that they did.'

Marcus nodded.

'Still, the more I see the more I feel that we and the Eihlans – and even the Nullmaurs – must originally have sprung from the same place,' he observed.

Rhea shook her head.

'It's hard to believe, isn't it?'

Eventually they arrived at the main lodge. It was a simple but ingeniously built space. Four centre posts rose to the roof. Their bases stood at the corners of four low brick walls. These enclosed a log fire with a bubbling cauldron resting on it. Curved rafters rose to meet the centre posts from all around the edges of the lodge. Rods of hazel stretched between the rafters in a dense criss-cross pattern, creating a frame. This was, in turn, daubed with glazed clay, which formed the lodge's outer wall, insulating it from the cold.

A low bench ran all the way around the lodge, flush against the wall. It was smothered in animal skins that slithered off it to merge with the woven rugs thickly strewn across the floor. Cooking smoke, both sweet and acrid, flavoured the air.

Every muscle in their bodies aching, the Cloudfarers sank on to the floor with a chorus of ecstatic groans. After the freezing beach, the suffocating tower of basalt and the juddering floor of a heavekairt, the layer of animal skins felt blissfully comfortable.

While they all settled themselves, the Eihlans served them a vegetable stew with freshly baked bread. They fell upon it, displaying – even by their standards – a complete disregard for dining decorum. Though the Eihlans refilled their bowls without hesitation, they began to cast doubtful glances towards the cauldron and to murmur between themselves when the second serving vanished as quickly as the first. Clearly they were wondering if they would be able to provide enough food to satisfy these creatures' insatiable appetites if they stayed for more than a few days. Also, any beliefs they might have been clinging to about their guests' divinity were banished by the gusto with which Jarrid and Denihr in particular stuffed vast chunks of bread into their mouths, splashing gravy over their soiled tunics and dribbling it down several days' growth of beard.

Still unable completely to abandon the table manners in which he had been rigorously trained for so many years, Marcus ate with slightly less gusto.

'So,' he said to Rhea, 'how long do you think we should stay?'

'Well, not too long, for the sake of the Eihlans – otherwise the biggest threat they face won't be from the Nullmaurs, it'll be from starvation.'

Marcus smiled, then his expression darkened again.

'And every day that goes by Titus will be tightening his grip on Heliopolis,' he pointed out.

'I know, I know. But if the ascent of the Ins'lberg is

going to be anywhere near as difficult as we imagine, we'll need all the rest we can get.'

As if to demonstrate her point, the Cloudfarers, being so tired and having eaten so much so quickly, began to fall asleep where they sat. Their heads nodded, their conversation grew desultory and then they toppled gently sideways one by one, as if tranquillised. Eventually even Rhea succumbed.

Having rested a little more than they had and having eaten less quickly, Marcus stayed awake for longer. He finished his meal in silence, surrounded by slumbering bodies. Breah entered the lodge and, after being served a rather meagre bowl of stew, wandered over and sat beside him with a groan.

'My mother will *not* leave me alone,' she said. 'She seems to think that if I'm out of her sight for more than a few seconds a Nullmaur will swoop down in one of your wooden birds and pluck me from her grasp.'

'Well . . . better than having no one to look after, surely?' said Marcus, in as gently reproving a tone as possible.

Brought up short, she gave him a concerned look. In spite of her apparently indomitable spirit, he could tell that softer emotions never lay far from the surface of her nature. Beneath an exterior toughened by an upbringing in which struggle and the death of neighbours were part of the daily routine, there was a surfeit of warmth and empathy.

'Oh . . . Yes, I'm sorry, I didn't think.' She paused. 'You must miss your father so much.'

Given the grief he still felt, such words would normally have elicited tears before he could stop them. But as she spoke she placed her slender fingers on his forearm. It was the most fleeting gesture of condolence, yet it had a profound and immediate effect upon him, as if she had offered him an infusion of her own strength.

'Yes, it's difficult ... I suppose I feel that I've not just lost him, but that I never really had him. I mean, I know he loved me, but, like I said before, he was always preoccupied with affairs of state. There never seemed much time to spare for us to be together. And ... in a way I feel a little angry too, that he allowed all this to happen.'

'Could he have stopped it?'

'No, Titus would still have been a cruel, ambitious man no matter what. But I can't help feeling my father should have kept a closer eye on him and have known better what was happening in the rest of the citadel. Then again, when I think that I immediately start feeling guilty and disloyal and ... it's so confusing. I just wish he hadn't left such a burden on me.'

She nodded pensively, clearly struggling to comprehend such complex emotions. In spite of a sadness he'd thought incurable, he couldn't help but feel consoled at being able to speak about these things with someone who seemed to possess such imperishable courage. It made him feel slightly braver himself. And it helped him to cast off some more of the inhibiting formality that his upbringing had imposed on him, like many layers of ornate but suffocating ceremonial robes.

They talked on a little longer, mainly about life in the

Eihlan village. She offered droll accounts of disputes between her and her sister, from which she always seemed to emerge the more at fault. And she confessed to fears that the other Eihlans her age – overprotected by perpetually anxious parents – would not be prepared to resist the Nullmaurs when they reached maturity.

Though intrigued by all of this, Marcus was eventually overwhelmed by tiredness. Smiling, Breah bade him goodnight and he lay down to rest. The smoky air and the Cloudfarers strewn around him, muttering in their sleep, reminded him of his first night in this world. This time they weren't huddled together nearly so tightly. But the sense of companionship, of bonds forged through danger faced and overcome together, was so much stronger. It enveloped them all in a warmth that Marcus knew would persist through the night – long after the fire in the centre of the lodge had crumbled into smoking embers. Consoled a little by this thought, he drifted into a long and peaceful sleep.

XVIII

The Nullmaurs attack

Marcus slept late the next morning. The instant he awoke he felt youthful high spirits bubbling up automatically within him, only to be quashed a few moments later when he remembered all that still lay ahead: all he still had to do. The lodge was empty. Only a scattering of deep indentations in the rugs showed where the Cloudfarers had lain. He stood, shook out the creases in his cloak and stepped outside.

The smell of fresh air, seasoned with the tang of moist earth, was invigorating as he wandered along the meandering trenches. Occasionally Eihlan women passed him, still averting their eyes. At other times, tiny Eihlan children, rounding a corner some way ahead, shrieked with an exultant mixture of fear and excitement when they saw him and scurried away. Smiling, he eventually found some steps cut into the wall of one of the trenches and climbed them.

Reaching the top, he stretched extravagantly, grateful for the feeling of liberation, and looked around him. The compound was bristling with activity. Eihlans hurried back and forth, absorbed in various chores. Some bore baskets of sophorus-coated wood to replenish the bon-fires. Others paced around the inside of the stockade, testing the defences, or climbed on to the roofs of the lodges with torches, glazing the clay and patching the moss where required. But there were other types of activity going on too.

In one place Rhea sat cross-legged with Nestor and Magnis. Discarded bowls of what must have contained breakfast were piled beside them. Heads lowered, they were stripping down a crossbolt – the barrel, shaft, stock and flash pan lay around them. Not far from them, Lucis, Jarrid, Denihr, Tafril and Persis were training a group of Eihlans in swordcraft. Slowly and exaggerated-ly, they performed different types of feint, parry and riposte, while barking the names of each. The Eihlans copied the moves intently. They were far from fluid, but they were growing more assured all the time. Their feet, repositioned for each stance, scuffed swirling patterns in the earth. Marcus watched them for a while, until he felt someone nudge him. He looked round, saw nothing, then looked down. Breah's sister, Eithné, was proffering a bowl. It contained a pale, glutinous substance and had a wooden spoon resting against the side of it. As she gazed up at him Eithné had an expression of barely sup-pressed fear on her face.

Taking it, he smiled and said, 'Thank you, Eithné.'

The instant her hands relinquished the bowl she scur-ried away and rattled down the steps into the nearest trench.

The bowl contained a lightly spiced maize porridge

that was warming and nourishing. Delving into the bowl with his spoon, Marcus wandered over to Rhea and crouched beside her. One long, thick strand of hair hung down over her face as she worked on one of the crossbolts.

'How's it going?' he asked.

Pushing the strand from her face, she raised her head and nodded at him.

'All right. We're just trying to get an idea of what materials we'll need to make more of these. Wood isn't a problem, obviously. But we need something stronger to reinforce the shaft. The best thing would be the iron struts that brace the bulkheads of our aëro:cruisers. There are some in the church. I've asked Aònghas if we can cannibalise them.'

'What did he say?'

'Well . . . he looked a bit startled, but he's going to speak to the other elders and see what he can do. If he agrees we could use the fire in the main lodge to heat the iron.'

'It's not just the shafts,' said Nestor. 'We need iron for the tips of the bolts too.'

'Let's take things one step at a time,' replied Rhea. 'If I were them, I wouldn't be happy about strangers plundering my most sacred objects, would you?'

'No . . . I suppose not,' said Nestor.

'Maybe we could persuade them that the bolts will be suffused with divine power,' suggested Magnis, with a faint smile.

'Well, maybe,' replied Rhea. 'But we have to respect

their traditions if we're going to fight alongside them.'

Marcus glanced over at the Eihlans training with the other Cloudfarers.

'They look as if they're picking it up pretty well,' he observed.

'Yes, they're keen to learn,' said Rhea. 'I only hope Lucis and the rest can get enough of them properly drilled before the Nullmaurs attack again. I mean, we may well be gone when it happens – then we'll have our own problems to deal with.'

Marcus sighed.

'Rhea?'

'Hmm?'

'Do you think this plan is crazy?'

'Which part exactly?'

'All of it.'

She considered this question for some time.

'I think it's just crazy enough,' she said eventually.

Several more days passed and the ebb and flow of village life re-established itself, after being disrupted by the new arrivals.

The Cloudfarers who would be staying behind continued to drill the Eihlans and make new weapons. As well as the crossbolts, they showed them how to fashion halberds, which looked like spears, with long shafts and twin blades jutting at right angles from a sharp tip. These, they hoped, would be useful in countering blows from the Nullmaurs' flails at close quarters.

For their part, the Eihlans grew less wary of them;

instead of avoiding eye contact all the time, they gazed steadily, even fervently, up into their faces, as if all their hopes were now invested in these larger beings. Indeed, no matter where the Cloudfarers went a group of inter-changeable children trotted after them and studied their every move – eyes wide, mouths slightly open.

The grashiels were fed twice a day. They were still tethered to the copse, but showed faint signs of becom-ing less ferociously anti-social: instead of devouring the arm of whoever brought them food, they now only tried to bite off his hand.

With Aònghas's help, Marcus took charge of making up packs of supplies that would help him, Rhea, Theus, Magnis and Nestor on their ascent.

'I can show you how to make strong ice axes,' Aònghas told him. 'Our ancestors used them in the little climb-ing they did on the lower parts of the Ins'lberg – as far as the glacier. We can use the . . . what did you call them? On the walls of the church?'

'Impellers.'

'Yes. We use them to fashion adzes.'

'What's that?' asked Marcus.

'The adze is the blade of the axe. It should be slightly curved with a flat head for biting into the ice. This is attached to the haft – which is the handle.'

'How?'

'We carve a slot in the haft then bind the adze to it with sinew. It is a simple method, and an even simpler tool.' His voice bore a faint trace of defensiveness. 'But effective.'

'Sounds very useful,' Marcus replied. 'Let's do it.'

So they set to work. While they were heating the iron in the main lodge and beating it into new shapes, Marcus asked Aònghas, 'How long will it take us to reach the . . . Ins'lberg?'

'Two days. Our people do not travel widely, as you know. But I have been there once before. I know the route.'

'Is it difficult?'

'There are several gorges to negotiate. They are blocked by snow in the winter, but I am hoping they will still be clear. There will be beasts abroad also, searching for food before they hibernate – we must be vigilant.'

'What about the Nullmaurs?'

'The Nullmaurs will be abroad, no doubt, to find out what happened to their comrades. But that is a risk we cannot avoid if you are to return to your people before winter. Soon the gorge will be impassable.'

Marcus nodded pensively then lowered his head again to resume work.

Nearly a week passed in the same routine, with the Eihlans growing more adept at swordcraft, while preparations for the ascent progressed. One morning Marcus woke earlier than he had in a while. As always his clothes were thick with the cloying odour of wood smoke, but he had come to find this comforting. He stretched and rubbed his face. Then, when he stepped out of the lodge, he found the trench brimming with ground mist.

He edged along it and eventually, by falling up them, located the steps that led to the compound. Here he discovered that the ground mist merged into an even greater opacity, as if the cloud layer had descended to smother the land.

Groping his way through it for a while, he eventually seized an arm that turned out to belong to Theus. The pilot's hair was lank with moisture and his moustache was drooping even more than normal.

'Oh, sorry,' said Marcus, removing his grip.

'That's all right,' replied Theus. 'Good morning.'

Marcus gazed around him, still disorientated.

'Is it often like this first thing?' he asked, trying to keep a plaintive tone out of his voice.

'Apparently so, according to Aònghas.'

'But how do the Eihlans get anything done?'

Theus gave a thin smile.

'Very slowly, as far as I can tell.'

It grew no clearer for several hours, but everyone continued with their tasks as best they could. Wreathed in mist they looked like a band of industrious ghosts. Marcus and Magnis hauled from the church one of the long planks of sturdy, straight-grained wood that the Eihlans had used as worshippers' benches. They chopped it into smaller pieces, which they then planed down to create snow stakes. These, they hoped, would help them to steady themselves as they crossed the Ins'lberg's glacier. Every now and then Marcus sat up straighter and twisted his head from side to side to ease the ache in his neck.

When the mist did begin to disperse it seemed to do so in stages, as if a series of curtains were being raised between the village and the distant plateau. Raising his head again, Marcus squinted at the receding whiteness. After a few moments he noticed something odd about it. It looked thicker here and there, as if it had gathered together in certain places. He frowned, rubbed his eyes and looked again. There could be no doubt about it: three pulsating shapes seemed to have formed from the mist. They were still indistinct, but there was something horribly familiar about their remorseless motion.

At last he understood what he was seeing. He leaped to his feet, pointed a quivering finger and yelled, 'They're coming!'

Everyone in the compound stopped what they were doing, their heads snapping round. Though most of the Eihlans didn't speak Marcus's language, his tone left little room for misunderstanding. Those who were being drilled all froze in the same posture, swords raised above their heads. They stared up at the blades – still beaded with moisture from the damp air – the realisation dawning on them that they would have to use their new weapons much sooner than they had hoped.

After a few seconds' stunned silence the compound erupted into frantic activity. Female Eihlans hoisted unattended children on to their shoulders and ran for the cover of the trenches. Lucis and Persis – with Aònghas hurriedly translating – assembled the sword and halberd-bearing Eihlans three deep at the entrance to the stockade. Male Eihlans who had been absorbed in other tasks snatched up tools and hastened over to flank them. The rest of the Cloudfarers, led by Rhea, shouldered the working crossbolts and clambered up ladders to the platform that ran around the inside of the stockade. Grabbing a satchel full of spare bolts, Marcus followed them. Nestling the barrels of their weapons between the pointed tips of the thick wooden posts, they crouched down to train them on the approaching aerial attack.

From the platform Marcus could see the three lead ornithopters growing more solid and acquiring distinct outlines, while more appeared behind them. They lost height in a series of banking turns – they were clearly preparing for a very low sweep across the compound.

But the ornithopters weren't all that was approaching the village. Lowering his gaze a little, Marcus saw something else emerging from the trees on the last tilted shelf of rock that led down from the plateau: grashiels, many, many grashiels, yoked together in pairs. Leaving the trees behind, they galloped across the low, bare hills with their usual rolling, determined gait, as if they were shouldering their way between invisible obstacles. Attached to the yoke that joined each pair at the neck was a set of reins. Drawn taut, it stretched all the way between their straining torsos and was gripped by a Nullmaur crouched on short skis behind them. Feet firmly wedged, dragged by the pair of beasts, he was able to slew his way across the snowy, undulating terrain.

Marcus began to count the grashiels: twelve pairs, with more emerging from the pines. Among the

Nullmaurs they towed he spied Gorloch – identifiable by his grey beard and more vivid attire. In spite of his greater age, the Nullmaur chief seemed no less agile than the others. As Marcus watched, he crested the top of a hill in a flurry of snow, legs spread wide, then slammed back on to the downward slope without a single spasm of awkwardness.

Meanwhile, another wave of ornithopters also swooped into view above, the wings of each one trailing twin vortices of mist. The Cloudfarers on the stockade straightened up a little and glanced worriedly at each other.

'What do you think, lieutenant?' asked Magnis. 'We can't bring down the ornithopters *and* those beasts at the same time. Which ones do we go for?'

Rhea frowned, her gaze flicking between the two targets.

'Aim for the ornithopters,' she replied. 'Our swordsmen will have to take care of the others as best they can. Just remember to keep your nerve and fire at the last possible moment.'

The three leading ornithopters drew closer still, drifting into single file. The Cloudfarers gripped their crossbolts even more tightly – the stocks pressed hard into their shoulders – and squinted down the barrels.

'Wait . . . wait . . .' Rhea told them.

The ornithopters made one final predatory swoop out of the mist.

'Now!' she yelled.

The Cloudfarers loosed a salvo of bolts as the

ornithopters sped towards them. Many arced fruitlessly through the air, but others struck home, splintering the wooden frames of the wings and puncturing their canvas skin. One of the ornithopters pitched sharply leftwards. A few seconds later it slammed into the steep bank that led up to the stockade and tumbled diagonally across it, strewing fragments in its wake.

While the Cloudfarers crouched to reload, the other two ornithopters, though they also pitched and yawed a good deal, swept through the upper part of the stockade's entrance, just above the heads of the Eihlan swordsmen. With a spasm of panic Marcus saw several clay pots tumble out of them and land in the bonfires on either side of the entrance, sending up a shower of sparks from each – incendiary bombs. He knew only too well what would happen next and – worse – that nothing could prevent it.

'Back everyone!' he shouted. 'Get away from the stockade!'

With scant regard for how jarring his landing would be, he threw the clanking satchel of bolts towards the compound and leaped after it. Fumbling with their weapons, the Cloudfarers looked up, confused. But, sensing that this was no idle warning, they swiftly followed. A few seconds later the bonfires erupted. The posts on both sides of the entrance buckled inward. Some were even uprooted and hurled, ablaze, twenty or thirty feet across the compound by the force of the blast. One impaled itself through the roof of a lodge. Persis, Lucis and the Eihlans flattened themselves against the ground as a fireball swept over them and lapped at the edge of the nearest trench.

After a few moments everyone struggled to their feet again. Though the fireball had receded, smoke still rolled across the compound. The gap in the stockade was now three times wider, the posts charred and blistered on either side. Coughing, eyes smarting, Cloudfarers and Eihlans alike stumbled towards it. They waved smoke from in front of their faces and saw, to their horror, that the grashiels had drawn much closer. They were now thrashing through the marsh. Though they stumbled occasionally between the pools, they were barely slowed down and churned the oily water into discoloured surf with their splayed claws. The Nullmaurs they towed twisted between the tussocks and cleaved the surf with their skis.

'Take aim!' yelled Rhea.

With Marcus distributing bolts amongst them as quickly as he could the Cloudfarers continued their frantic reloading. Meanwhile the Eihlans, corralled by Lucis and Persis, reformed their defences with halberds rather than swords. Going down on one knee, they gripped the long shafts in both hands and raised them at a forty-five degree angle, in the hope that some of the grashiels might be impaled on them.

The beasts gained the near side of the marsh and hauled themselves out of it. Then, with a final surge of brute strength, they galloped up the bank and barged into the assembled Eihlans. Bodies tumbled in every direction, limbs flailing. Only a few of the halberds found their target.

Crouching behind the grashiels' rumps, the Nullmaurs – Gorloch among them – were able to skim, untouched, through the entrance. As soon as they were inside the compound, they dropped the reins and slewed to a halt. The grashiels went marauding through the village, vaulting the trenches. The Nullmaurs, meanwhile, kicked off their skis, unsheathed their swords and whirled round to face the astonished Eihlans.

Gorloch sneered at them.

'Your "gods" cannot protect you now,' he bellowed. 'See how weak they are against our might!'

Marcus tensed at hearing this. But hardly any of the assembled Eihlans understood their sacred language. This taunt did little to confuse them or temper their resolve. And there was no time for Gorloch to spit out any others before the village's defenders snatched up their own swords again and rushed at the Nullmaurs. Battle was swiftly joined. Within moments the antagonists grew so enmeshed with one another that they seemed to become one creature. Many-legged, with blades protruding from it like lethal quills, it staggered back and forth across the compound's scorched earth, emitting grunts and snarls that rose steadily in pitch and volume.

While this seething mass of Eihlans and Nullmaurs fought together, several female Eihlans scrabbled up the sides of the trenches and tried to put out the fires smouldering in the roofs of the lodges. Above them the ornithopters swept on across the village. When each one reached the fields beyond, it banked steeply then returned for another pass.

'They're coming back!' Marcus shouted to the Cloudfarers as, heads bowed, they fumbled the last of the bolts into the barrels of their weapons.

They shouldered them and took aim again. The ornithopters wheeled over the village. With immense skill their pilots not only threw more incendiary bombs at the compound but also managed to bowl some along the trenches. After a few moments' silence the doors of one of the lodges disintegrated in flames, gouging out a substantial part of the trench on either side. Marcus scowled – the Nullmaurs were intent on slaughtering Eihlan children too, as part of their revenge.

The Cloudfarers loosed another salvo. Each weapon juddered as a succession of bolts tore from it. This time a larger number found their target. The starboard wing of one ornithopter disintegrated. Its remaining wing still beating furiously, it spun sideways and slammed against the stockade. Another was skewered through the tail. It didn't flinch from its course, flying low and straight over the compound while ejecting several more bombs. But once it had crossed the marshland it failed to make the expected turn; the bolt had jammed its rudder. Its wings sagging, it glided serenely on and eventually dashed itself upon the side of the plateau.

More ornithopters were brought down but others continued to strafe the village. Marcus was desperate to do more than just feed ammunition to the Cloudfarers. But he knew the crossbolts were too heavy for him to hold and fire accurately. He looked around. His eye lit on the heavekairts. They were parked at the side of the compound, next to the copse, resting on their stubby runners. The tethered grashiels had, with uncharacteristic timidity, retreated as far into the copse as their ropes allowed. Dodging craters and smouldering spars of wood, he dashed over and leaped aboard the smaller heavekairt.

Grabbing the handles that protruded from either side of the stock, he tried to hoist up the barrel of the swivel gun. But it too was much heavier than he had expected. He continued to struggle with it – frustration squirming in his chest – when he heard a voice say, 'Here, let me help.'

He glanced round. Breah was peering over the side of the heavekairt, her face flushed. As eager as he to repel the Nullmaurs in some more meaningful way, she had spotted him dashing towards it and followed, guessing what he intended to do.

'Get back inside!' he told her in as stern a tone as the slender gap in their ages allowed. 'It's dangerous out here, or hadn't you noticed?'

'Marcus, I have been living with danger just beyond my door for as long as I can remember,' she said reprovingly. 'This is no different.'

Ignoring his exasperated sigh, she clambered into the heavekairt.

'You cannot aim well enough to bring down one of those flying machines on your own,' she continued. 'But two of us might have the strength to do it.'

Marcus found it hard to tell which was the more galling – the fact that she was right or the fact that she clearly knew she was. He glanced up. Several ornithopters were still strafing the village.

'All right, all right,' he said testily. 'Let's try it.'

They wrenched the swivel gun upwards and sought a target. At first each wanted to aim at a different one and they kept on pulling in opposite directions. But eventually they agreed on a strategy and began to sweep the barrel back and forth with increasing assurance as ornithopters flashed by.

At last Marcus yelled, 'Now!'

Fingers interlaced, they yanked the rope attached to the firing mechanism. Gun and pedestal alike juddered with the force of the recoil. The bolt sped towards its target while the cable attached to it uncoiled in a blur at their feet. It lodged in the underside of the ornithopter, where the wing joined the main fuselage. The ornithopter convulsed with the impact.

Marcus slammed a bunched fist into the palm of his other hand.

'Yes!' he exclaimed, while Breah beamed.

Such was their elation at hitting their target they were completely unprepared for what happened next. Though damaged, the ornithopter flew on. The rope that trailed from the bolt was still attached to the swivel gun. It grew taut, the barrel twitched sideways and, a few seconds later, the whole heavekairt jerked forward, hurling both of them to the floor. When they pulled themselves upright again it was to discover that they were careering across the compound, dragged along by the ornithopter. They scrambled up either side of the heavekairt and threw themselves out, rolling over several times as soon as they landed. Eventually the heavekairt collided with the stockade. Its stern reared up then slammed back on to the ground. Finally unable to fly any further, the ornithopter dipped towards the marshland as if pressed downwards by the palm of an invisible hand and plunged into the dark, viscous water, foundering immediately. Moments after it submerged the pilot broke the surface again in a surge of bubbles and clawed his way towards one of the tussocks.

Struggling to their feet, Marcus and Breah brushed themselves down and grinned at one another with a mixture of triumph and acute relief. Then, smiles fading, they surveyed the conflict that still raged around them. The thrashing creature that the Nullmaur and Eihlan forces had seemed to form when they first engaged one another had now split into several creatures that were smaller but still many-legged and bristling with blades. Marcus saw Denihr leaping back from the vicious sweep of Gorloch's flail and counter with a series of short jabs from his sword. Close by, Jarrid blocked another Nullmaur's flail with a halberd. The chain instantly wrapped itself around the halberd's shaft. Jarrid wrenched at his weapon, pulling the flail from the Nullmaur's grip, then lunged at him.

Their crossbolts spent, the rest of the Cloudfarers had unsheathed their swords and barged into the fray as well. With these new reinforcements the Eihlan, to their evident surprise, began to look as if they might prevail. A number of Nullmaurs had already been felled. As soon as they had caught their breaths Marcus and Breah ran back to the remaining heavekairt and fired again at the circling ornithopters. After a few failed attempts – which forced them to laboriously reel in the bolt – they managed to bring the others down.

The downing of the last ornithopter seemed to sap what little ferocity the reduced number of Nullmaurs still possessed. They parried the Eihlans' and Cloudfarers' blows but offered few ripostes as they backed through the charred gap in the stockade. Gorloch fought on longest, but eventually even he retreated. When he and the others reached the edge of the marshland, they ran, hopping from one tussock to the next, thrashing onwards regardless of whether they fell into the water.

Reaching the other side, the rest of the Nullmaurs kept on running. Gorloch, however, turned back, wounded yet still defiant, and yelled, 'You will not win! You will not control Daldriadh. Your "sky gods" will avail you nothing. We will destroy you every last one of you. We will raze your lodges. The trenches will brim with the blood of your young!'

Standing at the centre of the sundered entrance to the stockade, Marcus couldn't help retort. Lent a desperate eloquence, he shouted back, 'When will you learn? We do not want to control these lands; we only wish to return to our citadel, to put right the ills that have beset it. But we will *not* let you kill these people.'

Stepping forward, Aònghas pointed to Marcus and the Cloudfarers, and added, 'These beings are brethren to us both. Why not accept that and seek to learn from them.'

But these fine sentiments were lost on Gorloch. He merely raised his arms in a frenzied gesture of dismissal then followed the other routed Nullmaurs, staggering towards the plateau.

Chests heaving, limbs trembling, the victors watched the Nullmaurs flee. Many Eihlans buckled where they stood, now that the desperation that had borne them up could be allowed to ebb at last. Their faces were smeared with grime and their clothes mottled with blood from flesh wounds.

Taking Rhea's hand, Aònghas bowed gravely to her.

'You have saved us,' he said.

'You've saved yourselves,' Rhea replied.

Aònghas shook his head.

'You may say you are not gods . . . I will believe you if you wish. But by your presence you have granted us a strength we would not otherwise have possessed.'

'All we did is fight alongside you,' Magnis pointed out. 'And make you believe in yourselves.'

'And what is that but an act of faith?' asked Aònghas, with a smile. 'You have explained how you came to be among us. And I realise that your knowledge of both worlds is far greater than mine could ever be. But perhaps . . . perhaps you *were* sent to us, for reasons that are beyond even your comprehension.'

Normally Rhea and the other Cloudfarers would have flatly denied it. But at this precise moment – in the midst of victory and all the attendant feelings of elation and relief – Aònghas's view seemed more than plausible.

XIX

In the shadow of the Ins'lberg

First the survivors, though bloodied and exhausted, sorted through their fallen comrades. Their movements ponderous with grief, they stumbled between the crumpled bodies, rolling each one over to check if it still breathed. Five Eihlans had been slain. Marcus and Rhea exchanged anguished looks when each new fatality was discovered. But their anguish was nothing compared to that of the dead Eihlans' loved ones, who knelt beside their corpses, rocking slowly back and forth, and setting up low, soft murmurs of lament.

Eventually the bereaved were coaxed away from the corpses, which were then wrapped in shrouds and carried, in a swaying, keening procession, to the burial ground on the far side of the fields. Marcus, Rhea and the Cloudfarers followed at a respectful distance, heads bowed. Aònghas recited the funeral oration. It was spoken in the Eihlans' sacred language – the one learned from the remnants of the Heliopolitan books – which meant that the Cloudfarers understood it but most of the Eihlans didn't. For some reason Marcus found this unspeakably poignant: almost as poignant as the graceful efficiency with which the Eihlans then interred their dead. They had been through this many times before.

The rest of the day was spent clearing up the village. Cloudfarers and Eihlans laboured side by side, both grateful to be absorbed in such practical tasks. The Nullmaur dead were disposed of with much less ceremony: piled just outside the stockade and cremated. As they watched the corpses burn, Rhea said to Marcus, 'Gorloch underestimated us this time and paid the price. It won't happen again. The Nullmaurs will return before long in greater numbers.'

Marcus nodded. He imagined Gorloch and Titus – two implacable dictators, sitting in their throne rooms in two utterly different worlds, but both nurturing violence against anyone who stood in the way of their determination to extend their power. He sighed. It was all so onerous to contemplate.

'Well, we just have to hope that by the time they attack again more of the Eihlans will be better trained to repel them,' he said.

The compound was swept clear of debris, the craters filled in and the wattle and daub on the roofs of the lodges patched where it had been breached. The trenches were also cleared of the earth that had collapsed into them where bombs had exploded. By evening, though the village still looked pitted and charred, its defences were once again secure and everyone could afford to rest a little.

They all ate together in the main lodge. The barrier of language between the Cloudfarers and most of the Eihlans was as impenetrable as ever. But their shared struggle had bred a new ease between them and they communicated more freely through gentle nods and melancholy smiles. Presently Aònghas joined them, sitting between Marcus and Magnis. Breah was elsewhere, helping her mother to comfort the dead Eihlans' families.

'When your people have tried to climb the, uh . . . Ins'lberg before, what happened?' asked Magnis.

'No one has attempted it for many seasons,' replied Aònghas. 'But it is written that those who did climbed only a short way into the clouds before having . . .' He frowned, gesturing to his chest. 'They had blood from here and . . .'

Tafril nodded.

'Altitude sickness,' he said. 'It has affected Cloudfarers when they take part in aithernautics – trying to reach the upper parts of the atmosphere. But that still doesn't explain why no one who has climbed down from Heliopolis has ever returned. After all, we know now that apart from fairly mild barotrauma . . .'

'Barotrauma?' asked Marcus.

'Discomfort in the ear caused by pressure differences between the inside and outside of the eardrum,' explained Tafril. 'We know that apart from *that*, sinking into the clouds doesn't disable us.'

Rhea sighed.

'Well,' she said, 'I suppose these are mysteries that will

have to wait for the future to be solved – if we get home and do . . . all we have to do.'

The others lapsed into moderately silent chewing for a while. Then Magnis, during brief gaps between mouthfuls, said, 'You know, I've been thinking. There might be a way to make the climb less difficult. Or less impossible, at any rate.'

'Hmm? What's that?' asked Rhea.

'Well, there's so much canvas from the air sacs draped around the roof of the church. There's even some galley stoves, amongst all the other –' He paused, seeking a diplomatic word, '– uh . . . relics. They're a bit battered but we might be able to get them working again. They run off proleyne like the burners aboard the aëro:cruisers and they use intake hoses and heating coils just the same way. I've checked them and they still have some fuel in them. I think we could top it up with oil distilled from the marshes. Then, with a bit of ingenuity we could make some new air sacs. They'd be a lot smaller than the ones on the aëro:cruiser of course, but still . . .'

'And how would that help?' asked Lucis.

'We take them with us to the base of the mountain, right?' said Magnis. 'We inflate them there, using air heated by the stoves, then tether ourselves to them. They won't be able to lift us up through the clouds, I realise that. But they could give us a bit of extra buoyancy as we climb: make us feel lighter. And if anyone lost his grip they would slow his fall.'

Marcus glanced at Aònghas, wondering how he would react, but he seemed resigned to the idea of the church being stripped of yet more décor. Rhea tilted her head one way then the other, as if contemplating the plan from different angles.

'What do you think?' she asked Marcus.

'I think it's certainly worth trying,' he replied.

So Marcus and Magnis scavenged the reliquaries of the church once more for suitable materials. They also borrowed various cooking utensils from Breah's mother, to cut and score the canvas, as well as tough thread to sew it with. While they worked, Marcus asked Magnis to describe his experiences of climbing the Cydonia chain and explain basic climbing terminology.

'Chimneys – those are narrow clefts in the rock, kind of like a gully,' he said. 'And flutings are the same sort of thing, only in ice, often with sharp edges. Then, sometimes, if you have to climb sideways instead of straight up, you call it a traverse. And where part of the mountain gets much steeper, above the glacier, that's the head wall.'

Marcus sat cross-legged and listened intently while he worked. After a few days he and Magnis had managed to create five air sacs, with simple harnesses attached that would anchor them to the climbers. All were fairly robust, even if they did tend to bulge in unexpected places when inflated.

Finally the day of departure arrived. Marcus and the Cloudfarers woke early and, though slowed by the swirling ground mist, began their preparations. Over at the copse, Magnis, Jarrid, Denihr and Lucis lifted the first of the two smaller heavekairts on to their shoulders – one gripping each corner.

'I have new respect for these beasts,' gasped Lucis. 'I'd be in a bad mood all the time too if I had to toil around with this weight on my back.'

While the four Cloudfarers stood there – grimacing and trembling – the others untethered two grashiels, led them over one after the other and harnessed them again. The same process was repeated with the other heavekairt, after which both were loaded with packs containing food, blankets, climbing equipment, Magnis's improvised air sacs and many lengths of rope. Then the grashiels – obdurate as ever –were led, by a somewhat meandering route, towards the stockade's charred, buckled entrance.

At last those who were leaving said their farewells to those who would be staying behind to help the Eihlans defend themselves from further Nullmaur attacks. Jarrid, Denihr, Amik, Lucis and Tafril all hugged Marcus and murmured words of support to him.

'I have to admit,' Lucis said, 'I would never have believed you could do the things you've done unless I had seen them myself.'

'Not so much the spoiled brat any more, eh?' asked Marcus with a smile.

'We never saw you as a spoiled brat,' said Tafril. 'It's just that . . . well, we were concerned about carrying out our mission while having to protect you too.'

'I know, I know.'

'Find a way back,' added Amik. 'Defeat Titus. Draw his poison from Heliopolis. Then return for us. He may have perverted the Cloudfaring Corps' traditions in our world, but we'll continue them in this one.'

'I will,' said Marcus. 'I . . .'

He paused, worried that what he most wanted to say next would sound pompous, fraudulent. But he pressed on anyway.

'I'll do everything I can to prove myself worthy of you.'

They hugged again. During this leavetaking Persis hung back. But then Rhea, turning from Denihr, found herself face to face with him. He searched her expression, waiting to see how she would react.

Eventually she said, 'Well, I suppose I should thank you for staying behind to fight with the others.'

'I don't expect thanks,' replied Persis. 'But there is one thing you can do for me.'

While Rhea hesitated, Marcus said, 'Yes, what's that?'

'If you get home and you see my family, please tell them why I had to serve Titus – please explain it was because . . . because I loved them.'

'We only have your word . . .' Rhea began testily.

'I will,' Marcus assured him. 'You've got to understand, Persis, that your part in what happened to bring us down into this world is hard to forgive. But I . . . it has forced me to think a lot about the way we live in Heliopolis: the divisions between us, the way Titus could easily hurt those below without anyone else from above knowing. So, if we do get home and if what you've told us turns out to be true, then yes, I'll explain to your family that you were forced to do what you did.'

'Thank you,' said Persis.

Aònghas stepped forward. Placing a hand lightly on Marcus's arm, he said, 'Please, it is time.'

The last farewells were said. Marcus looked around for Breah, but couldn't see her. Frowning, he clambered aboard one of the heavekairts with Aònghas, Magnis and Nestor. Rhea and Theus piloted the other, with most of the supplies in it. Aònghas jerked the reins and his grashiels lurched forwards with the usual torrent of unwilling grunts and snorts, the other following. Marcus was resignedly settling himself down when – to his surprise – Breah's breathless face appeared beside him. She was standing on tiptoe on the edge of the stern, gripping the pedestal of the swivel gun for support.

'Where *were* you?' he asked.

'I hate goodbyes,' she explained. 'As long as I can remember people in my life have vanished, killed by the Nullmaurs, without any chance for leave-taking.'

He nodded.

'I understand.'

Perhaps because she had appeared so suddenly, he felt as if he were seeing her again for the first time: her wispy fair hair ruffled by the breeze; her heart-shaped face and slightly pointed chin; her delicate mouth, which puckered at the corners when she smiled.

'I wish you could come back with us,' he told her, before he could stop himself.

288

Only a slight faltering in the steadiness of her gaze showed him that she understood the implication behind what he'd just said.

'I could not survive there,' she replied, in the even tone of someone well used to dealing with unalterable reality. 'But I shall pray for you – even though I'm no longer quite sure where my prayers go.'

'Thank you.'

'And if you do survive, please do not forget about ... us. Please remember the friends you have in this world too.'

'I shall. I promise.'

She kissed him gravely on the cheek. Magnis and Nestor looked away with impeccable diplomacy. Then – nimble and fleet-footed as ever – she jumped from the heavekairt just before it breached the marshland. While the grashiels lurched on through the tussocks and oily pools, she retreated to the entrance of the stockade and stood waving with the other Eihlans gathered there. Her slender outline and straight-backed posture seemed to symbolise all the fragility blended with strength that Marcus now associated with her. He continued to wave back until the heavekairts began to ascend the first ledge of rock and were swallowed by the pines.

The heavekairts crossed the plateau once again, though in a different direction this time. They encountered few of the same phenomena – no geysers, no dervishes. Instead they crossed a featureless terrain that lacked even the expanse's tracery of ridges. Having ascended nearly a thousand feet, they found themselves at first in the same freezing mist that had earlier enveloped the village. But this was a strange, granular kind of mist: one made of countless tiny ice crystals suspended in the air, like sand swirling in water. If you drew your hand across your forehead, Marcus noticed, you felt the roughness of them for a few moments until they dissolved.

He recalled his first journey in this world. This one was slightly more comfortable, but also more subdued. He and the Cloudfarers no longer twisted their heads round every few seconds to gaze, rapt, at some extraordinary feature in the landscape. Instead they drew their cloaks around them and stared at the knots and whorls on the wooded floors of the heavekairts, privately contemplating what lay ahead.

The first night fell. They were still on the long descent from the other side of the plateau, half-way down a gentle, thickly wooded slope. Aònghas and Rhea slowed the lumbering grashiels to a halt in a small clearing and allowed them to sink to the snowy ground for a rest. Then Marcus and the others lodged sophorus torches in the snow and lit them, creating a perimeter of fire to ward off eildritches or any other predators. Everyone settled down to sleep on the floor of the heavekairts – except Magnis, who took the first shift manning the gun at the stern of his heavekairt and squinting into the dark recesses between the trees.

The night passed without incident and they pressed on at first light through the mist-laced forest. It ended abruptly and presented them with another frozen lake.

Much smaller than the one they had traversed before – the expanse – it widened and narrowed frequently along its whole length, encroached upon on either side by steep ridges denuded of vegetation. If the rocks on the coastline had reached into the water like outstretched fingers, these ridges were more like the knuckles of two clenched fists. In the places where they almost met, the passage between them was only about twenty feet wide.

Soon the heavekairts were out upon the ice, exposed once again. A familiar, barbarous wind buffeted them. All the passengers huddled close together. In Marcus's heavekairt he, Nestor and Magnis swathed Aònghas in extra blankets to stop the extreme cold from paralysing him. In the other Theus did the same for Rhea. When they passed through the first narrowing of the lake, snow and ice scoured from the ridges were conjured into a storm that tormented the air between them. It didn't take long to pass through this phenomenon, but it was so dense and violent that exposure to it was almost impossible to endure. Both Aònghas and Rhea ducked right down behind their respective prows, wrestling with the grashiels' reins. The reins grew rapidly stiff and ice-encrusted, but the protesting creatures continued to struggle forward, heads bowed. The passengers lay flat on the floor of the heavekairts, cloaks thrown over them.

When they all stirred themselves to peer over the sides the lake was widening again and the storm growing sparser.

'It will take us several more hours to reach the other

side of this lake, though the ridges do not encroach all the way along,' said Aònghas, glancing over his shoulder at them. 'When we reach the mouth of the first gorge we will be more sheltered.'

Marcus nodded. All too soon he and the others were bracing themselves to pass through the wall of tortured air between the next pair of ridges. Throwing his cloak over his head again, he huddled against the side of the heavekairt.

Closing his eyes, he muttered to himself, 'Then we climb.'

At last they left the lake behind and, as Aònghas had promised, entered the first of the narrow, tortuous gorges that would take them to the base of the mountain. Two vast walls of rock reared up on either side of them, topped by crenellated ridges. They were so sheer that they seemed to lean inwards, as if threatening to crush the heavekairts at any moment. The crevices that rent them all the way down were filled with monstrously twisted columns of ice. These, Marcus guessed, must be frozen waterfalls. He shuddered. The enclosing walls inflamed the old feeling of oppression that this world had provoked in him when he first plunged into it. The enveloping warmth of the close-knit Eihlan village had soothed the sensation. But now it returned more acutely than ever.

For the rest of the day they travelled along a succession of gorges. When they camped overnight the wind, sweeping up from the lake, howled as it blundered through each twist and narrowing of the rock walls. They pulled a canvas over each heavekairt and tethered it against the sides to offer themselves some protection. The grashiels, hunched on the gorge's floor, heads bowed between forelegs, seemed indifferent to it.

They set off again at dawn and not long afterwards the walls became less sheer, leaning back from the heavekairts. The last gorge widened into a valley. Then the valley floor curved upwards and the boulders that littered it grew larger and more numerous.

'The rocks and sediment are carried down into the gorge when the fringes of the glacier melt during the mild seasons,' said Aònghas.

He had to slow down to thread his way between them. Rhea followed suit. When the valley became impassable in certain places, they drove the grashiels right up the sides and round the obstruction. Even with their claws clenched, the beasts scrambled to hold their footing on the steeply sloping rock. Indeed, there were times when his heavekairt tilted so far that Marcus was convinced it would topple over. But it stayed upright through all these manoeuvres and brought them at last to the end of the valley.

Immediately before them a crescent-shaped slope stretched upwards, curving away as far as they could see on each side. It was littered with gravel. Beyond it lay row upon row of huge, swollen masses of rock, which Magnis called buttresses. They had narrow gullies between them. Above these loomed the glacier – a great mass of ice with a curved back, heaving itself upwards. And above the glacier was the Ins'lberg proper, its sheer side vanishing into the clouds. As the grashiels scrambled to a halt, Aònghas gestured ahead of him.

'These are the scree slopes,' he said. 'They're covered in small rocks swept down from the glacier, just like the boulders back down in the valley – except those roll much further because they're heavier. From here, you must walk.'

While he and Rhea kept a tight grip on the reins of the grashiels to stop them growing restive, Marcus, Theus, Nestor and Magnis leaped down from the heavekairts. They landed awkwardly on the loose surface, their limbs stiff from hours of confinement. Once they had unloaded the supplies they unharnessed the grashiels that had borne Rhea's heavekairt, allowing the heavekairt itself to land on the scree with a crunching thud. The grashiels bolted from the loosened straps and wheeled around. Their slavering jaws swung dangerously close to Magnis and Theus, who sprang back, drawing their swords. But soon, exulting in their freedom, the beasts scrambled back down the scree slopes. The other grashiels grew even more agitated at the sight of their companions being liberated and strained against their harnesses, but to no avail.

Watching the freed grashiels galloping down the gorge, Aònghas said, with grim satisfaction, 'Any Nullmaurs who might be following us will have an unpleasant surprise, I think, when they meet them.'

Rhea and Nestor severed the empty harnesses for use as extra climbing ropes, then everyone crouched down

to shoulder their packs. Magnis's, containing the unin-
flated air sacs and the proleyne stoves, was by far the
heaviest. He staggered when he straightened up at first,
eyes wide with alarm, until the others reached out to
steady him.

Marcus jumped aboard the heavekairt, where
Aònghas still stood, and reached out to shake his hand.

'Thank you,' he said. 'Thank you for all you've done
to help us. I ... I'm so sorry for all the trouble our peo-
ple have brought into your world for so many years
without knowing it.'

Aònghas inclined his head and smiled.

'Well, you have,' he replied. 'But you have brought
new hope to us also. That will sustain us until you return
with more of your people to help us drive away the
Nullmaurs for ever.'

The fact that he said this in so quiet and plain a tone
– as if there were no doubt at all that it would come
true – moved Marcus beyond words. Aònghas embraced
him and all the Cloudfarers, receiving murmured words
of gratitude and support from each one. Because he
stood in the heavekairt and they on the slope he was
taller than they were, which seemed only just, under the
circumstances. After the last farewells were said he
jerked on the reins, swept his grashiels round in a broad
circle and headed down towards the valley, waving as he
went.

'I hope he'll be all right on his own,' commented
Marcus.

'He has no extra weight to carry now,' replied Rhea.

'So he'll travel a lot faster. I think he has a good chance.'

Marcus nodded. He looked up at the succession of buttresses. Their width and the creases between them made them look like a furrowed brow, as if the mountain were frowning at them in a monitory way.

'A better chance than we do, perhaps,' he said with a sigh.

They set off up the scree slopes. The route looked deceptively easy at first. The slopes were neither too steep nor covered in especially large rocks. But the loose surface made the going unsteady. Each of them fell at least once, grazing palms and shins, only to be helped up by the others.

Slipping for the third time with a resigned groan, Marcus set a small avalanche of gravel in motion and fought to avoid following it all the way back down on his hands and knees. He struggled to his feet again, and rubbed his gravel-caked palms against his trousers. Looking at him, Magnis said, 'I know it'll be a bit slower, but if we walked up diagonally we might slip less often.'

Rhea and the others considered this.

'Okay,' she said, 'let's give it a try.'

They set off again in this way, zigzagging up the slope. They still fell, but less often. For many hours, as they trudged on through the ice-encrusted gravel, it seemed as if they were barely making any progress at all. But, during the middle of the afternoon, they stopped to rest for a few minutes. Marcus dropped his pack and squatted down beside it. Looking back, he saw that the valley they had travelled up was now far below and actually lay between two mountains. Indeed, there were many other peaks – smaller than the Ins'lberg, but imposing none the less – clustered around it, like its brutish offspring.

After walking for several more hours they found themselves in the lee of the great rock buttresses. Already what little colour the terrain boasted was beginning to fade – the first tell-tale sign of the onset of night.

'What do you think?' said Theus. 'Do we look for a gully and hope to get up it before the light goes completely?'

Rhea gazed at the bulging wall of rock.

'No,' she said. 'Let's camp here tonight. We'll press on at dawn.'

So they settled down, seeking some shelter under the buttresses, and unloaded their packs. Magnis lit one of the battered stoves to heat spiced tea. Theus unwrapped oaten bread and cured meat. He tore chunks of each and passed them round. The bread was so dense and heavy that each chunk had to be chewed vigorously before it could be swallowed, but was very filling. After eating they spread out a groundsheet, weighing it down at each corner with a small rock. Then everyone wriggled into flaxen blankets, each one of which had been sewn up to form a kind of cocoon. Now that the last of the light had faded the wind grew stronger again, raking the scree slopes and whipping fusillades of gravel over them. Wincing, Marcus squirmed deeper into his blanket.

★

When he woke at dawn he first grew conscious of the lumps under the groundsheet, closely followed by the dampness seeping through his gritty hair. Though he had slept soundly the ache in his back and shoulders meant that he hardly felt rested at all. He sat up and rubbed his eyes. He had spent many days in this world now, but he still felt vaguely surprised when it presented itself to him each morning. And, though he hadn't expected it, he felt dispirited to notice that there was no contrast of brightness and shadow amid the surrounding peaks, nor any shafts of sunlight glancing down on to the face of the glacier. The dawn brought with it only the grudging retreat of darkness.

The others had, as always, risen before him. Rhea was still rolling up her blanket while Nestor took his turn to brew tea. Marcus joined them and they all sat hunched on their packs, eating more oaten bread. Then, heaving a collective sigh, they tossed out the dregs of their tea, stowed away the tin mugs and set off again.

They began by skirting the foot of the buttresses, looking for a suitable gully to climb. The gullies were almost vertical, with rough walls covered in loose, easily dislodged outcrops.

'Does it matter which one we choose?' asked Magnis, after Rhea had passed three – gazing up at them for a few moments then moving on.

'Aònghas told me that many of them narrow and close about half-way up. We don't want to get stuck. We'd have to come back down and start again, or traverse across the buttress and look for another gully.'

'So we go for the widest one?' asked Marcus.

'Yes . . . I think so.'

They kept on searching until they found a gully with a fairly wide entrance that looked like the best prospect. Taking the lengths of rope from their packs, they knotted them all together into one long rope. This was then wound round the waist and looped through the belt of each climber: first Magnis, then Rhea, then Marcus, then Theus, then Nestor. When they were finished they checked one another's belts, making sure the knots were secure. Looking around at the rest of them, Marcus announced, in as casual a tone as possible, 'I should go first.'

'What? Why?' asked Rhea.

'Think about it,' he said. 'I'm the lightest. If I fall the rest of you will be able to bear my weight. But if Magnis falls he could easily take everyone with him. It should be me first, then you, then the others.'

'But that's not the point. You're . . .'

He sensed that she had been about to say something like, 'You're more important than the rest of us,' then realised that this would only make him more determined. And she could see, from a purely practical point of view, that the idea made sense. She frowned and ran her fingers through her hair then said, 'You're more likely to be affected by the cold than the rest of us.'

'I'm more likely to be affected by the cold if I stand around debating this much longer,' replied Marcus. He pointed to the others, who were hugging themselves and stamping their feet. 'We all are.'

'All right,' she said at last. 'We'll try it. But if it doesn't work we'll switch round again.'

'Thanks.' Then he added with a smile, 'I'll try not to let you down . . . in any way.'

After various contortions, they all managed to untie the ropes from themselves then retie them with Marcus and Rhea at one end of the line and a vaguely disgruntled-looking Magnis demoted to the other.

Stepping up cautiously to the entrance of the gully, Marcus tested the footholds with light kicks and tapped the rock above his head with his axe to determine its looseness. Only when he reached up did he realise that his hands were trembling. The true test was about to begin.

XX

The ascent begins

At first they inched upwards. Marcus dug his axes into the corners of the gully and kept his legs splayed. His inexperience meant that for every time the blades of the axes lodged in the rock, there were several more when they simply gouged out a trickle of fragments as soon as he tugged on them. Quite often he thought that he had a secure stance only to lurch sickeningly downwards when the adzes gave way. Each time this happened he had to brace his feet even more firmly against the side walls. He winced as a juddering pain shot up both legs.

'Are you all right?' Rhea asked from below.

'Yes!' he shouted back, loath to reveal how much of a struggle he was finding this first stretch.

He grew a little more confident as time passed and now needed only one or two attempts to lodge his axes into the rock. The others followed him closely, burrowing their fingers into the holds he had created. But progress was still agonisingly slow. In spite of the cold his clothes felt clammy against his skin and the handles of the axes slippery beneath his clenched fingers. Then, as he was chipping into the corners, his feet gave way. Yelling out in alarm and fear, he lost his grip on the axes, both of which remained firmly lodged. He tumbled down the gully, past Rhea, who shrank to one side to avoid being knocked off by his flailing body. He fell past all the others too, until the length of rope connecting him to Rhea pulled taut. She cried out at the sudden weight, but managed, with supreme effort, to keep a firm stance.

Marcus was left dangling upside down about ten feet below Magnis, spinning slowly and swaying from side to side. The gully's walls slid past his vision. They were replaced for a few moments by the peaks of the surrounding mountains, now a craggy roof to his inverted world. Then he found himself staring at the walls again. His head bumped against the rock as he spun. The rope had ridden up and was like a vice around his chest. He reached down, gasping, and tried to prise it a little looser. His fingers trembled and all the sweat had chilled on his skin.

'Can you get back up?' asked Magnis, peering down at him anxiously.

'I think so,' he gasped.

He kicked against the gully's walls, a little lower each time, first to stop himself spinning then to right himself. Once he had succeeded he paused for a moment, legs splayed. His pulse thudded in his temples, as if he were being struck simultaneously on either side of the head, and grey dots swarmed around the edges of his vision. He closed his eyes for a few moments and pressed his forehead against the rock. Then he started to crawl back up the gully. The Cloudfarers shuffled sideways to let him pass. When he drew level with Theus, the pilot offered a doleful smile and said, 'Well, you were right about one thing: none of the rest of us fell.'

'That's a great comfort,' Marcus muttered.

Once he had retrieved his axes he and the Cloudfarers resumed the climb. Progress slowed for a while. Marcus took much more time to find secure holds, struggling against the looseness of the eroded rock and the caution that his recent fall had bred in him. But gradually he regained confidence and their movement upwards became much smoother.

They continued on like this for many hours. Every now and then they tried to rest. But remaining poised in the gully with feet pressed against the side walls was almost as awkward as climbing, so they didn't stop for long.

Late in the afternoon Marcus looked down at Rhea and said, 'If we're still in the gully when night comes it's going to be pretty difficult climbing in the dark.'

'I know,' replied Rhea. 'But we won't have any choice. It's not like we can make camp here.'

So they pressed on. But before they could consider how to deal with this problem a new one confronted them. Peering upwards, Marcus saw that the gully narrowed and closed about twenty yards above. It was impassable. He shouted the news down to the others. It was greeted by a chorus of groans.

'We can't go back,' Nestor shouted up. 'It'll be dark before we even get a quarter of the way down.'

'Yes, but there's no way we can stay here all night. We'll weaken and fall eventually,' Magnis pointed out.

Rhea shook her head.

'The only thing we can do is traverse across the buttress and try to find another gully,' she said. 'It'll be risky, but we have no other choice. Marcus, do you think you can lead off?'

'I'll try.' He leaned back as far as he dared, trying to peer round each of the side walls. 'I think it might be easier if we go to the right.'

'Okay.'

He took a deep breath and slipped the handles of the ice axes through the loops in his belt. Then, his stomach tightening with fear, he removed his foot from its hold in the left side wall and twisted his body to face the one on the right. He kicked his left foot against it, seeking another hold. Once he had found a secure one he stretched his right arm and leg round the corner of the side wall and edged on to the rough, friable surface of the buttress. Peering up at him, the others followed suit.

Only when they had climbed out of it did Marcus realise how sheltered they had been in the gully. On the buttress they not only had to concentrate on finding secure holds but also contend with the icy, barging wind. They struggled sideways none the less, crossing several more buttresses. All the gullies proved to be too narrow to climb, but they sought shelter briefly in each one. They said little to one another since it was almost impossible to shout above the wind's howling.

They had been climbing now for seven hours without

a proper break. Marcus felt weak from hunger, as if the emptiness in his stomach were transmitting itself through his limbs, making them weightless. He worried that his grip would soon fail him. But he knew he couldn't afford to stop. They *had* to find another gully. He kept on edging sideways.

Just when it seemed that their situation couldn't grow any more perilous he heard a low rumble. The sound seemed to come from deep within the mountain, as if it were groaning with displeasure at having such tiny, pestiferous creatures crawling over its haunches. Marcus stopped and peered upwards, craning his neck back as far as he dared while his straining shoulders trembled. He could see nothing beyond the brow of the buttress except the sheer rock and ice walls of the mountain in the far distance. The vast glacier that lay in between was completely hidden.

The rumble grew louder. Something was happening, but *what?*

The answer – abrupt and shocking – came a few seconds later. A barrage of stones swept downwards, bouncing and spinning over the buttress.

'Look out!' Marcus shouted down to the others.

The stones were only a few inches across. As long as Marcus hugged the buttress with his head lowered they stung his scalp and hands without threatening to dislodge him.

'Is everyone all right?' he called out when the barrage had abated somewhat.

'Yes!' came a chorus of breathless voices.

But the small stones proved to be only a harbinger. A few seconds later the buttress seemed to shiver beneath Marcus's clenched fingertips as boulders several feet across came tumbling down it, smacking against the rocky outcrops.

This time Marcus had no chance to yell a warning. Like the others he was forced to twist his body this way and that to dodge the boulders while trying not to lose his grip. The vertical line of climbers undulated like a writhing serpent against the buttress. At the opposite end of the rope from Marcus, Nestor lunged too sharply out of the path of a boulder that was hurtling diagonally towards him. He lost his grip with an anguished cry. For a few moments he clawed frantically at the buttress with his bare hands then his footholds gave way and he plummeted past Magnis.

Hearing Nestor cry out, Rhea shouted 'Brace!' – just as she might have during an especially violent manoeuvre aboard an aëro:cruiser. Everyone tightened their grip and flattened themselves against the buttress to bear Nestor's weight. When the rope grew taut between him and Magnis the latter grunted as he began to be dragged downwards. He kicked hard against the rock and dug his fingers in as deeply as he could. Doing so tore the skin from his hands, but it also slowed his descent. Howling with pain, he clung to the buttress in this way until Nestor managed to find holds once again.

Marcus's eyes, like Rhea's and Theus's, repeatedly darted between his struggling comrades below and the threat from above. At one point, when he glanced up, he saw a boulder careering right for him. It was too close and moving too fast for him to dodge it. His first impulse should have been to screw up his eyes, before the impact that would surely split his skull and wrench him from the buttress. But some kind of paralysis seized him. He stared at the approaching lump of rock, mesmerised. Then, when it was only inches away, it struck an outcrop. The outcrop wasn't large, but it was solid enough to send the boulder spinning just clear of Marcus's head, ruffling his hair.

He immediately looked over his shoulder to see if it had hit anyone else. But the others had edged far enough sideways, one way or the other, so that there was no one directly below him. He watched the boulder plunging down the buttress towards the scree slopes, where it would doubtless trundle to a halt and accumulate with the others at the top of the valley.

At last the deluge stopped. It turned back into a shower of pebbles – vexing but not life-threatening – which trickled down collars and into the sleeves of outstretched arms. For a short while everyone clung, motionless, to the buttress, trying to absorb the fact that although they were all bruised and Magnis's hands badly cut, they had somehow survived.

'I'm so sorry,' said Nestor, looking more anguished at the trouble he had caused than by his own fear at falling.

'Don't worry, it could have happened to any of us,' replied Marcus.

'Can you still climb?' Rhea called to Magnis.

'Not easily,' he told her, wincing.

'Wait, wait . . .' said Nestor. 'I think I can help.'

He climbed up beside Magnis. Removing one hand from the buttress, he unwound his scarf from his neck and tore it in two along its whole length with his teeth. Then, manoeuvring himself closer still, he wrapped the strips with great care around his comrade's lacerated hands, while the tips of Magnis's fingers trembled in their crumbling holds.

'This won't stop the pain,' he said. 'But it should make it bearable for a while.'

'Thank you,' Magnis replied, in a low yet tremulous voice.

Marcus looked at Rhea.

'Maybe we shouldn't try to find another gully,' he suggested. 'Maybe we should just climb the buttress. We might reach the glacier faster.'

'We're more exposed out here,' she pointed out.

'I know, but rocks could fall down a gully just like they did here. And if they did it would be much harder to dodge them in a narrow space.'

'It'll be nightfall soon,' Theus added. 'I think speed is the most important thing now.'

Rhea considered this then nodded.

'Okay, we just climb.'

They continued vertically up the swollen contours of the buttress, with Marcus still leading. They were conscious of Magnis's injuries, so their progress wasn't fast, but it remained steady. Frequent showers of pebbles made them tense and lower their heads, but none turned into anything stronger. Every now and then Marcus paused and risked leaning away from the rock to see if he could glimpse the glacier. But the curve of the buttress meant that it remained hidden; he had no idea how distant it was. The only thing he could tell for certain was that the underbelly of the clouds didn't seem to be drawing any closer. Feeling more and more dispirited, he resumed climbing.

The light grew enfeebled. Marcus knew that the longer they climbed the likelier it would be that one of them might founder again. He kept this fear to himself. But he sensed a sagging of spirits amongst the others too, as if the rope that bound everyone together made him privy to their thoughts. It became darker still, and colder. His fingers had grown almost completely numb. As he watched them struggle blindly across the rock it seemed to him that they were alien five-legged creatures, crawling on ahead, unconnected to the rest of his body. This sense of disconnection was dangerously appealing. It would be so much easier for him and the others to let gravity drag them down to their fate.

It seemed that luck had abandoned them, that the mountain would soon shrug them off. But the next time Marcus paused for a moment, wondering if he would have the strength to start again, he glanced up to the right with a weary, unfocused gaze and saw something unusual. About fifty yards above there was what could only be described as a large, coarse bulge on the side of the buttress, as if it had grown inflamed in one place. Its sides were steeper than the curving rock around it, but it looked as if it might contain just enough space on top for them to cram themselves on to.

He shouted down to Rhea, who had also paused. When he had her attention he risked removing one hand from its hold and pointed.

'Look at that. Maybe we could stop there for a while. I know it won't be flat on top like a ledge. But we might just be able to rest on it.'

Rhea squinted past him.

'Let's try it,' she said.

They all shuffled sideways then began to ascend to the outcrop. Reaching its lower portion first, Marcus reached out gingerly and tested for handholds. The rock was even more friable than that on the main buttress. But after tugging at it a little he guessed that it could hold his weight. Awkwardly he twisted round again – from the face of the buttress on to the outcrop – and continued to climb. The others followed. Chunks of rock crumbled away with worrying ease when they kicked at it to gouge footholds, but no one fell.

One by one, they hauled themselves on to the humped back of the outcrop. As Marcus had guessed, they were just about able to sit on it, though they all had to face outwards, each person's back propped against another's. They dug their heels in and pressed their palms against it too, just to be on the safe side.

As darkness deepened around them, it brought with it the realisation that they wouldn't be able to lie down for any real rest, or wriggle into the blankets to seek protection from the bitter night air.

Sitting beside Magnis, Rhea said, 'Here, let me look at your hands.'

He proffered them and she slowly unwrapped the makeshift bandages. Dried blood had stuck the last layer to his skin. Magnis grimaced as it was peeled away, but didn't protest. After examining his hands, she said to Marcus, 'Aònghas gave me a pot of ointment to soothe wounds. Can you get it out of my pack?'

'I'll try,' replied Marcus, who sat with his back to her.

His features twitching with concentration, he reached behind him and fumbled with the straps of Rhea's pack. Then he wriggled his hand about inside it.

'Can you find it?' she asked.

'Not yet.'

He fumbled around some more. Eventually his fingers closed round a small clay pot, wrapped in a piece of linen secured with string.

'Got it!'

Very carefully, not wanting to pull anything else out of the pack that might tumble away down the buttress, he withdrew his hand and passed the pot over his shoulder to Rhea. Rhea's fingers grasped the air for a few moments until they closed around it. Resting it on her lap, she opened it and began to smear the ointment over Magnis's hands.

'This should take the sting away and form a protective layer over the wounds,' she explained.

'Thank you,' he replied, the tension lines on his face

growing less deeply etched already.

Once Rhea had attended to Magnis, Theus said, 'So, do we stop here for a while then try to press on or do we sit out the night here?'

'Climbing the buttress in daylight has been bad enough,' commented Nestor. 'I can't imagine how we would survive it in the dark.'

'If we stay here we daren't sleep,' said Marcus. 'It's far too precarious.'

Rhea glanced over her shoulder.

'One of us could,' she said. 'One of us could sit on top and rest against the buttress, with the others sitting round them so they won't slide off.'

They immediately nominated Magnis to do this. After a few feeble protests he clambered on top of the outcrop. Cloak drawn around him, each hand slid under the opposite arm to warm and protect it, he closed his eyes. The others shuffled around the edge to sit two on either side of him, facing out into the abysmal darkness.

Now beside Rhea, Marcus said in an undertone, 'I'm beginning to wonder if it might take us another whole day to reach the glacier.'

'I know, it's worrying me too,' she replied. 'Well, we knew when we started this it was going to be difficult.'

'Yes . . . yes, *everything* is difficult.'

His voice kept its light pitch as he said this, but even he was surprised by the note of weary resignation – many fathoms deep – that lurked in it.

'We've come a long way, Marcus,' Rhea reminded him gently. 'And we wouldn't have made it even this far

312

if it hadn't been for some of the things you've done. Don't despair.'

'It's okay, I'm not despairing. It's just . . . I'm just beginning to realise that if we do get back to Heliopolis we've got an even greater task ahead of us after that. And given what we've been through just in the past few hours we're probably going to be in pretty poor shape when we get there.'

'Well, I think those are things we can only worry about when we confront them. For now we just have to concentrate on making it back to Heliopolis alive. And if we do, remember, Magnis is from the Farmers' layer. He might be able to make contact with a family who can hide us for a while.'

'That's true.'

'And while we're recovering there we can start to think about a plan to defeat Titus.'

'Yes. Yes, I suppose so.'

'Then restore everything to the way it should be: the way it was before.'

Marcus took a deep breath and let it out extremely slowly. He felt compelled to say what he was going to next, but he knew it would shock her.

'No, that's not going to happen.'

'*What*? Then why are we . . .'

'Rhea, I've been thinking about a lot of things since we first fell into this world – mainly about my father, but also . . . Persis was quite right, you know. Titus couldn't have planned his coup the way he did if it wasn't for the way our citadel is built: everyone in their layers, everyone told to accept their lot, people in the palace – people like me, my father, Synvadis – knowing nothing about the lives of those below. It's all wrong. It's . . . *unjust*. I don't care if this makes me sound pompous or worthy or just ungrateful, but if we ever make it home, I can't become the ruler of a place like that, not after all I've been through. It's time for the people to choose their own leaders and for the leaders to live among the people and understand them, instead of being so distant, so cut off far above them. We might think we're more advanced than the Eihlans, but the way they live is so much fairer.'

Rhea frowned deeply and looked away, as if flinching from a blow he'd just dealt her.

'*That's* how we can get the ordinary citizens to rise up against Titus,' he continued, tugging insistently at her sleeve. 'We have to show them that although they might have been made to feel powerless over so many centuries there are far more of them than of the people above. Think about it: the layers they live in are much bigger and more populous than the ones above. The whole way the citadel is built has always meant that those in the lower layers have the greatest power – it's just that they've never realised it. I know it won't be easy to persuade them, but if we can give them some-thing to believe in, if we can make them see they're fighting for their own freedom, I think we might just manage it.'

Rhea was now looking down at her lap, not exactly wringing her hands, but kneading each with the fingers of the other.

'I know it sounds strange: me of all people talking about revolution,' he added, with a melancholy laugh. 'Believe me, I wish I'd never realised these things. I wish my father was still alive. But I . . . I really feel that if we can try to make life better and fairer for our people then somehow . . . he won't have died in vain. And it'll become more bearable – to live without him.'

'I suppose I understand,' she replied, nodding reluctantly. 'I have to admit hearing you talk about these things, it's . . . it's a little hard for me to take in. I mean, traditions – the traditions of the Corps – are what myself and the others have been trying to uphold since we've been in this world, to defy what Titus has done to them . . .'

'No, I realise that, I do,' Marcus assured her. 'I'm not talking about getting rid of all the traditions, just the ones that are unfair, the ones that keep us apart from one another in our different layers, instead of feeling like we're all . . . one family.'

At these last words Rhea smiled sympathetically, as if she had glimpsed, just for a moment, the years of loneliness and yearning for a more normal life that lay behind them.

'Yes, Marcus, I see what you mean.'

They talked on for many hours, Marcus trying to draw Rhea further into his vision of a new citadel, she offering questions and, eventually, tentative suggestions. In this way they sat out the darkness until dawn brought its familiar torpid light.

★

As soon as it was light enough to see they ate a little oaten bread and prepared to set off again. They tugged at the loops of rope that hung between them to test the knots. Then Marcus rose gingerly on the side of the outcrop – one leg straight, one leg bent – and reached up for the buttress, searching for the first holds.

Hesitant at first, they began to climb again. They agreed to waste no time searching for another gully. Instead they pressed on up the buttress. Each climber's progress was slowed occasionally when a hold gave way and they lurched downwards. But this time no one fell more than a few feet. And by midday the curve of rock grew less steep and brought them to the fringes of the glacier.

The ice here was twisted and ruptured by the head of the buttress. But then it swept upwards in a smooth, snow-covered plain – the glacier. This was topped by a series of corniced ridges. Beyond these lay the head wall – a mass of sheer rock, corrugated with ice, that marked the beginning of the mountain proper. They stood and gazed at this forbidding vista for a while, absorbing the realisation of all they still had to overcome.

'I think we should trek up diagonally, like we did on the scree slopes, then try to find a gap in the ridges,' said Rhea.

'Do we untie ourselves?' asked Magnis, raising a loop of rope.

'No, we stay together. What happens to one of us affects all the others – that's the way it should be,' said Rhea. She smiled at Marcus. 'Isn't that right?'

'That's right,' he replied.

Everyone shouldered their pack. Then, unsheathing the snow stakes to give them extra balance, they set off, the rope trailing between them. Trudging upwards, Marcus noticed that the glacier's mantle was etched with narrow fracture lines. Some of the sections of frozen snow carved out in this way covered nearly an acre and were slightly raised or sunken compared to those surrounding them.

Though progress was easier than on the buttress, torrents of spindrift, swept down off the ridges, harried them, forcing them to stop occasionally and bow their heads, as if in acknowledgement of the mountain's latent power. After everything that had happened to them already, Marcus grew superstitious, feeling that they might avert further disaster by paying homage to it in this way.

When they reached the half-way point, several hours later, such notions proved false. Just as he raised his head after the latest torrent of spindrift had abated, Marcus felt his foothold growing slacker – almost liquid. He looked down again. Though the featurelessness of the snow made it hard to tell what was going on at first, the sensation was unmistakable. The section of the mantle he walked on had detached itself from the rest and was sliding down the glacier. He broke into a frantic stride, but soon realised that it was hopeless. While he struggled upwards, the broad, flat chunk of frozen snow sped downwards. He was running on the spot, watching its top edge draw closer, unable to stop it. There were cries of alarm behind him. The others lost their balance, crashing to their hands and knees.

XXI

The head wall

Throwing his snow stake aside, Marcus wrenched one of the ice axes from his belt and hurled himself forwards. He slammed the adze of an axe into the glacier. But it just chipped the ice then skipped across it as he and the others were swept downwards, growing faster and more entangled all the time.

Juddering along on his stomach, Marcus gathered all his strength then began to hack at the ice with both his axes. At the same time the others twisted on to their backs and tried to dig their heels into the ice to slow themselves a little. For what seemed like an eternity nothing happened. Then the axes bit. The part of the rope that connected Marcus and Rhea grew taut. She spun through one hundred and eighty degrees then came to an abrupt halt. He felt as if his arms were being wrenched from their sockets, but he kept his grip on the handles. As soon as she stopped moving she stabbed her sword into the ice to brace herself. A few seconds later Theus did the same. Eventually the others slowed and stopped too. Everyone lay motionless. Though their lungs were well able to cope with the thinning air, their exertions had left them gasping.

For a while they all sat recovering, knees drawn up protectively. As they watched, the section of mantle they had been standing on surged downwards, splitting into smaller pieces, then dashing itself against the head of one of the buttresses. A pall of powdery snow rose above it.

'You know, it's ironic,' observed Nestor. 'When I lived in Heliopolis I used to think of the rock below my feet as the most secure, most durable thing possible – it would never change, never diminish, not like the clouds that swirled around it. Yet here we are trying to climb it and it crumbles and slides and does everything it can to cast us off.'

They all pondered the humbling truth of this. Then they rose, retrieved their swords and, with an exaggeratedly heavy tread – to keep a firm grip on the newly exposed ice – they continued upwards. There was little they could do to prevent a repeat of what had just happened, except concentrate hard and exercise even more vigilance every time they placed one foot in front of the other. This slowed their progress once again, but brought them by late afternoon to the banked-up snow at the foot of the ridges.

'We'll have to stop here for the night,' said Rhea. 'If we start to climb again now after trekking up the whole glacier we'll tire and make mistakes. And if we find ourselves stuck on the head wall with nowhere to rest we'll be in real trouble.'

'I was under the impression we'd been in trouble ever

since we arrived in this world,' commented Nestor dryly.

'Well, even bigger trouble.'

'We're a good deal higher up now than we were on the outcrop,' Theus said. 'It's going to get even colder with nightfall and we'll be pretty exposed. Maybe there'll be more shelter on the far side of the ridges?'

'But we don't know how difficult it might be to cross them,' countered Rhea. 'If it gets dark while we're trying we could easily get stuck.'

She gazed up at the boundless height and girth of the mountain, thinking.

'No, we'll dig a hole in the snow,' she said at last.

'A hole for five people? Won't that take an awfully long time?' asked Marcus.

'Not if we all dig together.'

So, raising their swords, they began to alternately slash and burrow at the banked snow until they had excavated a hole just large enough for them all to squeeze inside. Then, before the last of the wan light expired, they ate a little and brewed some spiced tea.

'I suppose tomorrow will be the start of the real test,' observed Theus as they squatted around the stove, hands extended to catch a little warmth from it.

'I fear so,' replied Rhea. 'Scaling the head wall is going to be . . . well, a lot more interesting than climbing the buttresses. There won't be any handholds. We'll have to hack out every one from the ice.'

They all nodded. No one said anything else for a while. Marcus guessed they were all thinking the same as he: if anyone fell on the next stage of the climb the others would have little chance of bearing his weight while trying to grip a sheer wall of rock and ice.

'You know what's even more amazing?' asked Magnis.

The others shook their heads.

'Well . . . all of this.' He gestured around him. 'What we've seen and travelled through – it's only one small part of this world. I mean, think how different from ours the citadels closer to the equator are. Think of all the exotic fruits they have and how lush their pastures are. Winter there is nothing – it merely soaks the grass. The southern parts of *this* world must be just as different. There must be plants and flowers and animals and insects there that would seem so alien to us.'

They all murmured agreement with this. Then, after some more ruminative chewing, Theus said, 'It's strange – I know we're still a long way from Heliopolis. I know there are all sorts of hazards still ahead of us. And I *do* want to come back to this world some day, to see other parts of it. But I can't help starting to think about the things I might do if I get home – and if we do find a way to defeat Titus.'

'Like what, Theus?' asked Marcus.

'Well . . . seeing my family again more than anything else, of course. But also, as everyone knows, I was about to retire. I'd planned to spend some time doing paintings of the cloudscape. In fact, I was hoping to get a dispensation to paint in one of the palace towers a couple of days a week.'

'I'm sure that could be arranged,' said Marcus encouragingly.

322

'All I want is to be back with my maps in my room below the observatory,' said Nestor. 'It gets a little dingy sometimes and my routine may seem a rather dull one, but whole hours can go by without anyone trying to kill me.'

The others chuckled at this.

'What about you, Magnis? What would you like to do?' asked Rhea.

Magnis looked vaguely embarrassed. Then, slipping his hand inside his tunic, he took out a piece of cloth. Unfolding it, he shyly revealed the neatly arranged cuttings of various plants and semperennial flowers nestling inside it.

'I have all these cuttings I've taken on our journey,' he said. 'I'd love a patch of garden of my own – maybe even in the Hortoreum – where I could plant them, see if I could make them grow in our thinner mountain air.'

They all smiled at the image of the burly Cloudfarer hunched over the tender shoots of some new plant, patting down the surrounding soil. Theus and Magnis looked expectantly at Marcus, waiting for his description of what he would most like to do. But he glanced instead at Rhea.

'And you?' he asked her.

She pursed her lips.

'Playing with my nieces in the Hortoreum,' she said. 'Seeing them enjoy the open spaces. But also, just the chance for all of us to be together in peace.'

The others nodded. Theus raised his mug.

'To comradeship,' he said. 'And friendship.'

'To friendship,' they all repeated, raising their mugs.

Warmed a little by these thoughts, they packed away their supplies and huddled together in the snow hole.

When Marcus woke the next morning he felt disorientated at first by the milky white glow that bathed him. The others lay huddled next to him, cradled by the snow hole's curving sides. More showers of spindrift had swept down in the night and sealed it completely. Marcus punched through where the glow was brightest and struggled back out on to the glacier. Hearing him do this, the others woke with a succession of groans, then followed him out on hands and knees.

After a hasty breakfast they toiled up towards the ridges. The overhangs of snow that topped them looked impossibly precarious; they gave the impression that they might collapse if you expressed your astonishment at them in too loud a voice. Marcus and the others edged gingerly along, searching for a spot where the ridges were eroded.

Eventually Rhea said, 'It's no good. We'll have to cut our way through.'

Raising their swords high, Theus and Magnis started to slash at the ridge, the others following close behind. The overhanging powder snow crumbled instantly. But they continued to struggle onward, even when it piled waist high, or in Marcus's case chest high.

Their exertions brought them to the other side at last. They emerged from the collapsed ridges looking like creatures made of snow rather than humans who had just carved a path through it. They shook the snow off then gazed up at their next challenge. The head wall was covered in vertical flutings of ice with razor-sharp edges and between these lay gullies – shallower than the ones on the buttress but much smoother and even more treacherous looking. The ice that clad both had, from a distance, seemed colourless. Now Marcus could see rich seams of blue and green, as if there were sapphires and emeralds trapped in it. There were even stray patches of amethyst purple. As Rhea had pointed out, there would be no natural holds here; they would have to hack all of them out with axes.

'Okay,' she said, taking a deep breath, 'let's do this.'

They trekked along the base of the head wall, as they had done below the buttresses, searching for the widest gully to climb. Being the lightest, Marcus led off again. He stepped towards the gully they had chosen, ice axes raised.

With Marcus hacking into the ice and the others fumbling for the holds he created, they continued upwards. If before they had scrambled over the mountain's haunches, now Marcus felt that they were ascending its torso – a torso with ribs of ice and muscles of bulging rock. He was so acutely conscious of the mountain's immense size that he felt as if the head wall was pushing back against him as he clung to it. But he kept such thoughts at bay by focusing on small, achievable goals: moving up another twenty feet then having a brief rest.

Several hours later, to his surprise, the gully they were edging up split in two. After a certain amount of indecision he took the right-hand branch. He was now climbing at a slight angle and had to restrict the movement of his legs and arms slightly to ensure that they weren't cut by the serrations of ice that fringed the gully. When its sloping sides receded a little at one point he leaned back from the head wall and saw, with a sinking heart, that they were now negotiating a complex vertical maze, etched into the face of the mountain. Everywhere he looked, gullies veined the rock, all of them branching off in several different directions and intersecting one another. Rhea and Theus crawled up beside him and surveyed it.

'This is going to complicate things,' said Theus.

'If we head up the wrong gully at any point,' added Marcus. 'We could get hopelessly snarled up.'

'We have to take that chance,' replied Rhea grimly. 'We've come too far to stop.'

So they pressed on. Until now the ascent had been just a matter of endurance. Now there were agonising decisions to be made every few hundred yards about which route to take and Marcus struggled with them almost as much as he did with the sheer physical effort of climbing.

When, for the third time, they had to shuffle back down a gully because it closed further up, he felt a helpless paralysis overtake him. The strength of his lungs should have meant that he had little trouble breathing. The fact that he had spent his whole life above the clouds should have meant that he had no fear of heights. Yet the freezing air seared his chest each time he breathed it in and the wind clawed at him. He closed his eyes and pressed his forehead against the ice-clad rock for a moment. But there was nowhere to rest. Despair wove itself around his aching body, making his limbs feel heavier and heavier.

'Are you all right?' Rhea shouted from below.

His muscles tensed at the sound of her voice. He couldn't let the others down. He couldn't let himself down. He burrowed deep inside himself, groping around for memories that might sustain him. He remembered Asperia hugging him with all her pent-up devotion on the landing stage. He recalled the Cloudfarers doing the same just after they had liberated themselves from the Nullmaurs – and the enveloping warmth of their joy and admiration. He recalled Breah's grave kiss and the sight of her and the other Eihlans waving goodbye. He drew strength from all these memories. Then, flexing his arms and legs, he shrugged off despair and prepared to start climbing again.

'Are you all right?' Rhea repeated.

'Yes!' he shouted back.

Some time after midday Marcus looked up and saw, with a sense of dread, a huge overhang of ice looming above them. It was far too wide to go round. Tears of frustration sprang into his eyes and froze on the lashes like tiny jewels. His vision spangled with them, he cast around desperately for some other route. Then, to his right, he saw a ridge of rock, split from the head wall. It looked as if it had peeled half off, like the rind from a piece of fruit. The gap between it and the head wall was deep, but not wide. And where it led there was no maze of gullies, just the blank face of the mountain. He motioned Rhea to come up beside him.

'Look,' he said, pointing awkwardly. 'Surely we could head up there?'

'How?'

'We can put our feet on that ridge, brace our hands against the head wall and move up it sideways.'

'It'll be awkward.'

'But it has to be faster than climbing . . . and less exhausting.'

She peered up at the ridge for a while, glancing between it and the hulking overhang.

'Okay. Let's try it at least.'

With immense care they manoeuvred themselves around the edge of the fluting then traversed across it towards the chasm. Once they were poised above it, Marcus, his axes still embedded in the ice of the head wall, lowered his feet on to the ridge of rock. Like the edges of the gullies it was razor sharp. If any of them lost their footing and fell on to it they would most likely be split in two. None the less, the feeling of standing on something solid, after hours of clinging to contorted gullies, was blissful.

So, shuffling sideways, arms raised high and palms flat against the head wall, as if imploring the mountain not to grow any more treacherous, they continued their journey. Gradually the ice thinned, merely streaking the rock then vanishing completely. Every now and then Marcus looked up at the cloud layer. The blandness of its underside made it impossible to tell just how near or distant it was, but some vague apprehension told him that it had drawn much closer. Indeed, small threads of vapour, separated from the main layer, huddled against the rock and wove themselves round some of its outcrops.

He was just allowing the belief that they might be making real progress to creep into his mind when he heard a sickening crunch and a yell of alarm from the other end of the line. The ridge was crumbling beneath Theus's feet while his hands scrabbled against the head wall. Finally he lost his footing and plunged. Marcus knew that within a few seconds the rest of them would be wrenched from their stance by his flailing body. But as he fell, Theus managed to throw his arms out and grab the part of the ridge he had been standing on. It crumbled some more then held steady. Deprived of its sharp edge it failed to cut his arms. Magnis and Nestor shuffled together on one side of where he hung; Marcus and Rhea did the same on the other. Then, turning round so that their backs were pressed against the head wall, they hauled Theus back up – all the time trying not to brace their feet too hard on the ridge, lest it crumble even more.

Theus slumped against the rock, arms tightly folded, grimacing.

'I'm sorry,' he gasped.

'It's all right,' said Marcus. 'We're safe.'

'Can you keep going?' asked Rhea.

'Yes, I'm just bruised. It could have been a lot worse.'

'If we stay on this ridge it might well be,' Nestor pointed out.

Marcus squinted up at the head wall.

'There are no gullies now to protect us,' he replied. 'I think free climbing would still be even more dangerous – remember trying to scale the buttress.'

'Okay, let's carry on,' said Rhea. 'We'll just have to take it slower.'

They shuffled up the ridge again. After another hour they entered the cloud layer. As soon as they were sealed in its grey opacity, snow began to swirl round them. The rock grew swiftly soaked with water vapour and slippery to the touch. Marcus could see no more than three feet in front of him. Any sense of elation at reaching the crucial stage in the ascent was obliterated by the realisation that their task had only become more difficult.

The ridge peeled away even further from the head wall. They had to lean forwards at a more and more perilous angle to keep their hands on it. When Marcus looked down between his fully extended arms he saw the chasm gaping below him, fathomless and unknowable. Soon the ridge also grew steeper, making it impossible to negotiate any further. He felt despair beginning to envelop him once again.

'It's no good,' he said to Rhea, his voice echoing down the chasm. 'Nestor was right: we need to start climbing again.'

'Okay.'

Drawing out his axes, he wedged them into the rock and hoisted himself back on to the head wall. He kicked hard at it, summoning up all his frustration at the mountain's obduracy: the way it kept on thwarting them at every turn. Once he had found secure footholds he began to hack a route upwards again, the others following.

They continued as they had on the buttress, contesting every inch of the way against the manic wind and the crumbling rock. Then, after an hour or so, one of Marcus's axes – extended, quivering, above his head – swiped at thin air. He frowned and peered up, arching his back painfully to see as far as possible.

'What is it?' asked Rhea.

'It looks like some kind of alcove. It's got a bit of an outcrop jutting from it,' he reported.

'Maybe we can rest there. What do you think?' he shouted to Rhea above the howling of the wind.

'Maybe. Let's try it.'

He hauled himself on to the outcrop and looked around the alcove on his hands and knees. It was wide but shallow, with concave sides. Small stones littered its surface. Sweeping his hand lightly over them, he frowned and looked up at the mountain. Only a few feet were visible before it vanished into the cloud. The others clambered after him. Shuffling to his side, Theus said, 'I'd imagine there are a lot of small rock falls. The stones must gather here.'

'I suppose so,' said Marcus.

Once they were all in the alcove it didn't seem quite as wide as it had before. But the Cloudfarers slumped against the sides with sighs of relief and loosened the rope around their waists. No one said anything; they just stared out into the void. After a while it thickened, almost imperceptibly, from pale to mid grey.

'Night'll be coming soon,' Marcus said to Rhea.

She nodded.

'We'll rest here. We can sleep in shifts.'

So, after everyone had eaten a little, Marcus and Rhea lay down first, legs tucked under them, making a cocoon of their cloaks, while Theus, Magnis and Nestor talked quietly and fought to stay awake.

In truth Marcus didn't get much sleep. Though the others had created as much space as possible for him and Rhea, his brain found it impossible to ignore the fact that he was lying directly above a drop of many miles. He would drift off to sleep for half an hour or so then lurch back to wakefulness with a plunging sensation, convinced that he had just rolled over the edge of the alcove. When the time came for Theus and Magnis to replace them he was somewhat relieved.

They performed the changeover with care, since the night, combined with the thickness of the cloud, meant that the blackness around them was absolute. In spite of this each one of them was still elbowed in the head or chest several times. While Theus and Magnis finally settled down Marcus patted his way to the side of the alcove and sat there with his legs dangling. He heard Rhea shuffling over beside him.

'I can't believe we've made it even this far,' he said in an undertone, not wanting to disturb the others' slumber.

'I wouldn't recommend sharing that sentiment with the others, but I know what you mean,' Rhea replied.

'Do you . . . do you think we might really do this?'

'Well, if the head wall stays clear of any more gullies or chasms we should be able to use Magnis's air sacs at last. Hopefully they'll make the ascent a lot less difficult . . . always assuming they work.'

'Hmm.'

They sat in silence for a while, staring sightlessly into the night.

Rhea sighed.

'You know, I've been thinking a lot about what you were saying before, about the way things should change in Heliopolis if we defeat Titus, about . . . democracy. It's taking me a while to get used to the idea, I must confess, but if it really did happen, what about *you*? When we were talking about what we'd like to do if we got home and defeated Titus, I noticed that you didn't say anything. The others noticed too, of course, but they didn't want to embarrass you by mentioning it. What *would* you do afterwards?'

'I don't know, Rhea, I really don't. I mean, my life was always so organised for me before, the path ahead always looked set. And now it's changed so much from how I thought it would be and I . . . I can't even imagine a future for myself, to be honest. Since Titus's attack my whole world has been turned upside down – literally. At last I know what it's like to feel like you're in the lowest place – to look up at the rest of the world and feel cut off from it. I've seen things from a point of view that my father never did. I'll always love him and honour his memory and I don't mean to sound like I feel superior to him. But I keep thinking back to what Asperia told me about his Prince's Test – how he scaled the palace walls without being in any real danger at all. And . . . after all the things I've been through, including this, and all the things I've learned that he could never even have suspected, I almost feel as if *he's* the son and I'm the father. Does that make sense at all?'

Rhea nodded gravely.

'But do you wish you hadn't learned those things? Do you wish your life hadn't changed?'

'No, no, I'm grateful for what I've learned. I'm grateful to have found out that there's a world below the clouds, just as there's a world above; that they're both really part of the same world and connected in so many ways. It makes everything seem more . . . complete somehow. And, even if it sounds strange, I'm grateful for what I've been through with you and the others. All the time we've been struggling to get home I've felt part of something for the first time in my life. It's just . . . I wish I could have gained all that without losing so much too, without all this pain. I wish I could have learned it but still have my father here and things the way they were.'

'But Marcus, life isn't *like* that. Happiness and things staying the same don't teach you anything – they just confirm what you think is true. The really valuable lessons, the ones that stay with you longest are usually the painful ones, I'm afraid.'

'But I don't want to be alone. That's the only thing I really fear – more than confronting Titus, more even than dying.'

'You won't be alone, Marcus, not as long as we're around. I promise.'

He felt her hand seek his in the darkness and squeeze it.

The night seemed to last for ever. But finally the clouds began to work their way through their familiar palette of grey, each shade just a little lighter than the one before. The wind had died to a murmur. Theus woke Nestor, the last to sleep. They all ate quickly, then Magnis crouched down and opened his pack. He pulled out the uninflated air sacs and the gas stoves. After tethering each stove to an air sac, he lit the first one. Marcus held the air sac above the burner. Peeling its narrow aperture apart, he tried to lower it close enough for the hot gas to be conducted into it but not so close that the burner would singe either it or his fingers. The wrinkles in the puckered skin of the canvas quickly smoothed out and it began to swell with a plaintive creak. Before long it was rigid and buoyant. Marcus tied the harness to it while Magnis hugged it to himself with evident pride.

Marcus slipped his arms through the harness's looped straps. The air sac bobbed above the quietly simmering stove and the stove itself hung about a foot above his head. He felt the effect immediately. He knew he was in no immediate danger of floating off up the head wall; climbing it would still be hard work. Nor did he feel any definite sense of buoyancy. It was rather as if he had abruptly lost weight: as if a couple of stone had been subtracted from his body within an instant. He hopped slightly a couple of times, savouring the sensation.

Rhea nodded encouragingly. She and the others inflated the rest of the air sacs and slung on the harnesses.

'Secure the line,' she said, 'and let's get moving.'

Air sacs clustered, jostling, above their heads, they all bent down to tie the rope around their waists again. Nestor, still half-asleep, stood fumbling with it, trying to cinch his knot. Just as he was about to turn towards the head wall, Marcus was startled by the most chilling sound he had ever heard – a dissonant screech that rent the misty air. He froze and peered into the cloud. A dark, throbbing disturbance was just visible for a few moments before disappearing again. It reappeared twice more, once lower, once higher. The third time it appeared, a powerful surge of air swept across the alcove, causing them all to stumble backwards. Nestor fumbled more urgently with the rope.

Marcus bent down with difficulty, the air sac quivering above his head. This time, instead of sifting his fingers across the pebbles, he raked deeply through them. He raised his hand. Pebbles trickled from it, but amongst the pebbles there was something else: small fragments of bone. He looked up at Rhea.

'This isn't an alcove,' he said, his voice hushed with fear. 'This is a nest.'

XXII

Furies unseen

Barely a second after he said it, they heard the screech again, much louder this time. In a flash of talons, Nestor was hoisted up into the cloud, where he vanished instantly.

The rope that bound Nestor to Magnis grew taut, stretching upwards. Magnis grabbed it with both hands. But, lightened by the tethered air sac, he began to be dragged, helplessly, towards the edge of the outcrop.

Nestor's screams melded themselves with the now exultant cries of whatever creature it was that had him in its grip, as if they were joining in some hideous duet. The downdraught of its furiously beating wings conjured a blizzard of pebbles and bone from the surface of the alcove. Screwing up their eyes, Marcus, Rhea and Theus sprang forwards and grabbed the same section of rope as Magnis. But such was the flying creature's strength that all four of them were soon staggering towards the edge.

'Cut the rope! Save yourselves!' yelled Nestor. His voice sounded resolute, but, at the same time, besieged by fear.

'No!' Marcus shouted back, tightening his grip on

338

the rope, its coarse fibres chafing his palms. 'We're not losing you. Hang on!'

While their struggle with this invisible foe continued, the already swirling cloud began to throb in other places too. All the different disturbances soon converged on the first.

'There are more!' screamed Nestor. 'They'll kill you all. Cut it! *Cut it!*'

'No!' yelled Rhea.

No one expected what happened next. The sounds the newly arrived creatures made – more strident and numerous all the time – took on a disputing tone. They were fighting over who should claim Nestor's body as their prize. Magnis, Marcus, Theus and Rhea inched closer to the edge, digging their heels in to no avail. Then, without warning, the cloud was drenched with a sickly sodium glare and a scorching shock wave slammed them back into the alcove. The creatures' raucous cries grew piercingly distressed, and the frantic beating of their wings carried with it gusts of burning feathers. The severed, blackened end of the rope flopped down on the lip of the outcrop.

'Nestor!' screamed Marcus.

Without thinking he leaped towards the source of the cacophony. But Magnis seized his arm and held him back.

'There's nothing we can do,' he hissed. 'Nestor must have punctured the stove's tank with his knife – made all the fuel combust to take those creatures with him . . . and stop them from attacking us.'

The sounds quickly faded, spinning down into the void. Marcus continued to strain in Magnis's grip until Rhea placed her hands on either side of his head, twisting it round, forcing him to look at her.

'He's gone, Marcus,' Rhea told him. 'But more of those creatures might be here any minute. We *have* to save ourselves.'

His eyes blazed. But he could see the truth in what she said. He stood shaking and stooped with anguish for a few moments, in spite of the air sac's buoyancy. Then he turned and reached up blindly for the head wall.

He climbed in a trance. So did the others. They all climbed throughout the day. The face of the mountain remained clear of any serious obstacles, as if it had finally accepted that it could not throw them off and had grown impassive, indifferent. They were borne up it not just by the air sacs but by a surge of intense fear. To Marcus it seemed almost obscene that his body should have been lent such buoyancy when his heart was so ponderous with fresh loss. Night came, but they continued to climb without even debating the fact. When someone reached up to open the valve on their stove's burner, the air sac above it glowed in the dark like a lantern, its outline blurring and fluttering in the snow. This was an eerily beautiful sight, but they took no joy in it.

Dawn came more swiftly than it had for some time. His eyes focused on the rock right in front of him, it took Marcus a while to notice that faint shafts of sunlight – just diffuse slivers, like the last ones he'd seen before the *Noble Quest* plummeted – were filtering through the cloud. Pausing to absorb this, he also noticed that the rock face didn't seem quite as precipitous as it had before. The mountain was no longer sheer-sided. And, as he resumed climbing, it grew steadily less steep. His stove was almost out of fuel, hissing thinly.

Within another couple of hours he and the others were able to crawl upwards on their hands and knees – what buoyancy the air sacs still possessed making them look curiously hunchbacked. They paused at last for rest. Rhea came up to join Marcus. They turned round and rested with their backs against the mountain and their heels jammed into a couple of off-widths: meandering clefts in the rock, too narrow to be chimneys. The cloud, though still thick, was now a luminous pale grey. Marcus looked above for stray smudges of blue, but there weren't any – not yet.

'I can't believe Nestor did that – sacrificed himself that way,' he said.

'We couldn't have saved him,' replied Rhea. 'He realised that.'

'I know. But he was trying so hard – to conquer his fear, to get past his lack of experience, just like me. I really thought we'd make it through together.'

Rhea nodded miserably.

'I swore to him that I'd keep him and the others alive – in both worlds. Now, whatever happens next, I've broken my word.'

They lay side by side in silence for a while. Theus and

Magnis were slightly further down to the left, each struggling to deal with Nestor's death in his own way.

'Do you know what "Nestor" means in our ancient language? I remember Asperia telling me once in philology classes,' said Marcus.

'No, what?'

'Homecoming.'

Rhea winced, tears gathering in the corners of her eyes.

'If we do make it back,' she said, 'we'll have a memorial for him.'

'What about his family?' asked Marcus. 'Do we tell them how close he came to getting home?'

She considered this.

'No. It's enough that they know how brave he was and what he did for the rest of us.'

Theus peered up at them. In his drawn features was etched all the pain and exhaustion that Marcus himself felt.

'Time to lead off?' Theus asked, without much enthusiasm.

'Yes,' said Rhea, sighing.

As they turned awkwardly to face the rock again, Marcus said, 'Well . . . if nothing else I suppose we can guess now why no one climbing down the mountain has ever returned. Those creatures probably infest the middle air.'

'But I wonder why we never see them above the cloudscape?' pondered Rhea.

'Perhaps like the Nullmaurs and Eihlans they can't

survive above a certain altitude,' replied Marcus.

'Hmm.'

They resumed their scramble upwards. They began to feel warmth on their backs and shoulders and drew strength from it. After mile upon mile of sheer-sided desolation, they entered a new landscape of boulders and sparse shrubs that sloped even less steeply. Trekking through it for several hours, they were soon perspiring heavily, the backs of their tunics damp where their packs rested. Each stove's supply of fuel was now spent and all the air sacs had begun to sag and pucker. Like the others, Marcus slipped out of his harness and stamped on the canvas to deflate it before carrying on.

Stopping to wipe sweat from his brow a little later, Marcus noticed a round, pale object, lodged between a large boulder and a smaller one. It looked like it might be an egg from one of the monstrous creatures that had carried Nestor away. But, as Rhea had said, if they ventured so far up into the cloud layer, why had they never been spotted from the citadel? With some difficulty he pulled the object free and turned it over in his hands. It stared sightlessly back at him, teeth locked in a perpetual grimace. It was a skull. He dropped it with a gasp. Now, everywhere he looked, bones, more skulls, even whole skeletons − sprawled in contorted positions − seemed to leap into sight.

'Our dead,' said Rhea, joining him. 'Hundreds of years of Heliopolis's dead, cast over from the fields. This is a graveyard.'

Marcus shuddered.

'We've cheated death already,' he replied grimly. 'We don't belong here . . . Come on.'

They hastened onwards. The incline grew shallower still and they moved swiftly, assuredly, standing straighter. With a growing sense of anticipation, they loosened the rope around their waists, unknotted it and threw it off. The shafts of sunlight were thicker and more defined than ever. Then, abruptly, the clouds parted and they were drenched in crisp early winter sunlight. From horizon to horizon stretched an immaculate span of blue. They all stopped and turned to face the sun, eyes closed, arms loose at their sides, letting it bathe them in its beneficence. After a while Marcus pushed his fringe out of his eyes with an almost languid motion then turned to gaze up at the mountain peak.

They were standing at the fringes of the orchard. Fruit that had fallen and rolled away before it could be picked lay rotting at their feet. Tendrils of cloud snaked upwards, curling between the tree trunks. Beyond the orchard lay the gentle slope of the fields – ploughed into fresh, glistening furrows after the harvest – then the first of the citadel's fortified walls. Its battlements were patrolled by more sentinels than Marcus had thought possible, but the cloud that lapped the orchards was just thick enough to conceal him and the others from view, as long as they crouched. Meanwhile, the guards in the fields actually outnumbered the Farmers they were supposed to be observing.

The rest of the citadel looked majestic, its contours sharply defined in the high, clear air. In spite of all he had said to Rhea earlier, seeing it from such a humbling perspective for the first time was overwhelming for Marcus. Everything he had been through up to this point – all the disasters and triumphs – had unfolded in stages. He'd had time, even if only a little, to get used to each trial before the next was upon him. But now, staring up at the citadel, he felt the realisation of all the unsought changes in his life bear down upon him. His legs trembled, as if they were about to buckle with the weight of it. He'd given every morsel of strength he possessed to get this far – battled against the limits of his endurance. He'd been forced to show resolve, stamina, courage and indifference to pain and discomfort – all qualities that his sheltered upbringing had been so ill suited to instil in him. But right now he felt as if he had no more reserves to draw upon. He was tired in his bones. None the less, he knew that he had set himself and the others on a path he couldn't turn away from now. No matter what happened next, there was nothing to do but carry on – for better or worse.

So he straightened up, squared his shoulders then fell into step with Rhea, Theus and Magnis, walking towards the shelter of the trees and all that still lay ahead . . .

The writer acknowledges support from the Scottish
Arts Council towards the writing of this title.

Scottish
Arts Council